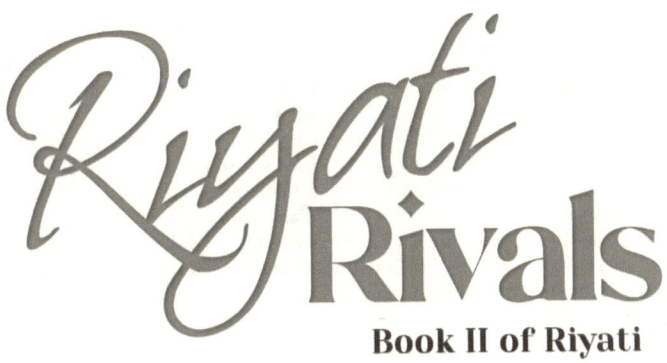

Book II of Riyati

Kai Zeal

Aquakat Publishing

Published by Aquakat Publishing
PO Box 656
Pinson, AL 35126
aquakatpublishing.com

First edition: May 2025

Cover Design by Kai Zeal
Cover Glyph Illustration by amagren
Edited by K Swindler

ISBN 979-8-9923922-3-4 (eBook)
ISBN 979-8-9923922-4-1 (Paperback)
ISBN 979-8-9923922-5-8 (Hardcover)

Human Creativity Badge by Conrad Altmann

content warnings

The viewpoints and actions in this book do not necessarily express the viewpoints of the author. **The following are depicted, described, or implied within this book:**

Abandonment, alcoholism, attempted suicide, blood, bullying, child abuse, classism, confinement, death, emotional abuse, emotional manipulation, extreme violence, gore, homelessness, human experimentation, kidnapping, misogyny, murder, parental neglect, physical abuse, poverty, self-harm, stalking, strong adult language, substance abuse, suicide, suicidal ideation, torture, toxic friendship, and trauma-based responses.

Reader discretion is advised.

To those continuing to struggle even when it seems hopeless,
to those who can only see an endless dark tunnel,
Don't give up, for you are worth more than you'll ever know.

table of contents

The Story So Far...

Riyati Rebirth

During a routine visit to the local city park with her childhood friend Jordan, Kylie encounters a life-threatening situation, causing her to have Activation (Act), which grants her the ability to use magic. Soon after, she discovers that she is the reincarnation of Kisate Riyati, crown princess of the now-destroyed magic kingdom of Riyati. Even stranger, her past incarnations and future self (Siani, often called "Sia") now share a body with her, each a distinct consciousness only she can hear. While every mage — an individual that has experienced Act — has a unique ability, Kylie is an exception: she possesses two abilities. The first is empathy, where she feels and senses the emotions of individuals around her; the second is sensory precognition, a type of clairvoyance that allows her to experience the future through non-vision-based senses.

The next few months of Kylie's life pass peacefully as she adjusts to magic in her life. That peace doesn't last, however, as multiple individuals attempt to kidnap her and bring her to a man named Asuza. Asuza was Kisate's — her original incarnation — primary servant and the man who murdered Kylie's previous two incarnations. During one of these kidnapping attempts, Jordan walks in and witnesses the attempted kidnapping. This causes his own Act to occur, and soon after, he's revealed to be affected by the same reincarnation spell as Kylie; his original incarnation is Takite Tanoti, Kisate's fiancé. Similar to Kylie, he shares a body with his prior incarnations (Takite, John, and Dmitri) and future self (Rotanu, often called "Rota"); unlike Kylie, he has the standard one ability — hypermnesia, the perfect recall of his memories since his Act. While Kylie is impartial to magic itself, only disliking how it has changed her life, Jordan despises it. Stemming from long-term low self-esteem caused by a lifetime of being bullied because of his family's low socioeconomic status and abuse from his alcoholic father, he views magic as another sign of being an outcast. This disdain is only increased as he frequently clashes with Rotanu, who he refuses to believe is himself from the future — in part because Rotanu is engaged to Siani, a reality Jordan refuses to believe he could possibly be worthy of.

Come late June, Asuza finally succeeds in kidnapping Kylie. Once Jordan realizes she's missing, he confronts Rotanu, who admits that she has been kidnapped by Asuza and that he even knows where Kylie is held. Jordan decides to attempt rescuing her and enters the run-down building Rotanu directs him to. Within the dimly-lit building, he sees a girl, similar in appearance to Kylie, dead on an altar. Many visions flash across his eyes of additional women that look like Kylie, all dead, and extreme pain manifests in his chest before further hallucinations play out in front of him — one of a reality in which Kylie never had Act. Jordan realizes what he sees is nothing more than an illusion. He breaks out of the spell and reaches Kylie before she dies. Together, they work to cast a spell forcing both Asuza and their previous incarnations to rest, triggering their wings — a form of "magic exhaust" for high-powered spells — during the process. Finally freed, Kylie heads back home and is greeted by her frantic mother and childhood friend Dani.

Chapter One

eleventh grade

Almost a month and a half since that damn bastard'd kidnapped her. Summer break'd already come and gone, the damn Georgia late summer heat and humidity as shitty as ever. As expected, hadn't really seen her much since she'd survived that day. Well. Guess it'd be better said as "remembered" for me and Kyle, but it'd been kinda obvious even without us having lived it once: there's no way Ms. Rae'd take Kylie going missing well, and she ain't exactly a woman that'd ever handled a lack of control with grace.

Now, it's the night b'fore school started back: the infamous eleventh grade year. A time I never wanted to revisit yet's at my damn doorstep already. I'd say it's too soon, but always'd be, if I'm honest.

Jordan pressed the doorbell — was mid-afternoon the Sunday b'fore classes started back. It'd been a completely strategic decision given Jenn typically started a week after the public schools, which meant Ms. Rae's typically at said community college for last-minute fall semester prep this time of the year. Kylie answered the door. "Oh, hey, what's up?" She said as she stepped to the side for Jordan to come in. Lights're on in the foyer and up the staircase, but only a cursory light on in the dining room. She hadn't been down on this floor, likely up in her room b'fore answering the door.

"Just, uh. Wanted to see how you're doing." Jordan moved his hand to his neck as he glanced away toward that frankly ugly-ass rug they'd always had in the dining room. He stepped inside, keeping his eyes from her.

It'd been over two weeks since they'd last seen each other. Kyle and me'd made *special arrangements* the other two didn't know 'bout, so we met more often, but it still ain't been great.

Kylie closed the door and walked up the steps that led to her room. Wanted to snicker as Jordan swallowed, unsure if he should follow. Ms. Rae's definitely not there, and typical Kylie, she thought nothing of two teenagers in her bedroom unsupervised. Jordan glanced around, as if waiting for a trap, b'fore trudging up the steps, through the hallway, and then into her bedroom.

Kylie sat on her desk chair backwards, chin resting on the backrest as her legs poked out from the back of the chair. "Mom's still barely letting me breathe by myself," she said, a huff to her voice. "I get why and everything, but I'm so tired of being in this house. Actually looking forward to school starting back since it's *something different*."

Jordan sat on the edge of the pull-out futon in the back corner of Kylie's room. I'd heard stories of Dani bitching 'bout it to Kylie, of how uncomfortable it was. While the actual bed part's put up so couldn't say there, the couch part's fine enough. Then again, anything with damn AC's a blessing in August, and the Rae Residence's nice and cooled. Too cool compared to outside, actually. Was whiplash, but I'd take it 'bout now. "Has... Nothing else's happened, right?"

She shook her head, though her eyes drifted down to her wrists, which still had scars from where the rope'd been too tight. "Just been me and Sia, like normal. Dani hasn't really been by much lately." And Jordan rarely came 'cause've how bitchy Ms. Rae got if she's here when he stopped by. "Mom's finally letting me at least check the mail now, but only when she's home. Practically stares out the door the whole time, so haven't felt fresh air in forever now."

"It's been hot as fuck out, so ain't missed much." Jordan moved his eyes back to the carpet. It'd been the opposite for him: barely seen Kylie but'd socialized more than ever b'fore. This past summer had more hangouts than he'd ever had, 'specially in AC'ed buildings. Could only pretend to read in the library so much b'fore they started getting bitchy, happened basically every year.

Kylie softly chuckled as she said, "I guess not." I wished Jordan knew how much of a jackass comment that'd been. He at least had the choice, ain't effectively on permanent house arrest. "Have you picked up your schedule yet?"

"Oh, uh, right." Jordan grabbed the piece of paper he'd folded and shoved in his back pocket. Dunno why he bothered — remembered everything on it, but his eyes scanned over it like he didn't. Refused to admit hypermnesia'd meant he didn't need the sheet of paper, still on his dumbass crusade against the magic that'd benefited his life. Was gonna save his life, even. "I've got Samson for homeroom, and fourth for lunch." He didn't bother mentioning the actual classes: he barely made current grade level coursework, and she's in all honors, even's in multiple AP class this year, though hadn't told Jordan yet. Was yet another weird-ass moment of watching my past play out live as Jordan's present. Kyle prob'bly had it a bit easier since no hypermnesia, but no way she ain't experiencing it to some extent too.

"Umm..." Kylie turned around, almost falling out of her chair as she did so, catching her balance at the last second. She flipped through her planner to a loose sheet of paper. "Albertson for homeroom." Her voice softened further. "And third lunch." While it ain't the first time, it's one of the core problems for this particular year: there're no shared classes or lunch periods. "Huh? Oh, sure." Kylie's eyes moved to Jordan. "Sia wanted to know what Rota's been working on you with lately."

Jordan rolled his eyes. "Dumbass's too much of a ditz to teach a damn thing." Ain't like he's the most eager learner here.

Just 'cause I didn't wanna fight his ass on every little thing, made it sound like it's on me.

I knew the sigh that came from Kylie's body was Kyle. Was too amused to have been from Kylie. "Until Mom lets up, I can't really teach you. You two need to work together here." She knew there's not a shot in hell that'd work as motivation; basically's her saying we couldn't bitch to her when Jordan didn't know shit Kylie did.

While Jordan nodded timidly, the only one who might've believed something'd come outta this's Kylie.

Speaking of, she gained control back, a softening of her gaze as her eyes didn't meet Jordan's any longer. "I, um. Guess we'll meet up after school then?"

"Oh, it's gonna be okay for you to be out again once school starts up?"

Kylie shook her head. "I doubt it, but Mom has a few evening classes in the fall so I can walk back home at least. I can't really linger but it's better than being stuck here all day."

She's desperate, and I wished Jordan got how much so. Wished he didn't nod and casually say, "Y-yeah, sure."

Wished this year would never start.

Chapter Two

promising start

Kylie | August 14
Opal Pines High School

I'd forgotten an important downside to being around people since I'd been under house arrest all summer: people are *loud*. I was pretty sure Sia handled more of my empathy than she normally did right then, and my head was still splitting. Didn't want to talk to anyone else, at least, no one that I couldn't complain about the *loudness* of people to. I somehow even picked what I was fairly certain was Jordan's emotions up despite us not sharing a single class — I wasn't sure if it was that my empathy had gotten that much stronger since we last had classes or if I was just better at picking out his and Rota's emotions or if I was misinterpreting the consistent emotions I'd experienced all day regardless of where in the building I was. Regardless, it wasn't just them — this whole high school had too many emotions. No longer just my neighbors or Dani and Jordan and Rota stopping by.

No one at school realized one of the "missing people" had been me, not even when I'd jumped at some freshman bumping into me. None of the investigation details about the kidnapping were public compared, unlike the cases of people missing in the forest back when all this started. While I preferred them not to know — was nice to not feel pity from everyone around me like had so often been the case since Asuza had kidnapped me — , I struggled to maintain the energy they had, that I once had.

Everything was removed, like I was an impostor here with all the normal high school students despite it being the school I'd been in for years now. School just didn't feel as important as it once had.

But I also had spent more than enough time in my room lately since it's all Mom allowed until my kidnapper was "caught." I understood why, but it was all the more frustrating when I knew he wouldn't come back, was dead, but no one else did. Well, no one outside of me, Sia, Jordan, and Rota. Technically Dani did too, but I could tell she didn't really believe what actually happened. Maybe she couldn't, since she wasn't there like us.

I wished there was a middle ground between "locked in house" and "locked in a high school full of emotions I didn't want to experience."

As I walked toward my last class, I saw Bethany wave at me. I waved back and bit my tongue as I hoped she didn't want to talk. I just didn't have the energy, especially not now.

As usual of late, I had absolutely no luck; she walked up to me. "Hey, how was your summer?"

"It... was. Not ready for more homework." Sure, that was the honors equivalent of talking about weather, but at least it was reliable: none of us ever wanted more homework.

She nodded enthusiastically. "I know what you mean. I was on the beach in Savannah a week ago, and what I wouldn't give to go back there now." The bell screeched out, causing me to jump. It happened every period change so far, the noise sending my heart racing as it took me unaware each time despite being the same bell they'd always used in this school.

"Almost out." When *Sia* consoled me, I knew I must've been in bad shape.

"Kylie?" Bethany's genuine surprise and concern wasn't what I needed filling my head right then despite being well-meaning.

"Yeah," I said under my breath. "Sorry, I have Wilson so

6

can't be late!" I rushed away, into the classroom. Thankfully, I wasn't the last one in. I could just forget any bathroom breaks between sixth and seventh periods; their classrooms were on opposite sides of the school basically and even the locker switch was a nightmare. I hated when the guidance counselor arranged my schedule like that.

I sat down in a first row seat toward the left side of the room. I felt safer seeing the door, something I'd never considered before spring of last year.

All the hushed gossip and summer catch-ups in the room quieted as Mr. Wilson came to board at the front. It didn't help that he had a *reputation*, and his AP Bio class had the recurring rumor of being an absolute nightmare. Our general hope was that the whispers going around about him retiring soon were true and maybe he'd chill these last few years. However, his emotions indicated anything but "chill" given he was possibly the only person in this school more done with today than me. At least, I thought it was him. It also might've been another student. I hated crowds, and a classroom was squarely in the crowd category. "Don't get too comfortable. We'll be assigning seats with your partners soon."

I bit back rolling my eyes. Seriously, he assigned seats in *high school*? Even better, he assigned our lab partner too. I glanced around the room, seeing almost all familiar faces outside of two people: a blonde-haired girl that I was pretty sure I'd seen around over the years, just never in my classes before, and a red-haired guy that I wasn't sure I'd seen before. I really hoped I wasn't paired with Samuel again; the last group project I had with him, I had to do *more* work than if the assignment had been a solo project because of how much I had to manage him, even for the simplest things like paper margins that had never remotely changed. Despite my efforts, he somehow *still* messed the basic format up where I was up half the night fixing things the night before that stupid English presentation was due. If I was stuck with him again, this time, I was doing it all myself from the start; I wasn't sure how he'd never gotten kicked out of honors, but my life was hectic enough without his *help* right now.

"We'll do roll call as I assign your seat, so everyone to the front of the room." I bit back my grumble, unlike a handful of other students who were more openly annoyed. We all did as he said though, cramming together at the front of the classroom. "As you may have noticed, the room is arranged in pairs of desks. The person your desk connects with is your partner for the year for all projects and labs. And no, I will not switch you because you don't like your partner."

I wished I could ask Sia how miserable this next year was about to be from my lack of judgment in believing his reputation was really that deserved. Instead, I glanced around the classroom and at the other students. Everyone was still feeling entirely too much, too loudly.

The other bad news: with my last name being far from the beginning of the alphabet, I was never at the top of roll call. So I stood awkwardly at the front of the classroom, watching others sit as there were fewer and fewer people beside me. Once again, it was like being chosen *almost* last, where, sure, I wasn't the only one left, but I wasn't far off either. It had always been this way for roll call, but usually I wasn't literally standing as slowly there was no one beside me. He called more names, finally down to the other R's.

He tapped a desk in the second row, beside the blonde-haired girl I faintly recognized. "Rae."

Okay, at least it wasn't Samuel. I made my way to the desk — Mom would not be amused if she saw I wasn't assigned a front row spot, but I'd take it; meant if I doodled or worked on magic stuff here and there, it wouldn't be as obvious. I couldn't get in trouble if I wasn't the one who picked this seat; she could take it up with him, and I wasn't sure who would win that parent-teacher conference.

I took my place to the right of my new partner. I felt her gray eyes on me, something in my stomach turning at the gaze. It wasn't from empathy, but something I couldn't identify, articulate. She had her phone hidden between the desk and her lap, seemingly left-handed like me. That was helpful: I hated elbowing right-handed people while taking notes, and I was on the side of the desk where it would matter. Part of the reason I appreciated any class I shared with Jordan was that even though

8

he was right-handed, he was also more than used to being elbowed by me; we'd grown up with it happening, and he didn't jump every time I did so like he had years back. He hadn't ever been big on touch, so I think he'd just gotten accustomed over the years. Unfortunately, we rarely shared classes now, and it'd been that way since mid-middle school.

I wondered how his day's gone? I mean, I sort of had an idea because of what I thought was his or Rota's emotions through empathy, but it wasn't the same.

Taking a breath, I noticed others were chatting since we were supposed to be introducing ourselves to our partners. "Um, hi there. I'm Kylie. Nice to meet you."

Irritation. Her gray eyes glanced up from her phone as her attention focused on me. "Lianne Payne." Her attention immediately went back to her phone, ignoring the rest of the classroom. She wasn't even that engaged. Just bored. This restlessness — or was that me? I couldn't tell at this point, my head splitting far too much. There were too many emotions, and I wanted out.

Even though I had no shot at actually comprehending anything said in the lecture, I was actually happy when it started: the chatter of everyone in the room couldn't further overwhelm me on top of empathy anymore.

How had I tolerated this so well back in May? Was it really just that my empathy was stronger? I'd ask Sia, but I most certainly wouldn't get a good answer.

Instead, I took notes that I had near no recollection of, too exhausted and overwhelmed to pretend to actually hear a word being said. It certainly wasn't the most promising start to this year.

Chapter Three

just like magic

Jordan | August 14
North Opal Pines High School

First day of entirely too damn many for this year's finally done. I stood a bit off from the school exit and waited for Kylie. Hell knew I ain't gonna be early, so this's basically the only time we'd see each other. Was different from sixth grade when this'd last happened. Ms. Rae didn't hate me as much then, and Kylie wasn't under effective lock-down. Another damn negative effect of magic on our lives.

Even I barely believed what'd happened back in June, and I saw it, was there. Could all too easily envision the wires attached to her, skin paler than I'd ever seen. How her back'd been nothing but dripping blood. How her wrists still had scars around them, even yesterday. How Rotanu'd fuckin' let it happen, knew the exact time and date and had said jack shit.

I glanced at the clock above the school entrance door — it'd already been ten minutes and she's still not out. A few of the senior girls're huddled around each other, whispering and giggling. I averted my eyes; Tiffany and Kelly in particular basically hated anyone below them, and I'm at the damn near bottom of that big-ass long list. Didn't want them making more snide remarks 'bout me than they already would this year, but would've been a lie to say I ain't curious what had them sound so damn excited. Whatever it was, they're laying it on entirely too goddamn thick to the person they wanted to impress. I kept my eyes on the dying grass beside the school walkway exit, away from them. It never worked, but maybe if I didn't see them, they wouldn't see me. They came closer and closer.

"Move," Kelly snapped at me, as if I hadn't been standing there b'fore her and had gotten in her way. Same shit, different day.

"S-sorry." I stepped to the side, just wanting them both gone. The problem with being stuck with the same people since elementary's that everyone knew everyone, and they'd long since decided they're above me. And they were, that ain't wrong, just...

"Oh." I knew that voice, but not from school. My eyes shot up, seeing a tall guy with long blonde hair, lips pulled to an amused smirk. Had on some type of expensive clothes I didn't know the names of — just too damn formal for high school since it was similar to, but not quite, a suit. "There you are, yo."

Richard?

"Uh... hi?" I didn't know what else to say. Looked more like a goddamn idiot than usual, but the fuck's he doing here? He went to some rich kid private school I'd never heard of b'fore meeting him: Asherton Preparatory Institution, he'd said. Definitely ain't in the uniform I'd seen back last April and May when he cut class, though. Tiffany and Kelly're on each side of him, almost pushing each other to get his attention, though they double-took when they realized he spoke to me. Didn't blame them, I kinda was too right then. Not 'cause I didn't know him, but 'cause he'd been someone I met outside of this hellhole; had been the blonde-haired guy I'd ran past the day after my Act, when I almost burned down the whole damn forest, and thank fuckin' god he hadn't realized I caused that shitshow. Since Kylie'd been on house arrest all summer, we'd hung out a lot past few months — he's first guy I'd ever been friends with. Well. First person in general outside of Kylie, really. And Rotanu typically left me the hell alone while with Richard, which's even better.

"The guy you said you're looking for..." Tiffany glanced from me to Richard, and while her tone's prob'bly the sweetest I'd ever heard it, there's a layer of disbelief under it I ain't sure I'd ever heard b'fore. Would've been fuckin' hilarious under different circumstances. "It's *him*? I'm sure it's someone else. He's *no one*." Even worse, there're hushed whispers from a few other classmates that're still here. More attention on me. Just goddamn great.

I averted my eyes back to the concrete, seeing where it cracked and needed to be redone and had needed redoing for like two years now. More steps, these coming closer and closer. Great, who else's joining in?

"Sorry I'm so late." That's Kylie, and not soon enough. She stepped beside me, saying, "Oh, hey, Tiffany and Kelly and... I, um, don't think we've met? But I'm Kylie. Nice to meet you." She then turned to me, wincing a moment. As I glanced to her face, I noticed she looked like hell. Hell's up for her to look so exhausted? "Sorry you waited... Mom's in the parking lot, decided I can't even walk home today. She's got night class tomorrow though, so I should be able to then." I noticed her phone's in her hand, lighting up. She huffed, rolling her eyes while mumbling, "Going, I'm going." Her attention refocused back to Richard. "Anyways, nice to meet you."

His eyes went between Kylie and me b'fore his eyebrow raised. "Richard, pleasure's yours."

Her head tilted. "Um, sure, likewise?" I hated I wanted to snicker with Rotanu at Richard's momentary frown, at Tiffany and Kelly near facepalming and instead gritting their teeth. Kylie'd earned the reputation of friendly, easy to work with and generally get along with... but denser than a damn rock when someone's coming onto her. It ain't an undeserved reputation at all: she'd never been interested in anyone. Part of why whatever's going on with Siani and Rotanu's a goddamn lie, 'cause outta all the guys she'd turned down, I sure as hell ain't the one that'd be different. I knew better, knew even having her as a friend's more than I should've had.

"*Woosh,*" Rotanu said. Bit down on my tongue 'cause I ain't getting caught laughing there, 'specially not from him.

A car beeped; Kylie jumped, the wind briefly picking up b'fore dying back down. That'd been her, Kylie shifting the wind as I'd done numerous times with fire and ice when startled. But shit didn't pass through Siani's control like it did fuckup-Rotanu's. Ain't even entirely sure how I knew it wasn't a natural breeze — maybe 'cause've the timing right after the car horn and her reaction to it. Maybe been me too many times, so shit clicked. But that'd definitely been Kylie. I turned, seeing her mom's gray SUV at the curb, the only car around. "Oh, for..." she said, half under her breath. "I'll see you tomorrow." She waved goodbye as she ran to the SUV.

I turned to wave goodbye back and was half through the motion b'fore I realized she's already in the SUV and talking to her mom, attention focused on Ms. Rae.

"Change of plans," Richard said, this annoyed tone in his voice. "You two." He glanced at Tiffany and Kelly. "Later. And you." His head nodded to me. "With me."

"Uh." The looks Kelly and Tiffany gave me're some of the biggest glares I'd ever gotten from them, and considering, that's an achievement in and of itself. "I, uh." I didn't wanna say yes. I went to this school, just wanted to be invisible and am 'bout as fuckin' far from it as possible right then.

Richard's gaze intensified as his eyes moved to Kelly and Tiffany. "They're leaving anyway. Now."

"R-right," Kelly said. "We are, definitely. Right now." She yanked Tiffany away. The hell's going on for *them* to take that type of shit from Richard? Never seen that b'fore.

He scoffed. Hit a button on his cell phone; Kylie had the same cell phone a few years now, was a *mid-range model* she'd called it, an upgrade over the phone b'fore her current one. Richard's was twice the size of Kylie's and pristine; ain't sure what it was since I'd never had a cell phone, but even I could tell it's a hell'va lot more expensive than what Kylie had. A black car beeped from the almost vacated lot. "C'mon," he said.

"But, uh, where're we...?" Usually we met up at the park. Was where I'd originally met him, and ain't like there's a ton to hang around at in this city; we'd been to a handful of cafes and shit where he ordered a lot and I didn't during the summer, but only once the park'd just been too damn hot. Still ain't sure why he'd befriended me when he's the type of guy that even Tiffany and Kelly backed off from. Was more confused than ever, really. His car's a perfectly glossed and spotless convertible, and quite frankly, I'm terrified to even touch its door handle. "Don't worry about it." The phrase'd been friendly enough, but his tone certainly ain't; basically's an order, and not one I wanted to argue with. As gently as I could, I pushed against the door handle, sitting down on the leather seats — they're the same texture as the gloves Rotanu's "alt form" for fighting had, so I assumed's real leather at that. Only a few high schoolers here had cars, even fewer had non-hand-me-downs. His's prob'bly the only essentially brand new one I'd ever seen, let alone ridden in. He drove outta the lot, the school disappearing down roads I rarely saw; pretty much walked everywhere, always had. "Hell you let them talk to you like that for?"

"It's fine." It'd always been that way. Just how life was.

He huffed, one arm on the wheel and the other on the rolled-down window. "Thought it'd be a hilarious joke to see what a public high school's like. Fuck around with David and Michelle." Speaking of other things no other high schooler did, Richard called his parents by first name and even though I knew the names, it disoriented me every time. Couldn't imagine calling Father anything than, well. Father. He'd beat my ass more than he did already if I called him "Calvin." "But this is a motherfucking disaster. Letting bitches walk all over you like that."

"It's fine." He acted like this's something new, something problematic.

He ignored me, turning music on, something with piano and no words. I didn't know where he's taking me, but ain't 'bout to jump outta a moving vehicle so I'm stuck on whatever hellride I'd signed up for.

Wish I'd known b'fore I agreed, had more warning what a headache I'd been involved in this time. Just like magic, another headache I ain't prepared to deal with.

Chapter Four

four hours

Siani | August 19
Rae Residence

Since the whole Asuza incident, I'd been sneaking out late on Saturday evenings to meet up with Rota. As Rota had noted more than once, there were potential *ethical concerns* about sneaking out when Jordan and Kylie's bodies needed rest and neither had exactly given consent, but this was something between Rota and me. And it needed to *stay* that way. As I'd done so many times in my life, I levitated just off the carpet as I shortcast the alt form spell so I could have my own appearance. I unlatched the window, climbing onto the roof while closing but not locking the window. Remaining levitated while on the roof to prevent any noise, I jumped onto the nearest tree branch before I released the levitation and then climbed down the tree.

For four hours a week, I spoke with someone besides Kylie. I was me instead of Siani and all the obligations and responsibilities that entailed. I could justify looking like myself as an indulgence, but I didn't dare teleport directly to the training house — Kylie's active supply definitely couldn't have handled it while she was already supposed to be resting, and I couldn't justify using anything but her active supply for non-serious events. I knew the risks and limitations better than anyone else, after all.

Besides, it was nostalgic to walk this path. I had done it so many times, I probably could've walked here without sight, the dilapidated building my second — well, more like third — home. I pushed the door in, seeing no lights on or auras nearby; I beat Rota today, which was unusual but not worrying. He was usually here first since Jordan slept earlier than Kylie, but Jordan didn't always get that choice with his home life.

I sat down in the far corner where Rota and I usually sat, turning on one of the battery-operated lamps that Rota had melted into the concrete flooring. More I thought about it, more I realized his control over fire had actually been rather impressive for that one, able to isolate enough to not fry the batteries or internal wiring while assuring it was *not* moving anywhere. Theft was too much of a headache, and it was one we didn't want to deal with.

His aura edged closer. At most, he'd shortcast alt form like myself. This was Jordan's aura, and subsequent mana supply, instead of Rota's much bright one. It didn't take much longer until I heard the door push open, curse under his breath before the door closed back.

He stood next to me before dropping down to the concrete and letting out an exhausted sigh.

"That well, huh?" I asked, chuckling.

"If I could physically strangle him, I would. Like, seriously, how much of a dumbass..." He made gestures with his hands, as if grabbing something in the air. "It's so, ugh. Doesn't connect that maybe things can't be exactly the same after all that bullshit, doesn't come check on her much 'cause too damn socially awkward, and then..."

I laid my head against his shoulder. He slid his arm around my back, pulling me even closer. "You're expecting a bit much from a teenager just trying to survive. He doesn't have the space to really self-reflect like you're wanting here." I didn't bother pointing out that Rota wasn't really that much better than Jordan on self-awareness. Rota's strength was knowing upcoming events, but really, they both had their hearts in the right place while not realizing how much they shoved their foot down their throat sometimes; both wallowed in useless self-hatred that did nothing to fix the actual problem. And both knew how to be passive aggressive to an *art*. I'd been on the wrong side of the latter more than once, and it was *not* a fun place to be.

"Someone didn't try to literally murder his ass."

I moved my right hand into his left hand. "Hm... Didn't you just say you would?"

"That's different." He returned holding my hand. "And you damn well know it."

These were the four hours I waited all week on. And at least for now, I enjoyed these moments with him holding me, calm, steady breaths from his nose. "And I'm sure training's been going well?" He grumbled, and I knew it was because he hadn't even tried. If it was a book he could instantly memorize, he did great. If it was something that needed actual dedication, I might as well have physically dragged him. Sometimes I had, admittedly, but that had *generally* been accidentally. Mostly. "You *need* to work with him. We won't be here forever. He needs to know a bit of theory to survive once you're gone, same as swordplay."

"Yeah, yeah..."

Like old times, almost. "Though I guess he's been busy with friends given the new guest at school."

"Both of them're dumbasses." He sighed, rubbing his eyes with his free hand.

I chuckled, running the tips of my fingers against the pads of his fingertips. "They're high schoolers, of course they're dumbasses. That's part of the description."

"That's not — fuck you, you know what I meant."

"Not now, or *yet*, I guess would be the time appropriate term technically."

That got a snicker out of him, a joke we wouldn't make in front of the older two. They might've thought we were blatant about our relationship, but we actually weren't at all — in part because we were just more private about our relationship in general, in part because it wasn't something they needed shoved down their throats more than would already happen. "How'd it feel? Seeing him, well, that him. I know it..."

I brought my knees to my chest, using my free arm to lay over my legs. "I thought it'd hurt worse than it did. It's funny, being older. He's just like them, really. Looking for a home. Being absolutely obnoxious about it, but what's new there? His emotions are clear giveaways of how dependent he is on Jordan, but she isn't experienced enough as an empath to put it together... maybe not mature enough in general."

His eyes were on me, watching my every breath. Even though there was no need, he was clearly concerned, as much of a worrier as ever. "You really think just standing aside's the best thing to do?"

I brought the hand holding his close, kissing below one of his knuckles . "I do."

My loyalty was to my Jordan, not to a revisionist past where we'd never have the chance to grow, to be with the people most important to us now. After all, our mistakes defined us, and I wouldn't let anything take that chance away from them.

Chapter Five

innocence

Kylie | August 19
Rae Residence

No one knew what had happened outside myself and Jordan —
and Sia and Rota, of course — , and to a far lesser extent, Dani.
Mom talked to Mrs. Alana sometimes, conversations I wasn't
supposed to overhear, about how to know if I was okay. Mrs.
Alana would ask if I said anything to help with the case, if I
remembered anything new.

I thought school would be a welcome change of pace, a
normality missing in my life since last May. But it wasn't:
everything around me felt slow, mundane. My mind raced three
times as fast as everyone around me. Nothing felt safe. What did
geometry matter when I still saw my scarred wrist every time I
glanced down? AP Lit was useless when it didn't provide me
with words on how removed everything felt. School drained me
the past week: it had effectively done the opposite I'd hoped. I
should've been relaxing, enjoying the weekend, but instead all I
could focus on was that I was back in my bedroom and still felt
suffocated by every emotion around me, crowding into my
mind without permission.

I heard the wind chimes from our front door through my open bedroom window. Wind. Fresh air.

Shaking my head, I took a deep breath: I needed to see something besides these walls that wasn't a crowded high school.

"We can wait a bit on practice, right?" I asked Sia. I didn't know why I asked since I couldn't do anything fun on weekends anymore; with Mom confining me to the house, most days I spent with Sia now. If I studied theory right now or two hours from now really didn't matter since my brain would give out before the sun went down regardless.

"Mm, sure."

Putting my tennis shoes on, I opened my bedroom door. Mom watched TV in the living room, likely had a stack of papers in front of her as she graded through them. She muted the TV as I walked down the steps.

"I'm going to go walk around the block for a bit," I said.

I didn't like that I heard her stand, instant anxiety swarming me before she'd made it over to the door. Why couldn't I have had hyper-whatever that Jordan had? Why empathy? "Do I need to pick something up for you?"

Shaking my head, I lowered my eyes. Her anxiety was consuming, my own heart racing from her fear. I just wanted fresh air. Why was that so wrong?

"I just need some air for a bit, I think."

She put her hand on my right forearm, warm against my skin. "Sweetie, it's just not safe out there. Not until..."

He was dead. The actually-dead kind, not the "dead but still walking around like still alive" dead that I still didn't really understand the logistics of. There was nothing that Mom or Mrs. Alana or anyone could "watch out for" anymore. I knew they didn't know that. I knew that she was just concerned, but...

But why was it so much to ask to not be punished for something beyond my control?

"Please, Mom."

She shook her head. "I can't let you, not until... What if something happens?"

"I walk home from school fine, don't I?" I was barely allowed to do that, and maybe I shouldn't have mentioned it since it'd draw her attention to the only space I had. I knew the only reason she allowed me to walk home is because she had classes and couldn't pick me up as she had the first day.

She shook her head once more. "Why don't I order in some pizza tonight? We could watch a movie."

I just wanted *air*. But I knew better than to talk back more than I had; I felt the warning signs not only through empathy but through her firmer tone, lacking the pity of moments prior. "I'm not really hungry. I think I need to lay down for a bit." I walked back upstairs, closing my bedroom door behind me.

While I had no intention of actually sleeping, I still fell back on my bed. The fan spun in a circle, around and around and around. Much like every day so far had been since the start of the academic year: go to school, come home, go to school, come home.

"How'd you even manage to *see* Rota to 'date' him when she won't even let me breathe near the front door?" It was a long-shot, but maybe Sia would slip on something actually useful. I'd also take her as a distraction from the rising frustration in my stomach or from Mom's exasperation on the ground floor that was entirely too easy to pick up on. Stupid empathy.

"Breathe quieter."

What did she even mean by that? How was I supposed to breathe "quieter" than I already did? I huffed, leading her to chuckle. No point asking her to explain herself; she wouldn't, and we both knew it. "All right, fine. Might as well do whatever you wanted because apparently this is where I'm going to live until Monday morning. Again."

Colors — they were distant, not something I could see, but visual all the same. I'd seen this a few times before, primarily when Sia had been unconscious right before Jordan's Act and when I had berserked. *"Auras are my next suggestion. First we'll work on how to 'block' them and then how to intentionally tune into them for environmental awareness."*

"I take it back." I wasn't in the mood for something overwhelming my senses more than they already were. I wanted outside to clear my head and get *away* from emotions and overwhelming senses, not feel even worse than I already did. "I'll go to bed instead."

"At one pm? New definition of going to bed early." She didn't remotely believe me, and really, she wasn't wrong that there was no way I was sleeping this early and generally hadn't ever been much of a nap person. But she didn't have to sound so amused either. Growing up, I'd been a bit envious of other kids I knew that had siblings, but I understood more than I liked why Jordan just grumbled about his now. I hadn't ever met them, but if he dealt with something similar to Sia his whole life, he had the patience of a saint.

"Yeah, well. Nothing else to do," I said.

She chuckled. *"For what it's worth, I won't completely release aura control to you yet. But I do think making some progress would be ideal since it's similar to empathy in that there will be an adjustment period."*

That was *lovely* to find out. One way or another, there would be even more sensory stuff, and no matter what she said, I wasn't actually getting a choice with this. "Fine..."

"So that vague yellow..." Sia said. I nodded, unsure how to place where it was. I could somewhat see my own aura as right at my proximity, but that yellow Sia referred to was away yet down, not near me at all. Also, I had used enough magic to know yellow wasn't remotely near my aura colors, which were clouded-blue and aquamarine. *"That's Mom."*

Oh. "Wait, it's not limited by sight?" That's why it was weirdly below me, as if below the story I was on: because it was.

"Completely different sense. There's a proximity range like with anything, but it isn't dependent on strict line of sight. If you take info from one sense and combine it with auras, you can get better understanding like any other time you use multiple senses, however." So what was I up to now — seven senses? I missed when I thought people only had five. I guess even most mages only had six; empathy just threw a wrench into things like it always did.

I never wanted to admit it, but this was more fascinating than I thought it would've been: a meditative challenge to hone in on these faint colors and tune everything else out. "I can barely make out a like...lilac?" The color was so faint, it was hard to concretely identify. A pastel for sure though.

"Mr. Thomas."

Sia knowing everyone around me's auras wasn't at all surprising but was helpful, more so than I would've thought. "What determines how bright? I feel like mine's...super bright. Is it because it's the closest?"

"To some extent. There's both proximity and range bias, but also, raw current magipoten bias." Was bias really the right word choice? Wasn't worth arguing, but "bias" sounded more like something wrong instead of just closer and stronger magipotens being easier to discern.

Orange and light red auras approached, definitely two people instead of a multicolored aura like Jordan and me had. Outside of my own, the light red was the brightest I'd seen today. I tilted my head. Who was here?

"Dani and Mrs. Alana."

"Then the red's Dani?"

"Correct. Hers is brighter since she's had Act, so has more active mana compared to Mom and Mrs. Alana."

I didn't want to entertain Dani, but I'm sure she was *invited over* to try to get information from me again. Even when Dani didn't want to admit it, she wasn't hard to read, not now: empathy gave away what her face didn't, especially since she still didn't really believe in my empathy still somehow. She always said I had a lucky guess or something was obvious.

I heard Mom greeting them downstairs and the door closing behind them, then Dani walking up the stairs. I tilted my head once more. "Dani's can kind of blot out Mom's and Mrs. Alana's. Can't see Mr. Thomas at all now."

"Mm. As you increase in proficiency and magipoten, you'll get better at discerning and having further reach. But even now, I can struggle with interference. Like Rota overshadows nearby people unless I'm very actively blocking him out, and even then, it's a struggle." Oh great, that meant working on this anywhere near Jordan was going to be about as fun as empathy work near Jordan. Just what I needed to deal with at school.

"So is this like empathy where it's just me, or is it something for Jordan too?"

"Jordan as well, though Rota only learned how to block them,

not interpret, so don't hold your breath on Jordan being more proactive in that department." If Sia admitted a future-related tidbit, it was so sure to happen that there was literally not a reason to pretend otherwise.

Though that wasn't necessarily true, with her saying she was engaged to — I heard a knock at my bedroom door. Sitting up, I said, "Can you, um...?" The auras disappeared. There was no way I'd focus on Dani with those active; dealing with two more empathy reads — one of them soon-to-be in my room with me — was bad enough and not something I was in the mood for. I already dealt with entirely too many emotions during the school week, and Sia had my empathy less suppressed than normal at home since there weren't as many people around as at school. "Come in," I said, voice louder since I wasn't speaking to Sia.

Dani opened the door before coming in and closing it behind her. "Rough week?" Given the pity coming from her, I guess Mom had called because I wanted to go out on a walk. Dani must've been meant to *appease* me. It wasn't as if Dani was a substitution for seeing something besides these four walls, no matter how much Mom wanted her to be.

"There's just only so much time I can spend in this room."

Dani sat on my office chair backwards, leaning against the back of the chair while staring at me. "She's just worried."

"I know." Quite literally, unfortunately. I knew better than maybe even Mom herself at this point given she'd kept me up at night with her anxiety more than once so far. I understood why she was worried. I really did, just...

"What even happened during then? Like, he left, then you're back hours later... Where were you even?"

"I don't know." I really didn't know where I'd been held. Sia hadn't volunteered that information, though I suspected she knew like she knew everything else about that event. Dani still didn't believe me when I said I didn't know much of anything, though. Yet again, I clearly felt her judging disbelief as she believed she was some grand interrogator that could get info out of me that no one else had. It really didn't help that the bits I had honestly told her, she thought I made up; my injuries were one example: I should've been more injured than just the scarring, she'd said, even though she'd seen and even used some basic healing magic herself.

Her finger rapidly tapped against my chair, a fast-paced drum that did nothing to ease either of our moods. "*I* can't even leave the house now. Mom's scared something'll happen to me too." Given how rash Dani was, that wasn't as unreasonable as she made it out to be. Even Sia had barely kept her alive when things happened that one time. "Oh! I met someone at school. She's like us." Dani's eyes moved to me. "Can use, uh. Yeah."

What? Another mage? There were mages other than Jordan and myself? Dani liked to think she was one, but her current magipoten was a fraction of Jordan's, and he had Act later than her.

I pursed my lips together, unsure what to say.

"Anyone can have Act and become a mage, keep in mind," Sia said. *"There's a greater likelihood of non-induced Act for higher magipotens, current and theoretical max, but it doesn't necessarily mean their magipotens are around Jordan and yourself. Best to assume closer to Dani."*

Helpful background context but frustrating information given that Dani's "aptitude" had been near nonexistent so far, and I didn't want someone else pretending they understood when they didn't at all. "You'll have to meet her sometime. She's actually really cool — helped me with that healing spell. I finally got it after she showed it to me. So much better of a teacher than *she* is." Dani *still* had been struggling with the basic heal spell? It really wasn't that hard. Modifications made it more difficult, but not the base spell. That was near to the simplest spell I knew.

Actually, there was something else she said that should've caught my attention more. "Wait you...?" Was it really all right to use magic in front of other people? Why did the thought make my stomach drop? It wasn't from anyone else — I didn't think it was, at least — , but all the same, the thought made all the hair on my arms stand up. Sia and Rota both had been far too purposefully subtle on magic usage to think that it'd been accidental or a coincidence.

Dani's eyes further lit up, excitement in her voice, her heart racing as if to entice my own to share in the moment. "Yeah, I was talking to her, and it came out and then found out she's the same. Well. I don't know how hers happened — wasn't like whatever *she* did to me."

"I warned her. Not my fault she didn't listen."

I rolled my eyes, not getting in the middle of either's comments. Momentum and excitement picked back up in Dani's eyes and voice as she said, "You gotta meet her — I'm sure I could convince Mom to have you over sometimes, us have a sleep over like old times, but with Amalia too."

This was an in, wasn't it? A way to possibly gain some control over my life in a way that hadn't been possible since that day in June. "Could we practice like we were doing before? I think... I think I'd really benefit from that."

Not from teaching Dani magic — that was sanity draining. But as unreasonable as Dani had been in teaching me martial arts, it was better than watching my ceiling fan go around and around. It was a way I could prove to Mom and maybe myself that if something happened again, I wouldn't be captured. I'd be able to save myself this time. I wouldn't — couldn't, maybe even — let June ever happen again.

"Oh, that'd be a ton of fun!" Dani said, eyes huge. An innocence in them I wondered if I used to have, and if I did, when exactly I lost it. I wondered when it'd become not about being enjoyable or fun but solely about survival. "You're gonna love her, she's so sweet."

I didn't care if she was nice or not. I just wanted to see something that wasn't my room and never have a repeat of June again.

Chapter Six

please

It's hard as fuck not backseating cooking. Hadn't realized how much 'til there weren't other incarnations to distract me, but he's damn seasoning wrong and it wasn't even from half-assing it. Didn't realize I'd gotten better over the years 'til the past month where not interrupting him every time he fucked another damn innocent meal grated every last nerve I ever had.

Jordan winced, hot oil from the pan popping out onto his arm. Moved the pan too aggressively, but he'd figure that one out all by himself after his ass got burned enough.

"I'm heading out," Elaine said as she stepped into the kitchen. Current apartment had the exit to the unit there for whatever dumbass reason. Prob'bly 'cause the kitchen and dining room and living room're all one room basically, but other units I'd lived at still didn't put the damn exit right beside the oven. "Nothin' I need to pick up, right?"

She wanted the answer to be "no" 'cause "yes" meant she had to walk it back. Intentionally picked moments where others're too busy to be able to note down shit so she got outta bringing shit back. Hypermnesia'd been *wonderful* for countering that damn behavior. "Eggs, milk, vegetable oil — "

"Dammit, slow down, I'm not 'membering all that. D'you have a damn list over there or something?"

"Nope, also, carrots, tin foil..." Jordan added more things to the list Elaine tried to scribble down; she hadn't been prepared again, much as'd happened the past few times she asked him. If Jordan'd been less of an ass, he would've written it down in advance and just handed the damn thing over to her instead of watching her attempt and fail at making a shopping list. He'd also learn that if he gave more than a few things, she'd *forget* the rest, 'specially anything remotely heavy. Telling her two things every day worked better than all ten things one day.

She huffed as she shoved the paper in her back pocket. "Whatever, I'm late." She slammed the door shut, not bothering to lock it. Jordan's eyes lifted to where he saw her walking out on the corridor from the kitchen window view of the concrete hallway. Incredibly charming scenery for sure.

Jewel's over at her boyfriend's, and wherever Thomas was, it ain't home. Just had the asswipe of a father and Jordan left, with said asswipe unconscious, snoring on the couch.

Jordan quickly turned, checking to make sure he's the only one awake despite the snores. Seeing confirmation, he took his shirt off, glancing over his arms. "Fuck..." The oil burn's one problem; the purple bruise on his collarbone's another. "Time for the one damn thing you contribute."

"I'm not your heal-slave. Learn to say 'please' like a damn adult."

"That splatter's your damn fault."

"Wasn't. That's you being too damn rough with the pan." Technically it's 'cause Jordan's physical strength'd increased, side effect of more mana, and I guess *technically* that made it not completely his fault. Was squarely his problem though and wasn't like he just rolled over and suddenly's so much stronger. Had been gradual like everything else. *"Though brings up a great point. Once you finish, gotta actually practice some shit."*

Crossing his arms over his chest, Jordan scoffed. "Yeah fuckin' right." It wasn't like I wanted to work with him any more than he wanted to work with me. Unfortunately, Kyle'd ride my ass even more than she already was if I didn't, and she wasn't *wrong* in that he needed to know how to block auras. To prove how *beneficial* learning to aura block would be, I quit doing so for him; was the first time in years I'd seen them myself — never bothered learning how to deal with the damn things since Kyle's so efficient. His postured stiffened, the dim pink-colored aura behind him now visible. "Fuck." More colors came into view — these apartments're effectively sardine cans, so he easily had twenty different auras outside of himself. "Put it — " He quieted as a mumble came behind him. He lowered his voice, "What's the damn use of you if you're offloading all your damn jobs onto *me*?"

Dense as a damn brick. *"I won't always be here, dumbass. What then?"*

Jordan stirred the overcooked chicken. Looked like it was well on its way to becoming jerky. I couldn't believe how shitty of a cook I used to be, was kinda insulted. "Make these damn things go away. I can't fuckin' see to cook."

"Sounds like a you problem. Unless that's asking to learn how to block them, that is." Damn snot-nosed dumbass didn't get that he actually did need to know this one. It wasn't even for Kylie this time, but's 'cause if he didn't learn now, then when he'd have to learn, he'd be in even more deep shit than he'd already be in.

"Ain't my life hell enough without you fuckin' it up?"

"Cause you so try to make your life better." As if he had no role in why his life sucked. Still pissed the shit outta me, got under my skin far more than I wanted to admit. I'd never been great at hiding my feelings though, something Kyle'd always given me hell over.

"Fine," Jordan all but spat at me. "*Please* make the damn lights go away so I don't set this whole motherfuckin' building on fire."

At least he admitted some fault in his own circumstances. He ain't the passive victim he thought of himself as, and it just really pissed the fuck outta me. Guess some things still stung like fuck more than I'd realized.

Chapter Seven

indiscretions

Siani | September 6
North Opal Pines High

"Hey, we're having a fall party next weekend," Theresa said. Before being back at this time, I hadn't seen her in years. I'd forgotten about her, which made the fact we'd been in classes together consistently over the years more than a little awkward; I probably should have at least wondered how she'd been doing since I last saw her at the end of this school year. Life had been busy, I guess, and these mundane things were so distant now. "You want to come? Most of the gang's gonna be there."

More people I'd never see after this year. People I'd spent my whole life with until then, given we'd all shared honors classes. Jordan and Dani had been my closest friends growing up, but especially without them in classes with me, I had reasonably gotten along with most of the other recurring honors students.

Kylie forced a smile, shaking her head. "I'm sorry, I can't. Mom's been really strict lately, and I've got a lot of other things going on. Maybe next time." It wasn't even a good lie, and it was one that Theresa obviously didn't believe. Kylie didn't want people to realize she'd gone missing, that anything had happened, but then she did things like that where it was obvious *something* had happened over the summer. But she wouldn't talk about it. Not to Mom. Not to Dani. Not to anyone but briefly to Jordan and Rota.

I'd never been the best at depending on others, and it really showed during this for sure: no one would've believed she was fine. But what could they do if she refused to talk about anything, refused to acknowledge anything?

"Oh... okay then. Next time for sure! You've sure been busy this year so far."

"Mm. Just a lot going on." She had a very booked schedule with things like staring up at the ceiling.

Though I wasn't completely fair to Kylie and what I knew were her struggles right then: how could she reach out for something that didn't happen? How could she ask for help about an incident that no non-mage knew? It'd become a more recurring problem for me, one I had my own solutions for now, but she had to approach things at her pace. And meanwhile... I had effectively run out of anything interesting to do, which meant I was back at playing "decipher that emotion." Alas, high school emotions were actually pretty boring as well: nothing outside of stress, anxiety, and fatigue. It didn't matter if said emotion came from a teacher, student, or staff, no one really wanted to be here, myself included.

"Are you okay?"

Kylie pushed her lips to a smile as she nodded. But I could feel the smile not reach her eyes, her lack of ability to sell the lie she thought she could convince others of. "Yeah, just getting ready for things, that's all." She just focused on being a mage, not an honors student, though that was a clarification she'd never provide, understandably. "I'll see you tomorrow in English?"

"Yeah... see you then." Theresa walked away, and Kylie's smile faded as she turned back to her locker. It was finally to the last class of the day: biology. We were both always more excited for the class than we realistically should've been because once it's over, we could leave the empathy-overloaded location called a public high school. I *really* couldn't wait until I only had my own empathy to worry about again instead of the double if not triple from empathy inception I sometimes had.

Kylie swapped out books in her locker, grabbing everything needed so she wouldn't have to come by after biology. But something caught her attention, her routine pausing as she placed a book into her backpack. "Huh."

"Hm?"

"Something's weird. Like..." Her voice softened as she spoke; even her locker mate beside her couldn't have heard what she said over the noise going on. "Lianne's aura's just... strangely bright — Jordan's the other one super bright here, but I get that one at least."

I chuckled. *"None of you are that high on mana, sorry. Only reason it seems so is because the school's so condensed."*

Kylie rolled her eyes. "It's something, okay? Let me have my small enjoyment."

"What, the routine high school emotion drama cycle not enough?"

She grimaced as she rolled her eyes. "Actually, I'd prefer you tune that one *down*, not pay attention to it." Speaking of things she'd try to tune out, who was making out this time? That's one *I'd* rather not experience. Most emotions I just didn't care anymore — had a degree of desensitization — , but I couldn't block out my empathy because Kylie needed to work on hers, and I still controlled her empathy so mine was active with it. I didn't have control of a physical body, so that part was nice at least, but my cheeks would've been flushed and I knew it. Kylie just didn't know how to put things together. Not yet, at least.

Turning around, Kylie's eyes searched for Lianne, wanting to continue her game of aura tracking, this time aligning Lianne's aura with her eyes. It was good practice even if completely unnecessary. Except... I should've guessed that one, actually: the one who'd been making out with someone was Lianne, a guy not in Kylie's classes with his lips on Lianne's neck as she pressed herself against him.

"Found her." I sounded more entertained than I was, but that's only because Kylie felt so incredibly awkward as she ripped her eyes away and started toward the biology classroom.

"Miss Payne," said biology teacher snapped from somewhere

behind us in the hallway; it wasn't worth remembering his name, so I didn't bother since that memory space was better used on spells or combat stances or near anything else, actually. "And Mister Stanley. Please act like the lady and gentleman both you are." The guy scampered off, but Lianne just had a scowl on her face as she glared at whatever-his-name-was. He sighed, shaking his head. Kylie didn't get away fast enough as I heard, "Why can't you be more like Miss Rae here, who's focused on her future?" He paused before saying one more thing. "I thought you'd turned over a new leaf with your newfound academics. That's why I paired you with Miss Rae to begin with. But now you're still doing these... indiscretions." That might've been the most roundabout way to describe her mid-hallway makeout. Not sure any of the other students actually cared — well, I knew none of them did actually, from the emotions in the hallway. It was kind of funny the teacher cared more than anyone else, but he was that kind of teacher. He thought he was *helpful* when really he's just a busybody.

Lianne rolled her eyes as she stomped ahead, not saying anything to Kylie, who she passed on the way to the classroom.

Kylie tightened her grip on her backpack strap. "'Focused on the future,' huh?" Her voice softened even further. "I wish I even could anymore."

Chapter Eight

far too familiar

Siani | September 8
Caloso Residence

Kylie almost skipped out of the car; it was the happiest I'd seen her in months now. Mom had finally agreed to let Kylie learn "self-defense" from Dani more formally, allowing weekly Friday sleepovers. She thought it was good for protection since she trusted the Calosos as longtime family friends, and that maybe it'd help with whatever "phase" Kylie was in.

Dani was excited too; I could easily discern that from their driveway, and I'd been suspicious it was Dani before we'd hit their subdivision. Mom drove Kylie here, again concerned about safety. It made sense in a way it didn't living through this as Kylie — Mom was scared, didn't know how to handle her only daughter coming back from a kidnapping event with no information and seeming fine yet not, traumatized but not scared of the attacker resurfacing. None of Kylie's reactions made sense. But I didn't blame Kylie either, who felt like she punished for something out of her control; I didn't blame her learned helplessness when arguing against me, knowing I was complicit then and could do something similar again, yet she needed me in ways she didn't want. After all, she'd be alone quite often if I wasn't present, and her thoughts running free was worse than being stuck with me.

She was my own distraction too, I guess.

Matching auras and emotions, I placed who was present and their probable emotion: Dani and excitement, Mrs. Alana and concern, Amalia — the pastel yellow aura I'd otherwise not know — and anxiousness. Dani's dad must've been off on another business trip, which was common since he was usually gone more than home. It had been that way since middle school when he got a promotion to upper management for an overseas branch.

Almost as soon as the front door opened, Dani pulled Kylie down to the gym. Kylie held onto her gym bag tightly, an anxiousness that hadn't been there last time she was here. This time, I hadn't forced her here, after all: it'd been her own choice to practice anything she could with Dani. This was an attempt to secure a safety she knew deep down was shattered.

Adding another layer of irony to the situation was that the last time she'd been here had been the fight between herself and Dani, over magic and Jordan. Dani barely seemed to remember it now, the new school year and gossip and getting to introduce Amalia far more interesting to her; she didn't notice that this time was different for Kylie, that this wasn't just a fun sleepover with benefits or something done to appease me. Observation wasn't exactly Dani's strongest suite, all things considered.

Kylie's eyes rested on the owner of the pastel yellow aura: blonde hair with dark blue eyes, pale cream skin. Amalia was around Kylie and Dani's ages, taller than myself, and she had on a sundress and clogs. I assumed she wasn't participating in said workout and training based off her attire. At least I hoped not, because that looked miserable to fight in. She stepped forward and hugged Kylie, who froze from the contact. Some people truly had no regard for empathic sensitives. "Kylie, right? I've heard so much about you from Dani!"

"Y-yeah, nice to meet you." Kylie's hands patted Amalia's arms, as if that subtle cue was going to be enough to indicate to Amalia that Kylie was uncomfortable with that much physical contact. It wasn't, as expected, and instead Amalia lingered a second longer. Something I hadn't realized as Kylie that I realized watching the exchange as "Sia" was that Amalia had been checking Kylie out, eyes lingering on Kylie's face and a bit lower, and even I wanted to fidget from that realization. As Kylie, I'd more or less put together that Dani had a crush on Amalia, but at the time I felt that it was a welcome change from her attention on me, even if I hadn't connected the dots between the similarities of Dani's emotions toward me then and her emotions toward Amalia.

I wasn't sure I exactly liked having more information in this case, which actually wasn't that rare unfortunately, and it certainly wasn't going to make any encounter with Amalia easier. I couldn't even blame empathy this time, though it certainly confirmed it.

Amalia lowered her hands from Kylie, stepping back around a foot. She then held her right hand up, generating a light orb. "You too, right?" That was more brazen than even I'd do — just walking up to a stranger and using magic like that. That confidence wouldn't benefit her going forward, and I cringed knowing how much of a mistake it was. I said nothing though; it wasn't my future to spoil.

"Something like that," Kylie said, a blush filling her cheeks.

Dani didn't like being left out, so she physically moved between Kylie and Amalia as she said, "Right, let's get started."

As before June, Dani moved Kylie's body into stances and positions. But this time, Kylie followed Dani's instructions more focused than ever before. She had a better idea of the stakes, of why each swing needed to be perfect. There was no "good enough." Kylie pulled her left arm back, pushing force into the swing, knuckles stinging against the punching bag. She panted, having thrown too much of her weight behind the swing when I felt a punch into my leg despite not having control, and it happened fast enough I didn't stop the attack from tripping Kylie's sensory premonition. It'd become harder the more her magipoten increased — said increases increased the likelihood she'd detect the same things as myself and thus made it a lot more difficult to keep out of her consciousness. She winced, dropping to her feet as her hand laid over her calf.

"Kylie? The bag didn't hit you, right?" Dani walked over and kneeled down.

Kylie shook her head, eyes tightening as the next hit slammed into her ankle. That could easily be a fracture, though she didn't realize that; she didn't have enough experience with injuries, not yet. "It's not..." Her chest heaved from her breaths, feeble attempt as it was at pain control. She clenched her eyes shut.

"*Let's swap*," I said. She nodded, and I took control. The intensity was about what I expected, and the sense-reduction between actively controlling the body and just existing inside gave Kylie the opportunity to regroup herself.

Dani's hand laid on my — Kylie's — shoulder. "Kylie?"

I swallowed. "She's done. This is where she has to call it." Damn, another hit back on that same calf again? Rota would be busy within the next few days, maybe even this evening.

"Wait, you're..."

Nodding, I stood. Taking a deep breath, I blocked the pain to tolerable amounts. "She had an attack, needs rest."

Amalia came closer. "I know how to heal, don't worry."

While she thought she that was a helpful gesture and that she could prove her worth and *I knew that*, her offer just gave me more of a headache than I already had, emotions I wasn't quite ready for myself, especially right then. She thought she knew way more than she did, and there was nothing to heal in a sensory clairvoyance attack.

"Nothing to heal. It's part of her ability."

Mouthing the word, Amalia squinted at me. "'Ability'?"

"The empathy-whatever right?" Dani interjected. "Never seen it do this b'fore. Are you *sure* the punching bag didn't sock her?" These premonitions put me in a bad mood even without the pain throbbing throughout my calves and ankles. I wanted to ignore the helplessness I felt in what the premonition picked up on, my inability to do anything about those times, and the admitted foul mood wasn't improved with my and Kylie's current company. They didn't know what it was like to be Kylie, and they needed to stop acting like I didn't know what I was doing with magic. Even more so, they needed to stop acting like they knew what was best for her. "Let me check your wrist."

It wasn't even the wrist that was the problem. Admittedly, it was a *tad* bit of an overreaction, but I was done: I drew my left fist back, punching the bag before kicking it off the railing; the strikes had been targeted to the gravity lever on the chain, knocking the bag straight to the floor. Dani backed up, glancing between me and the punching bag — guess she'd never done that trick. Amalia's eyes widened, her fingers going over her mouth that opened in surprise. "Yeah. I think I know a thing or two about punching bags. There's nothing to heal, and no, it's not her wrist: it's sensory precognition, and it's not exactly a pleasant episode." I don't think I'd ever had a *good* sensory precognition attack, but that wasn't something any of them needed to know. "We'll call it here, as I said."

I picked Kylie's gym bag up and then walked up the stairs, lying to Mom about how I think I pushed myself too much this week at school and was feeling bad. She panicked and was more than happy to take us straight back home so Kylie could get a nice long shower. It was on the way out I noticed, though... there was a bright red aura a few blocks off, far too strong to be one of the residents here.

But also it was far too familiar to be a stranger.

Chapter Nine

i love you

Another week'd passed already. I waited in the training house, only bothering to turn on one light near me. Had the entire damn layout so memorized, I didn't honestly need light here. Kyle prob'bly didn't either, aura being good enough for her to find her way over to me.

Right on schedule, she opened the door, a soft creak open and then close. She let out a sigh, walking over and then half collapsing down onto the concrete against me. "Something happen?"

"You'll have some healing to do within in the next forty-eight hours, if it hasn't already happened. Enjoy." Her tone's dry, humored almost, even if I knew she found little actual humor in said situation.

I hesitated at pulling her closer. "Should you even be touching me then, if...? And fuck, should you even be out here?"

"Probably not and definitely not, but the stupid damn premonitions aren't taking this from me."

Her tone more than established I wouldn't win any fight about her well-being. She was here and we were going to spend time together, consequences be damned. I sighed, opening my arm for her to slide closer, as she normally did during these evenings. She leaned back, head against my collarbone, my left arm across the front of her shoulders. Her back pressed against my torso, relaxing against me. "Still on-going?"

"Mmn. Just fatigue now. Will be fine once the body sleeps it off." It wasn't fine at all, but I didn't argue back, just increased my grip. Her left hand rose to hold on to my forearm. "'Sides," she said, almost a mischievous tone to her words. "I tracked an interesting aura earlier."

Nothing good ever came from her definition of "interesting." "What d'you mean?"

She took a breath, easing further into my grip. "It's about time for things to pick back up. She was most definitely tracking, trying to deduce patterns. Sloppily, might I mention. She'd fail on actual recon — " Kyle kept going off on how aura could be modified here and sneaking better there and a bunch of other shit that would've put me to sleep even ignoring it was way past my normal bedtime.

"About time" though... I didn't want that time to come, but she's right. In many ways, it'd already started, prob'ly one of the biggest fuckups of my life — no. The biggest. Where there're tons of warning signs and chances to turn things around, but I was too much of a self-absorbed dumbass to realize something outside of myself. "Kyle?"

"Hm?" Couldn't tell if she had empathy active right then. Was damn annoying she always had it up when Kylie's conscious, but I got why. When it's just us, could've gotten rid of it more, but didn't mean she would. She's notoriously bad 'bout that, honing into people's emotions without their consent when she didn't have to. I'd know, being the most recurring victim.

"This whole big shitshow ain't gotta happen. Is it really the right thing? Just to sit on our asses and watch?" We watched 'cause we didn't know what effect changes'd cause. We watched 'cause the risk's missing meeting some of the most important people in our lives. Becoming who we were right then. But would we meet those people, anyway? Already had, to some degree. Was it really something we couldn't change?

Her head moved, lips softly kissing my neck; I circled my arms around her tighter, yet again wanting more than we'd do in this time. Her head didn't move back, her warm breath comforting, tempting. "I love you." She's self-righteous and whenever she found a cause, would fight to the end of hell for it. And this's a cause she wouldn't back down on, no matter what. But... if suffering could be avoided, why wouldn't we do it? Why wouldn't we avoid a huge-ass goddamn train wreck if we knew it's coming?

She's willing to stand aside, let the past repeat, 'cause she felt like it's important to who we were right then. And she's prob'bly right, maybe it was. I'd never been as confident as her, no matter how much I admired and sometimes hated her damn stubborn streak. Couldn't say the ends justified the means, was certainly not sure this's the right thing.

I gripped her shoulder tighter, skin pressing against my fingertips; always removed the gloves, craving more contact than I'd be able to get and not wanting that bit I did get prevented by gloves I didn't need.

This time, I didn't know what to do: go with her plan or oppose her. "I love you too." For now, I just needed to focus on these few hours. Had the rest of the goddamn week to ponder.

Chapter Ten

confidence

Jordan | October 14
La Petite Bistro

I should've pushed for the park instead of this French food place Richard'd picked out. He had two girls — neither I'd ever seen at school so assumed he knew them from somewhere else. One had long black hair and the other with short red hair and freckles, both with rather tight, low cut shirts that made it awkward to glance anywhere in their general direction so I tried not to, seeing the ornate off-white molding at the top of the doorway. We're in this private party room, only making it even more awkward since just the four of us, could've easily held like twenty people, and we still had an entire dedicated waiter. Of course Richard's paying like he did anytime anyone went somewhere with him. For not the first time since we sat down, I wondered why the hell I'd signed up for whatever the hell this was.

Then I remembered it's like sixty degrees out, and they'd have the damn windows open at home to air out the alcohol smell. Always sucked when it was between seasons 'cause've that, too damn noisy.

"You're *so* smart!" the redhead said. He hadn't bothered to introduce them, or really any of the girls he fucked around with. Unfortunately, if I said I had somewhere better to be, it'd been an outright lie. I never saw Kylie on the weekends, us only walking part of the way to her house Monday through Thursday; Friday she spent the night at Dani's, something she'd done for years but pissed me off more than it should've since it interrupted the limited time I already got to see her. Was worried 'bout her, hadn't been the same since June. Didn't help that Richard very obviously didn't like her, and Rotanu had obnoxiously loud-ass opinions 'bout *everyone* he just *had* to share.

"Something wrong?" Richard asked.

"Huh? Oh, uh, nah. Just distracted."

"You," he said as he pointed to the redhead. *He* at least knew their names, right? I ain't sure and even less sure I wanted to know. I'd say he treated women like shit, but they're eating outta his palm and never given me the light of day. Must've been doing something right that I ain't. "You go sit beside Jordan, too crowded over here."

I got the iciest stare from fuckin' frigid hell as her dark brown eyes moved to me. "It's uh, it's fine."

She wiggled in her chair, as if to emphasize she wasn't moving in a playful manner. Richard raised his eyebrow at her. Her head lowered as she moved over to my side, pushing around me and sat down. She leaned away from me, clearly uninterested and pissed at me.

Richard put his arm around the shoulders of the black-haired girl, and I wondered if there'd be a cat fight from the looks the two exchanged, like the red-haired girl's punished while the black-haired girl won some lottery. I moved my eyes down to the white table cloth, silk fabric instead of a cheap cotton.

Wondered if Kylie's still at Dani's? She said it'd been helping. That she felt herself improving, and she'd been able to read Dani's moves compared to where everything caught her off guard. Just needed to improve her reaction time now, she'd said.

As satisfied as she sounded by that, I wished she didn't need to care to begin with. Wished magic hadn't fucked both of our lives over, made being teenagers more hell than it already'd been.

"You can both go eat over there," Richard said, pulling me from my thoughts. I lifted my head, pushing my chair back. He sounded pissed, and I couldn't really blame him as much as I'd been not paying attention. Wasn't really polite, 'specially not for him being the one to foot the bill and shit, but just had other shit on my mind. "Not *you*," he said, as if I should've known that. "*Them*," he added as he motioned toward both girls.

Oh fuck, I was gonna get my ass fuckin' beat by those two next time Richard turned around. If looks could kill, I'd be long past dead, as if I was in competition on their joint-date shit. Was fairly certain he's dead straight, 'specially since he'd been annoyed catching a few gay guys checking him out at the park months back. Wasn't his type, he'd said, but didn't know how women're his type either with how much he seemed to hate them. I felt their eyes on us from a table on the other side of the room. Couldn't hear what they said nor did I wanna hear it in the first place given I'm sure comments 'bout me're being said and none too happy ones at that.

"You need more confidence."

"Huh?" I asked, not expecting the contemplative tone from Richard; thought he'd been 'bout to bitch me out with how dismissive and annoyed he'd sounded with the other two around.

"Actually yeah, I agree with that one." No one asked Rotanu. I ignored him, as I wished I could always do.

Richard stared intently at me, like he was solving some puzzle. "Just dress nicer, be more confident. We'll work on your speech."

"I, uh." He said that shit as if it's the simplest in the world. Just blow money I ain't got for confidence I didn't deserve. Yeah, I'd get right on that once I could afford any of it. Was newly embarrassed by my patched jeans and old tennis shoes, of the accent I had that he didn't.

He crossed his arms over his chest, leaning back. "How bad is it? When's your last woman?"

I couldn't meet his gaze. "I, uh... it's been... awhile." Never, more like. He assumed everyone's like him, with girls throwing themselves everywhere he walked. No one went out of their way to talk to me. Well, no one but Kylie, and I guess him. Still not sure why I'd become his seeming pet project either. Of all the people he seemed to somewhat respect, it made no goddamn sense why me over the other people at school and these woman and everyone else really, given I knew I ain't nothing special.

"How long is *awhile*?" His tone's strict, like he's some parent disciplining me over a fuckup. At least, how parents on TV acted; Father ain't ever had that tone with me, never gave enough of a damn 'bout us. Richard's not a year older than me, closer to ten months, though's admittedly much more experienced in dating than me. Ain't like that's hard either though.

Keeping my eyes away from him, I shook my head. "Never, guess you could say." He seemed to be one of the few people that didn't get the memo on me being a failure at life, as oblivious as Kylie in this one regard. Guess to be fair, they had a handful of similarities: both stubborn, weirdly oblivious despite being smarter than me, and had some soft spot for me that's confusing as fuck.

"What?" There wasn't any anger or disappointment like I'd been expecting. His tone's flat, like disbelief, as if I'd said gravity didn't exist or the world's flat or school lunch tasted fine every day. "It's because you've been waiting for that bitch, isn't it? Don't waste your time. You're indulging her too much with those useless walks as it is."

I kept my eyes on my lap, not sure what else to do or say.

Confidence, huh? Sure didn't seem like it'd help my ass out of this hell of a conversation I'd found myself in right then.

Chapter Eleven

manipulation

Kylie | October 14
Rae Residence

I wouldn't dare ever say it to Mom, but homework was the least of my concerns at the moment. Those sensory premonitions had been growing more consistent, and Sia probably wasn't lying when she said that it was because my magipoten was higher than it used to be, but something still unnerved me about them. If they were the future, then what was I picking up on? Was there going to be another incident like June? I couldn't go through that ever again.

But things didn't line up: why was Sia here if there was peace from now on? I certainly still wasn't really like her, not her precision or intensity. Rota was still significantly more confident than I'd ever seen from Jordan.

Stretching, I took in a deep breath. I'd been scrolling on social media for like half an hour as a break between coming back home from Dani's and Saturday training. "All right, nothing exciting is going on." Nothing exciting ever went on with social media anymore.

"You sure? I think there were at least twenty more get together and break up messages if you kept going."

I rolled my eyes, leaning against the back of my chair. "Look, I like *pretending* I get a normal life sometimes."

"For all the romance you've always been interested in, of course."

Even if I knew she was just teasing me, trying to get a rise out of me, I still huffed. "I don't want to be lectured by *you* of all people." She said she was me, but she was not at all subtle about her so-called relationship with Rota. At this point, it was the biggest dissonance point to me. How she could date a guy she'd known since elementary school? And I couldn't even begin to think about marriage. Why be tied down? Friends were all I needed, and I barely handled that right then. I wished fewer people talked to me at school, their emotions loud and concerned and suffocating.

"Mm. Of course." Sia chuckled, the sound annoying me as much as it usually did for this topic. *"First, a bit of theory. After, I want to teach you how to pick locks."* Joy, she had a full scheduled planned. I glanced at the clock on my laptop, seeing it early evening already. *"Actually, since it's near dusk, I want to do something that'll pull a bit of mana before it gets too late."*

"Pull a bit of mana" was likely far more than "a bit," especially if I got a warning. Nonetheless, I nodded as I glanced out my bedroom window. The sun had already started to set. Sure, it was basically fall so the sun setting earlier wasn't that unexpected, but still. It was almost Sunday again already, almost another week of school to start back up.

Sia took control of my body, standing to where she faced toward my bed and then she walked around a foot away from it. She held my left hand out, eyes closed. Even without control of my body, I could sense mana in the air that hadn't been there seconds prior. I heard a thud, something falling onto my bed. Sia opened her eyes, showing a leather-bound book that hadn't been there prior.

"What's...? Is that what you just cast?"

"Mm," she said. "It's a book comprised of spells and related information I know."

"Wait, all this time you could've done that instead of having me handwrite?"

She softly laughed again. "Well, yes and no. Until recently, you didn't have enough of an active mana supply without the cast taking you out the rest of that day. As well, the handwritten notes were basics to get started and fundamental theory craft, not many actual spells, if you'll recall." She wasn't wrong in that I hadn't really learned any spells besides mana transferring, Isare's spell, alt form spell, the light spell, and basic healing magic. Sia picked the book up, flipping through a few pages as she nodded to herself. I saw a mixture of the Riyatian characters I'd learned from Kisate and English; many pages were structured with those characters on the left and English on the right with what I assumed were direct translations. "To give your mana that breather, let's start with shortcasting."

"Like it's a shorter cast than normal?" Everything I knew had a relatively short cast as it was — most of the time spent was gathering mana, and that seemed like a weird if not impossible thing to omit.

Sia flipped through the book to the beginning third, thumbing through it as if she knew exactly what page she wanted. It was disorienting that something physical could be produced out of literal air and mana as it was, let alone that Sia seemed to know the book by heart. Maybe she did, if she was telling the truth about its origins. "Essentially. The idea is that you use a mental shortcut of sorts for the spell. The trade off is power: think like half the spell's cast, so you only get half the spell in results."

"Uhm. Why's that useful?"

I didn't like that Sia chuckled. Well, I rarely liked any of Sia's chuckles, but especially not ones during magic practice. "Because you don't always need the full power. Same amount of mana, but quicker cast — for instance, when training with Jordan and you need alt form but aren't using magic, it lets you go into alt form without the full spell. Isare can be shortcast as well, for that matter. What if you wanted to deflect an incoming attack but didn't have time for the full spell?" I liked that Sia thought I'd ever get training with Jordan again, because there's no way Mom would let me wander off. I wish I could've. I missed Jordan, missed even that stupid oven of a training house where we could learn together, figure this stuff out and it wasn't me stuck in my room.

"Fine, I see the benefit." There'd never be a reason for me to use it because there shouldn't have ever been another incident, another attack though, right? I couldn't even bring myself to ask.

"We'll work on actual short casts either later tonight or tomorrow. In the meantime, let's switch over to air manipulation, water manip can be later." All I really knew how to do for air manipulation was make a light breeze near my bedroom window if it was open. It'd been great when I got overheated a few times in the past few months; the downside of living on the second level was all the heat rose up to my bedroom, and it's even worse with me almost continually having the door shut if Mom's home so she didn't hear me talking to Sia. "In particular, lock picking, since it's great for precision control testing." Sia dug through my desk drawers before pulling out a paperclip. Bending it back so that it was no longer a paperclip but instead a long thin piece of metal, she closed the bathroom door before pushing the paperclip into the lock. I heard the lock turn a second later, and of course, that's when I got control of back of my body.

"Really?" I hated when she did this "learn or suffer" philosophy: Mom was home, so if I needed to go to the bathroom, would have to awkwardly explain why I was using the half bath downstairs since there's no way Sia was unlocking the door for me. Maybe I wanted to go back to that theory after all if the alternative was bashing my head against this until I got it.

"It's easier to manipulate an object with contact than remote manipulation. So yes, really, because it's something extremely light on mana but good for control practice."

I took a deep breath.

Regardless of anything Sia said, I knew I was right to complain. I was in my junior year of high school, preparing for exams and college applications. I couldn't fail because mom wouldn't let me, would make my life more and more miserable until I succeeded. It had always been that way: she doubled down instead of asking questions. It didn't matter how little I slept or if I felt scared or trapped. Sia *was* my best chance, and she wasn't a great one by any stretch, likely hiding the truth if not outright lying. She was all I had though, the only chance I could learn about these changes to me that'd been unknown six months ago.

Rolling the paperclip between my fingers, I took yet another deep breath as I focused onto my mana. What would Mom think if she walked in on me trying to learn how to pick locks on my own bathroom door? What excuse would I give? Did it matter or would she jump to conclusions only partially wrong?

I did as Sia had done, sticking the paperclip into the lock. Nothing. I didn't even feel the tumbler. "Did you break my door?"

"Nope. Quit trying to listen. You need to feel for it, control the air around the paperclip instead of the paperclip itself."

I was so not in the mood for whatever game she was playing, but I had little choice: I had to play Sia's games, or else I truly had no security for the future.

Chapter Twelve

by her side

Why'd my last period gotta be on the exit side and hers wasn't? I hated being here any longer than I already was. Plus, it's cooling down even more, and it sucked: might've hated the damn summers but the cold sucked ass so much more, 'specially since the fuckin' heat's, at highest, the minimum required at the apartment. I rubbed my hands together in my old jacket; damn thing'd gotten too thin, needed another one on top of it. At least the gossip mill ain't 'bout me as much this year. And actually, didn't even hear anything 'bout Richard for once today. Everyone else loved gossiping 'bout what they thought he liked or who he was with or who his parents *actually were*. Had heard some pretty far-fetched shit so far too, like the only son of a mega-corp. As if someone like that'd be in *Opal Pines* of all places.

Instead, today's gossip's 'bout a blonde high schooler that's a miracle worker of some kind. Was saying things like she'd fix injuries that'd need doctors and even some mild ER type injuries, and it'd be right there on the spot, no medicine or anything. Reminded me of healing magic and the times I'd had it used on me, but I ain't jumping to volunteer that info to others.

"Waiting again?"

I glanced up, seeing Richard with Stacey and Erin from my math class near him. They're cute admittedly, seemed to be his choice of the week; wondered if he's determined to date every girl in the school b'fore the year's over, but I didn't dare ask. None of them lasted long. Once he got bored, he discarded them with no emotion and moved onto the next. None of the girls even seemed to care, the few days with him being a status symbol of being *chosen* or some shit. "Ah, yeah. S'fine."

He rolled his eyes. "I don't understand why you'd bother waiting around in the first place. Hundreds more where she came from."

"*Charming*," Rotanu said. Rotanu'd been quiet 'bout Richard b'fore he transferred schools. Since, however, he'd only been getting pissier and bitchier.

I ignored him; it ain't worth trying to sneak an answer when Richard's staring straight at me. "She's just on the other side of the school, and I don't mind." 'Sides me freezing my ass off, but ain't like she did it intentionally.

Richard made a "hmph," sound b'fore crossing his arms over his chest. I saw other students — girls and guys both — glare at me for getting his attention again. Most of the guys I'd known most my life, and I'd never had a clue were into guys b'fore Richard came here. I knew now beyond a doubt though based on their frigid-ass glares being just as damning as the girls'.

I wish he wouldn't talk to me at school, had been a fuckin' nightmare with even more people pissed at me existing, taking his attention away from them. They got even more hostile to me when he dropped them so fast, like their existence's beneath him, yet consistently stayed on good terms with me. Said he stayed here 'cause I needed him, and he'd actually made things even more hell than normal, but I wasn't gonna ever tell him that. "She's just a woman. Replaceable."

"*Abso-fuckin'-lutely* charming," Rotanu repeated, as if I hadn't heard him the first time. I wasn't that fortunate.

I saw Kylie thankfully hurrying toward me, Lianne with her

as they talked about something. Not something that held Kylie's interest though, as she quickly waved goodbye and jogged over. "Sorry... Mr. Wilson never lets us leave at the bell."

"S'okay," I said. I could finally escape this hell hole 'til I came right back here tomorrow.

Richard stepped between me and her as he looked directly at me. "This's how you do it, if you're so determined." Oh *fuck*, he wasn't, right? Richard wasn't the type to take "no" as an answer, and all Kylie knew was "no." Rotanu whistled, and if there's anyone I wanted to glare at, it's him for the unnecessary commentary. Richard turned his attention to Kylie, peering down at her. "You."

"Um, hi?" Her eyes're unfocused, like she saw through us all. Fuckin' hell, Siani wasn't controlling empathy, was she? The thought made my heart race: it wasn't her fault that her ability's invasive as shit, but I hated every reminder of it I regularly got. Hated that she felt things I didn't want anyone to know, 'specially not her.

"Let's go out."

Her head tilted to the side, still not meeting his eyes as she squinted. What's her empathy picking up on? Prob'bly something to do with Richard. My heart raced at hearing him say that, but I knew the outcome. I did. It'd be the same as always, so there ain't a reason to get jealous from him asking. "Oh, I'm sorry, I can't really take detours. I have to head straight home. My mom's a bit, um, much, and... yeah."

Even after knowing her for so many years, I genuinely didn't know if she intentionally misunderstood or not. Either's possible, 'specially since most of the guys that'd tried asking her out knew to be more direct: she had a certain reputation as the one nobody could land.

I didn't know what I'd do if Richard ended up different, if she said yes to him when she'd never said yes to anyone else.

"I meant as my girlfriend."

"Oh!" Her cheeks flushed as she glanced away, first to me and then to the grass nearby. "Sorry, I'm not really interested. You seem really nice though, I'm sure you'll find someone soon."

It went about as expected, her somehow not noticing that he

already had "someone" — the entire school's in a damn bloodbath over being on his arm, somehow. Rotanu's reaction wasn't wrong for once when he snorted, though how that worked as a consciousness, I still didn't fuckin' understand.

"What?" Richard's tone was flat, not angry or disappointed. Like he'd never heard the phrase, didn't know how to process it.

"Though, I really do need to be going..." Her eyes moved to me. "Is it all right if...?"

I nodded, waving to Richard as I walked off with her. Maybe now he'd understand why I'm content — lucky, even — to just be by her side. It's more than someone like me could ever ask, really.

Chapter Thirteen

a dangerous game

Siani | October 20
Caloso Residence

I wished I could nap more. There's absolutely nothing to do lately, and I actually sort of missed contact with the prior incarnations. Even if it was just toying with Kisate, it was *something* to do; the dead had their use after all, it seemed. Comparatively, I had me, myself, and me again to talk to when Kylie was with others; after all, Kylie could barely keep conversation with me when one person was around, let alone when she's trying to mock-spar with Dani like right then. And the downside of being from the future, I kind of wasn't exactly sitting on the edge of my seat unsure how things would go. It wasn't like how Rota experienced things; I couldn't remember minute by minute plays, but I remembered well enough to be utterly bored right then.

Dani relied too much on her ability — enhanced athleticism; if she was a stronger mage, it would've probably meant something. But Dani had close to the lowest possible magipoten, so I was pretty sure her ability was effectively a placebo. The only reason she and Kylie knew about Dani's ability was because I had told them, and the only reason I knew was because when I'd been Kylie, Sia'd told me. It was a bit humorous, actually, that her ability as enhanced athleticism could've all been a repeated stable timelooped lie.

That said, regardless of ability influencing skills, Dani *had* been practicing martial arts literal decades longer than Kylie. It'd been at a more casual pace and with less direct instruction — it was generally difficult to provide instruction as direct as someone else commanding a body to demonstrate how something should feel or be positioned — , but Kylie had a fair bit to catch up on. And Kylie knew she couldn't just play catch-up: she had to be *better*. Truthfully, the quicker that Kylie gained proficiency, the better position we were in. Unlike prior to June, Kylie was focused, terrified of the inevitable confirmation that the peaceful teenage life she'd had prior to March truly was gone.

She swung a left punch at Dani, who blocked and knocked Kylie's arm out to the right, leaving her torso wide open. Kylie moved back, wincing as she positioned wrong and tripped, falling backward with a yelp. Hadn't grounded herself when she swung, and that energy had been even more offset with Dani's block and Kylie scrambling for recovery. Kylie clenched her eyes shut, preventing me from seeing directly around, but I heard movement and saw both Dani's faint aura and Amalia's brighter one come closer.

"You okay?" Dani asked.

Kylie's eyes opened back as she pushed air into her lungs. "Ankle hurts, give me a sec." Taking the sparring helmet, gloves, and feet covers off, Kylie felt her ankle. Just a mild sprain — her natural healing would have it healed in minutes, if it even took that long.

"Just get some water. Your mana will probably have it corrected after a five minute break."

Kylie nodded, but as she moved to stand, Amalia came even closer. "Um?" Kylie asked.

"I can take care of it." I shouldn't say anything. I shouldn't. I couldn't tell Rota that we just needed to let things go and then say something here. And yet... if there was one regret I had while we were here, one thing I was willing to risk changing... it was this, wasn't it?

"I need to do something." I pushed Kylie from control, though she didn't fight me much — I got the effects of her windedness instead, so wasn't surprised she didn't complain. I knocked Amalia's hand away from Kylie's ankle. shaking my head.

Dani kneeled down. "Kylie? What's wrong?"

"You need to stop using magic so openly for every little scratch." I wouldn't say why, couldn't really. But this was one of the few warnings of the future I was willing to give. It wasn't something to do with the future at all really since any mage that'd been around a bit knew better than to be as brazen as Amalia was; it was a mark of how inexperienced she was. Yet another instance of Amalia's desire to *prove herself* and show off in front of girls she thought were cute.

Amalia's head tilted. "But you're hurt — I can help!" There was more force to her movement as her hand reached for Kylie's ankle, which for the record, didn't throb any longer. As I'd expected, her body had already healed up.

I shook my head once more. This wasn't a game, and even more so, wasn't one she would win: she was just one newbie mage that figured out a healing spell because she was more naturally attuned to healing magic by virtue of light elemental affinity. She couldn't even say why the spell worked or how it functioned, just raw instinct. This was just reckless raw instinct with no regard to the consequences, ones she didn't deserve. "Don't you think it's strange? More experienced mages like myself aren't rushing to heal every scratch of every passing by person regardless of more mana and more skill?" I couldn't protect her if she was caught, not without tapping into the backup reserves as I had planted for Asuza, and that wasn't something I could do lightly, if at all. Maybe if Rota and me were together and both pulled into the reserves again but... That wouldn't happen. It couldn't, if my past was still the future, as it seemed to be.

Dani moved herself between me and Amalia. She shifted from concern to irritation and possessiveness. "Why are *you* here? Where's Kylie?"

Where did she think Kylie was? Like every other time when I had control over Kylie's body, Kylie was still here. It wasn't like Kylie could run away as a soul and leave her body behind because we both would've done that if it was possible. I'd love to not sit through high school again, for instance. Once was more than enough. "Yourself as well. It's not something to use as a talent show entry." So help me I hope that didn't just give her an idiotic idea, and I should've chosen a different phrase.

"I don't know who you are," Amalia said. Dani had never bothered to explain that Kylie wasn't "like them" as far as being a random girl that had Act. I doubted Dani even explained that her own Act wasn't even natural but forced, or that Jordan also had Act and about Rota and myself. Dani never told Kylie about Amalia's past either, so I didn't know what triggered Amalia's Act; it couldn't have been pleasant given she was on the lower-mid magipoten herself, though. Her smile very likely hid emotions that came out when others weren't around, especially as desperate for company and approval as she was. Unfortunately, playing saint wasn't going to erase whatever she ran from. "But I'm just helping Kylie."

She technically wasn't wrong. Was in a more private area than I'd healed Jordan for his own injuries, in fact. It wasn't for this incident I said something. It was for the general mentality of putting all her self-worth on showing off a basic heal spell, not knowing the dangerous game she played every time she did so in public, how rumors had already started circling at North Opal Pines High despite her not even going there.

I knew the risks every time I healed Jordan in public; I knew how to minimize them by hiding Kylie's aura, how to use a more generalized healing spell to not need multiple heals. I didn't want Kylie in pain through empathy where they both suffered and admittedly didn't want Jordan in pain for something not remotely his fault. I hadn't really healed him in months now anyways: Rota could do so in much safer conditions than myself, but still. Every use of magic I did in public was a calculated risk, with as many precautions as I could. "Just think about it: why haven't you met any other mages outside of these two?"

"What are you getting at?" I wouldn't tell Kylie. Not yet. But the time would come before we left, even if I hoped it wouldn't. For now, I acted like I heard nothing.

"I only met Dani because I helped her." Amalia was soft-spoken but stubborn — reminded me of Rota and Jordan, funnily enough. I felt the anger rising in her chest, her sweet chirps contrasting the anger in her eyes at me seeing through the mask she'd crafted, at me calling out her desperate grasp for attention.

"And besides, we're *obviously* special. Will you give Kylie back *now*?" It was a bit humorous that Dani thought I was the enemy, all things considered. I'd take that title no regrets if it saved —. Well. I could only say what I'd said. It's on them from here, this being more of an intervention than I should've done to begin with.

Amalia glared at me before nodding at Dani. "I won't help Kylie anymore, Whoever You Are. That's good enough, isn't it?"

She damn well knew that wasn't what I had meant at all, playing innocent and like a victim. That was her answer though, and I couldn't change things after all, it seemed. "Have it your way."

Chapter Fourteen

officially broken

Kylie kept glancing at the clock, counting down the minutes and then seconds. Yet another day of Mr. Yap-yap and his hate of all things modern while teaching *science* out of all things. He made me newly nostalgic for my old computer science classes. Well, old to me; Kylie didn't even know she'd be taking those yet. Either way, this man just seriously must've hated his life to have this much pent up whining.

The bell rang, Kylie quietly shoving materials back into their home. He kept lecturing, but glared at the louder packers over her. "Kids these days. No one wants to learn." Pretty sure he said that once a week; it might've even been more often honestly — when possible, I napped during his class, so it was pretty likely I'd missed a few.

"Hard-ass," Lianne mumbled to Kylie. While Kylie said nothing directly in response, she did nod. Lianne tossed her long blonde hair over her shoulder, not bothering to quietly pack up. She had the boldness of a *not traditional* honors student, and to be fair, she wasn't one.

Kylie rushed out just behind Lianne, didn't wait to appease

the teacher's ego as some of the other lingering students did, as Kylie certainly would've the previous year. It didn't help that she knew Jordan would be waiting outside in the moderately cold weather he and Rota often whined about, and Kylie felt guilty each time they waited.

Swapping books as quick as she could, Kylie then all but jogged to the exit of the school. She saw Jordan huddled closer to the building exit than normal — likely trying to catch heat from the doors opening but not wanting to remain in the actual building longer than he already did. Richard was with him, a scowl on his face once his eyes directed to Kylie; it'd been an ongoing problem ever since she hurt his ever fragile ego by rejecting his not even serious dating proposition. Two girls younger than Kylie — maybe ninth grade if I had to guess, which was entirely too young for him since he was a senior — were standing near him, curling their hair around their fingers as they told him how funny he was. I disagreed: it was far more fun to laugh at him than with him. Even worse, they had the subtly of a freight train blaring sirens, but that was how he wanted it, suffocated in affection despite knowing none of it was genuine. This was just his form of protection against getting hurt, effectively dangling cheese in front of the metaphorical mouse, something I understood more than I liked. I hated giving him even an inch of an excuse, but I got it in a way Kylie didn't, couldn't yet. She just wasn't experienced enough as an empath, wasn't aware enough of others around her and how their lives all circled themselves, not her. It wasn't that Kylie was really self-centered, but most people saw themselves at the center of their story, and Jordan had always done everything he could to put anyone in the spotlight over himself. Maybe it was even part of the reason people like myself — like Kylie and Richard — were drawn to him, the quiet, loyal companionship reassuring in a way we couldn't be.

Kylie maneuvered through the crowd right at the exit, making her way to Jordan.

"Just leave her," Richard said to Jordan. He purposely waited until Kylie was in earshot, and I wanted to roll my eyes at the pathetic pettiness. Yet another subtle as a train moment from the technical oldest, at least outside of us from the future. "We could go hang out."

"Ah, uhm." Jordan lowered his eyes, uneasiness in his tone, let alone his actual emotions. Kylie didn't get — had never noticed — Jordan had always taken the role of peacekeeper. He didn't want fights, just wanted conflict defused because he knew all too well how conflict bred violence, pain. Peace meant going to bed without anything bruised or broken, without more pain.

"I'm sorry for the wait." Maybe Kylie mistook Richard's annoyance as Jordan's. It'd been so long ago, I wasn't sure now. Richard's poor bruised ego meant he was eternally annoyed at something, and that something was especially Kylie if they were together. But Jordan's emotions were louder, always had been and likely always would be. It was easy for me to decipher between the two — three counting Rota, who was annoyed as well actually, but that also made a fair bit of sense — , but Kylie might've assumed or even mixed them.

Jordan shook his head. "It's fine. He actually let you out on time?"

"Technically." It was a generous definition to call whatever the high school students all mass leaving at bell as being *released on time*. That class was another reminder that I wanted nothing more to do with high school. "Um, so then?" Mom should've been relieved that Kylie didn't walk home alone, that Jordan was often with her. But she wouldn't have been. If anything, she was even less tolerant of him than before, misplaced aggression and protectiveness against someone that actually helped keep Kylie safe.

"Y-yeah so uh, I'll see you later," Jordan said to Richard as he turned to follow with Kylie. I vaguely made out a snap at the girls from Richard, but not what he said. They got the brunt of his tantrum this time, but the fact that they were drooling over what was almost certainly not his sparkling personality made it difficult for me to feel bad. They just wanted to use his status and wealth, were willing participants in whatever pathetic game he played there. Jordan — and I guess me, back in this time — were the only ones dense enough to not pick up on the rules of

Richard's games. It'd been adorable to observe, even if Rota's whining indicated he was less than amused.

There was momentary silence as they left the school grounds, passing through the old school logo signage. A sigh escaped from Kylie, empathic noise lessening as the density of people thinned; only Jordan, Rota, and a few other students walking on the streets around them discernible to her now. "I'm ready for this year to be over."

Jordan picked up his pace while walking. Kylie hadn't noticed that he struggled to match her stride because it'd never been something that had really happened before, but it was another cute moment to observe. "What's going on?" His head turned to her, trying to watch for expressions or something to clue him in on what had made this year so bad compared to others.

The question caused Kylie to reach for her absorption device, her steps slowing to a stop as she glanced to the ring secured around her neck. "You remember me mentioning my bio lab partner, right? That she was a bit difficult to work with?" Kylie still didn't get that Jordan would *remember* near everything she said if he was even somewhat lucid. Hypermnesia really made little remarks like that funny. To be fair, Jordan didn't truly understand the scope of her empathy or sensory premonitions either. Things they'd both learn in the years to come; I'd make sure they had that opportunity.

"Lianne?" Jordan asked. I felt Rota want to reach out. He was too soft when I was involved, regardless of if it was me or Kylie. I might've been his biggest blindspot, and it had been that way for years now — maybe even longer than I knew.

"Mm. She goofed off during our lab time, and I didn't really get what was going on in the class, so I ended up with a C on one of the pre-lab assignments. Mom ate me alive about how I should've done both parts, and Lianne wasn't going to college with me."

Jordan had a slight anger to him, one he often had when Mom was involved; he was ever torn between the envy of a parent caring as much as she did and anger at Kylie being in distress from Mom's often a bit too serious attitude when it came to education. Something wasn't right though. Blending

70

with those emotions was a caution, a fear. Hesitance. And those emotions weren't from Kylie or anyone passing by because they were too strong of a read for me.

And if these strong emotions weren't from Jordan, the only one it could've been was Rota. An anxiety from his memories, no doubt, something about right then that had him so weary. I increased the diameter of aura scans around us outside of the amount I'd been training Kylie with, making sure to block her senses from noticing the increase — would overwhelm her to pick up closer to what I normally scanned, and I didn't want to alert her to anything. Not yet. Not until I was sure, but Rota's increasing restlessness sure gave me a theory as to the coming hour. "It's weird. She's always been in my classes. Well, 'in''s relative since she barely ever shows up. Hell'va weird to go from failing out to all honors over the summer. She's in even more honors than you, right?"

"Mm. I mean, basically the same, but I have Health this year, and that can't be honors or AP. She doesn't, has something else in there, but not sure what." Kylie hesitated, gripping her absorption device even more. Made it rather difficult to get a view of her surroundings, so I expanded the aura scan out even further. "There's just...something weird with her that I can't place."

"Like, uh, her emotions?"

Kylie shook her head. I begged to differ: Lianne's emotions were kind of strange too — jealousy, hunger, resentment — , but that was another hindsight moment. "No. It's like... more instinctive. Just a bad feeling."

It was funny how Kylie missed Jordan's neck rub as he glanced away. Likely agreed with her, but he didn't want to admit it. "I mean, anyone going from failing out to perfect student over summer break prob'bly had hell'va bad past few months." Perfect student was a bit of a stretch there — honors and smart did not equate to actually doing said work. Rota would know, being far smarter than he often let on, especially when it came to anything that worked with his hypermnesia.

Also... there it was, aura scan caught us a stalker, about two miles out. That aura's entirely too bright and certainly too familiar to be happenstance, especially following along the trail.

Two other strong auras were around there too, furthering my suspicions.

"I'm taking control," I said.

"What? But — I mean, sure, but why?"

Kylie didn't fight me for control of her body. I repositioned her backpack, my left hand shifting into a loose grip in case I needed to shortcast Isare ahead of my schedule. The odds anything would happen out in the pure open were low, even with them, but I wasn't in the mood to take chances. "We're taking a detour, beautiful weather for some forestry today."

"Huh, no it ain't," Jordan said. Any second Rota would likely take over. "And wait, Siani? But..." And the faster, the better, because so help me, Jordan was bad at catching *hints*. I didn't want them to realize anything was up yet, not enough to force their hand from the poor stalking attempt.

I pushed a smile to him, my voice with a bit of a chirp as I said, "Mom won't be home for a bit longer, we can."

Jordan's fingertips brushed against my left palm, a tap, then two, then another two. Rota was definitely in control now given that was a method of conveying target information we'd created over the years. Would put us in the center, with one attacker in front and two behind us. He must've remembered the angle they'd attack in, which made sense all things considered. I definitely didn't, admittedly. "Yeah, sure." He lied better than Jordan, but he still wasn't what I'd call a spectacular liar. It was endearing, even if not as much right this second.

"What's going on?" Kylie asked. *"Mom'll kill me if I'm just hanging out."* Mom normally made it home about an hour and a half after Kylie came back from school. We'd have plenty of time to get back, though less so to fully explain a few things to the about to be rather unamused teenagers we currently shared a body with.

"You'll see," I said as a mumble, barely heard the words myself; I didn't want to risk the lack of focus splitting my consciousness for a non-verbal reply would cause. The auras continued trailing us, closer and closer the deeper into the forest we went. By now, they likely figured we knew they were around, but that was fine. A few miles into the forest, and things would be obscured. Mostly. We weren't leaving any bodies behind today anyways. I sat Kylie's backpack down by a tree, Rota setting Jordan's backpack down beside Kylie's. Stepping away from the backpacks to keep them out of the incoming mess, I sighed before raising my voice. "All right, if you're going to stalk someone, can you at least be less sloppy about it?"

A woman with neon green eyes stepped out from behind one of the trees. One Kylie already had the joy of knowing. *"Wait, she was...? But how? How'd she find me?"*

Nimaka had been Asuza's right-hand woman, the one trusted to tie Kylie when he had her kidnapped. One I'd rather contently gotten slapped to the floor by Asuza a handful of months back and would one-hundred percent repeat if given the chance. "Big words for someone that hadn't noticed otherwise for months now."

I was mildly offended at that accusation; she'd been getting increasingly sloppy and more aggressive with her tracking, but I'd noticed the day of, thank you. It wasn't worth correcting her, but I wanted to. "Unfortunately, I have a life. Unlike you and your friends there, who are aimless lost puppies without your master."

"Kyle..." Rota's voice was low, defensive. He moved his back against mine. He'd never been one for verbal exchanges before inevitable fights; he preferred to get things over with to get on with life. He often really took the joy out of moments like these I otherwise would've really gotten to enjoy, especially given I'd already gotten under her skin again. She was an easy target to manipulate, all things considered.

Nimaka's cheeks flushed. "You bitch." I'd take that compliment with pride; it belonged on my trophy wall. "You killed him."

Licking my lower lip, I shrugged. "Ah, so you're pissed your battery got shut off. Sorry, I thought you loved him, but I should've known better, my mistake." Asuza's whole life extension replacement squad was here, all three of them. "You know you were just another replacement that'd never satisfy him. Just a tool, begging to be used." A rustle behind me, toward Rota. The shuffling had been an unintentional anger response from whichever one was that way but hadn't bothered to introduce themselves yet. Nimaka was the distraction, being the only one Kylie had met.

Unfortunately, I wasn't the Kylie they expected.

I ran a more precise aura scan on Nimaka. I had a specific goal in mind for our little meeting today; after all, I'd been waiting on this moment for a while now actually.

"You know nothing about him!" Yeah, yeah. Keep getting riled up. I needed her to stand there about thirty more seconds for this spell to finish. "He took us in when... and he loved us when no one else would." How could people not love her, sparkling personality of toxic obsession that she had? He definitely had a type though given the other two were worse about it if anything. "Gave his *life* to us."

"Unlife, at best, given how long he's been dead. Though will give him credit in that he actually pulled off multiple artificial extensions on undead mana. Given he didn't seem the type to pass theory in magic studies, it was impressive for him." Somewhere in her torso? Aura was strongest there. I needed the scan to be more precise, directly at the symbol. "But he still dropped you all like broken dolls the second he thought Kisate was around. You saw it, I know. The looks he gave me over the ones he ever gave even you." Upper torso, left side. Just a little longer. They were pissed and anxious, so I just needed to bait them a few more seconds. Rota's annoyance at our verbal exchanges was even more prominent as he backed further against me, understanding my strategy; I felt his shoulders against mine, more rigid than me as he usually was in fights. He couldn't read auras, but he had both his memory and other senses to work off of for sensing the two on his side. Also it wasn't like he *couldn't* aura read, he was just too lazy to learn.

Kylie was silent, all the assurances I'd never given about her being forever safe now making more sense than she ever wanted. The quiet question that'd been hanging in her throat she never wanted to ask abruptly answered: why was I still here if she lived a normal life from here on?

Jordan struggled to piece things together since he'd only met

Asuza, but he had more than figured out something wrong had happened. Really, this was his first time in an actual fight given that the only other time had been with Asuza where he just transferred mana without any actual combat.

"You won't live after what you did to him. We won't let you!" She really meant that, didn't she? Nimaka charged toward me, likely the signal for the other two given I saw Jordan's aura spike and heard metal clanging behind me as Rota had caught the other two's weapons with Nateka, the sword locking all of their weapons in a stalemate. His shoulder-blades were higher than a second before, so he must've shortcast both Nateka and alt form; it was just about time for me to follow suit so no blood ended up on Kylie's clothes — blood would have incited questions I had no interest in answering.

The spell finally finished: mid left breast, close to her underarm. That was all I needed from her today.

Ducking, I shortcast into my own form; Isare was the next shortcast, the comforting staff resting in my grip, blade release so close to my fingers and utterly tempting to swipe. Two shortcasts back to back was a *bit* much for Kylie's mana supply, but it was nice to get away with it now when I couldn't have a few months prior. "Remember," I said. "Play nice." Nimaka glared as she tried to use her lance to lock Isare as Rota had done to the other two. I'm not sure what that would've done since I'm more agile than her, but whatever. Rota grumbled a curse that I'm pretty sure was directed toward me, but I ignored it — him grumbling during a fight was rather commonplace; he just never appreciated a good spar. Well, this was more than a spar given our opponents wanted us very dead, but they weren't the most experienced in combat.

I saw a third woman — long red hair in a bun, brown eyes with the light green outer edge life extension glow Nimaka had — charge at me while Isare was locked with Nimaka's lance, some type of saber or other light sword in her right hand. Not bad, actually. Kylie and Jordan didn't know her name — Zimihe — , but they would. Just like they'd know Sase, who was stabbed by Rota through the arm tendon. I got to feel that one myself thanks to empathy. At this point, I'd be so confused if I didn't feel everyone's injuries, but Kylie winced, unused to the pain. I pushed my weight onto Isare as I kicked off the grass, swinging my foot into Zimihe's ribs and hearing a crack. Minor inconvenience, she'd live. Zimihe skidded back as Rota swung in my direction; I sidestepped as he stabbed Nimaka's collarbone.

"Careful," I mumbled to him. He knew exactly what I meant and yanked Nateka out of Nimaka before turning again as Zimihe approached. He was clearly unamused but didn't fight me, which I appreciated given I didn't need another variable *quite yet*.

Nimaka growled. "Ignore him — just her!"

Biting back a comment to Rota about how I was the popular one *again*, I used the two finger swipe on Isare to release the blades on the end. "Think you can?" She couldn't, but she welcome to try. All three rushed toward me. "I got it," I said to Rota.

Rota said something under his breath that started with "goddamn" and I probably didn't want to know the rest, just that it was clearly aimed at me and not amused. He ducked out of the way, dodging my backward stab with Isare into Sase's abdomen. I ripped Isare upward, slicing through a decent amount of stomach muscles and probably some organs in there. It was always hard to tell without seeing, but empathy helped estimate the damage there, and she wasn't going to be walking around for a while after that one. I ripped Isare out as I sliced into Zimihe's arm, stabbing down through her foot into and through her shoe. Shifted my weight onto Isare as I kicked Nimaka's wrist and then ripped upward, slicing through most of Zimihe's ankle and leg as I re-centered Isare, stabbing through Nimaka's thigh.

I would've preferred mines, but the amount needed would've been too much mana for Kylie's current mana to sustain. We'd proven the point regardless. Raising my eyebrow to Nimaka, I pushed further in.

Jordan and Kylie weren't experienced enough to realize Rota and me had given them the opening to escape, run with their tail between their legs. Nothing would be fatal if healed sooner than later, but they needed to make their tactical retreat if they wanted that to remain the case. The longer they waited, the more critical and systemic the wounds became.

"Withdraw!" All three teleported away, likely back to Asuza's castle or wherever they lived, because it certainly wasn't in Opal Pines. I could run aura scans for the entire town and routinely did so, and Nimaka's presence had been a newer one.

For now, peace was officially broken, and the actors were almost all in place.

Chapter Fifteen

problems

Rotanu | November 7
Boyle Residence

As usual, Jordan's a little whining bitch when it came to maintaining alt form, and it'd been old the first time months ago. Didn't need empathy to know he's pissed as hell at me, but I ain't in a great mood either now that I better understood the whole shitshow that'd just played out.

We let them walk. A clear conscious choice that stung like fuck. Kyle wanted them to live so more of our past'd happen, but fuckin' hell... how much would've been avoided if we didn't? If I'd just went for one of the numerous openings that'd been there, waiting. I'd say I ain't sure why I didn't go for it, to hell with her insistence on preserving the past but...

I knew why I didn't: she ain't wrong that we didn't know what'd change with each deviation. I ain't sure I'd end up with my best friend, effective brother if I did, and wasn't sure I'm willing to take the gamble. Was a coward still, after everything.

Shortcasting into alt form, I undid the glove buttons, afterwards moving to boots. Sucky thing 'bout this whole setup Kyle did's that the clothes refreshed each time, but body stayed in stasis. So needed to wash blood out of hair and off skin, unlike the clean clothes that'd been on the form. Didn't know why it worked that way — Kyle prob'bly did, but fuck knew I wasn't asking 'cause she'd never shut up on theory this and I should've already known that. I liked history, genealogy, sociology, politics, foreign languages, lots of shit really. But not damn magic theory and ain't gonna change no matter how much she bitched.

"This's gonna be your problem eventually," I grumbled to him. Unsurprisingly, he ignored me.

Folding the pants and shirt b'fore placing them onto the sink counter, I jumped into the shower. Had to heat the damn water 'cause the water heater in this apartment sucked ass, couldn't make it ten minutes. Missed forty minute showers by myself like hell right then.

"Did you know?"

"'Bout?" I held my right hand near to the water at the shower cap. Could somewhat adjust temperature without the mental link, but ain't in the mood to bother. Easier to use the mental anchor and sustain based on it. Even while heating the water myself, couldn't stay as long as I'd like since it'd be suspicious for Jordan to be the only one getting half an hour hot showers. If I was able to hear people coming and leaving over the water, could've used that to know when it'd be possible to sneak longer showers, but water blocked out all the sound so I couldn't take the risk.

"That attack. Your memory should've..."

"Yeah." Of course I remembered, just like I remembered every other damn thing for near to the past five years of my life.

"Hasn't magic fucked enough of our lives? She was fuckin' crying when we left yesterday. Not a heads up or god fuckin' damn anything b'fore? Seriously?"

I squeezed the shampoo bottle more aggressively than strictly needed. It ain't that I like saying jack shit. But...what else am I s'posed to do? "What, you wanted me to pick a fight in the middle of the street? We got your asses somewhere safe and kept either of you from getting a scratch."

"That ain't what I meant, and you damn well know it."

I didn't want him to have a point. Refused to acknowledge

that he did. Would've happened either way, better they didn't stress 'bout it 'til it's time.

...It's a weak-ass excuse, and neither of us believed it.

"Jordan! Hurry up in there!" Jewel yelled. "Some've us have actual work to get to!"

Rolling my eyes and grumbling another cuss 'bout how Jewel's being her normal bitchy, obnoxious self again, what's fuckin' new, I hurried up. Had to reasonably make sure all the blood's washed down the drain.

"Thought all that shit's behind us. Just stuck with the damn consequences of it, not we have a motherfuckin' round two all of the sudden. Couldn't mention that those bitches just might *be pissed their psychopath leader's dead since you and Siani seemed to know all 'bout it?"*

"We're still here, ain't we? Not my idea of a joyride being stuck with you either." He had no idea how often I got homesick. Didn't wanna be in this fucked up period of my life again, but ain't like I got an option, really. Ain't like any of us got options here.

"What, so you'll leave when all this shit's over then? That what you're saying?"

I said nothing in response: it'd never be over. There ain't such a thing. Couldn't be.

Jewel beat on the door even louder. I finished up, intentionally leaving the water on as I somewhat dried off and redressed — would have to go back into alt form later for hair to dry, but could do that somewhere more alone and without a woman trying to beat down the damn door like it ain't already on its last hinges. Dropped the form once completely redressed, pushing Jordan back in control as he ran his hair quickly under the still running shower b'fore shutting it off. "Out in a sec!" he called, as if he hadn't heard her the whole time. He then unlocked the door, opening it up. "Sorry, didn't hear over the water."

She rolled her eyes as she pushed past him. "Late 'cause've you." She didn't believe him to no one's surprise.

Jordan moved to the room he shared with Thomas in this apartment, flopping onto his bed. Wasn't quite early enough to go to bed, but not far from it either. I was tempted to pretend I went to sleep to get some space from him, but he wouldn't last much longer. He stared up at the ceiling. I remembered his thoughts racing 'bout the hell's going on. 'Bout being pissed at me and Kyle and I wanted to blame him more than I honestly did. 'Bout him feeling helpless as he had to leave Kylie once her mom's 'bout home, didn't need her seeing us with Kylie and her crying. Would've caused more problems than it'd solve, and we all knew it.

"Damn magic," he said under his breath. I had nothing to say. Was yet another time we're pissed at each other yet still stuck together. Didn't have Kyle's grace for handling all this. "Might as well," he mumbled, reaching for his backpack beside the bed. He pulled out his history textbook, flipping through it as he skimmed the pages.

Studying's different with hypermnesia. Far less frustrating when I remembered each page I saw, and Jordan'd figured that out within the first few days of this school year. Like hell'd he admit it's helpful even though obviously was — for the first time, he knew answers on tests and when called on. Still did jack shit on homework, but it'd been enough to take him from C's and D's and a few F's to mostly B's with a few C's; highest he'd had since like elementary school.

Like anything, just wasn't a simple good or bad. And really, didn't matter if it was that simple: he's a mage, whether he liked it or not, and he couldn't ever change that.

Chapter Sixteen

normal high school girl

Kylie | December 2
Payne Residence

I was going to be away from home more than at it this weekend, and part of me was so excited. This was a chance to pretend no one wanted me dead: a chance to pretend the past many months of my life hadn't happened. I was just a high school student visiting for group project work. That was all. Lianne and I had a group project that we needed to work on for biology, so I *accidentally* arranged for me to go to Lianne's instead of the other way around. Mom wasn't amused, but since it was for school, she grumbled and said she was taking me and picking me up. We planned on me spending the night so we would have enough time to finish up the project.

It was the rare Saturday I skipped magic practice with Sia since I wasn't stuck in my room. I was so sick of those walls, feeling more claustrophobic than ever. I'd never been in my room this much before: I'd grown up with Mom encouraging independence since she'd always worked and daycare was expensive. I was in pre-k as soon as she could enroll me, and I'd been home alone, walking back from school by myself, long before I was a teenager since Mom often didn't get seniority with the times her classes were offered. I'd walked from school around town with Jordan most of my life, and she'd never really gotten in the way since he didn't come over often. Maybe that's why I felt so suffocated now, since Mom watched me closer than she had in over a decade. Her anxiety sometimes swallowed my mind, a pit in my stomach even when I wasn't anxious. The only other people who I'd had louder emotion reads from were Jordan and Rota, but Mom's was different from theirs.

Anxiety was a frequent guest in my brain even without empathy though, as much as I didn't want to acknowledge it. Sia would keep me safe if she was awake, but what if something happened while she slept? What if someone kidnapped me again? Asuza had kidnapped me because Sia had been unconscious; I didn't know how to protect myself, not nearly good enough to fight like Sia and Rota had that day.

Taking a deep breath, I tried to push those thoughts away for now. It'd almost been a month and nothing else had happened. I tried to comfort myself with the possibility that maybe those women died after they disappeared that day. I didn't bother asking Sia; if she hadn't given a warning things weren't over at all, she wouldn't bother giving more information now. I'd say it was a reminder that she wasn't ultimately acting in my benefit, but acknowledging that just left me feeling even more helpless. If she wasn't looking out for me, then it'd just be me and Jordan, and I barely saw him for half an hour after school now, and not really at all on Fridays.

No. I deserved this weekend where I could be just a normal high school girl for once. I wasn't having this conversation *again* with myself... at least not right now. I saw Mom pulling into a driveway, a brick three-story house, white picket fence for the backyard. It was almost picturesque of the ideal upper middle-class suburban neighborhood house. Considering her rough edges, it was hard to believe Lianne lived here.

Verifying the address versus the one Lianne had texted me, I said, "This should be it." Hugging Mom goodbye, I grabbed my backpack, which had project materials and stuff I needed to sleep over. Closing the door and then waving goodbye to Mom

84

as well once she didn't immediately leave, I sighed as I turned around. She really *was* going to watch until I went in, more uneasiness in my stomach no doubt coming from her. I wished Sia went back to blocking that out; I missed the days she would limit almost all of my empathic reads, now having a majority percentage of it under my own control according to her. I didn't want it; empathy sucked, just less than the sensory precognition did.

Ringing the doorbell, a middle-aged man with brown hair opened the door. "Oh, you must be Kylie, welcome, welcome." He turned around, shouting for Lianne. I stepped inside, seeing nice laminate wood flooring and white walls, the rush of heat that led to me unzipping my jacket, a pleasant cinnamon scent in the air. Cheesy sayings about time with family being priceless were hung up everywhere in the foyer along with pictures of what I assumed was Lianne's family.

Before I could get a good view of the family photos, Lianne yelled back, "I'm coming already." She walked from the opposite side of the house, grabbing my wrist and pulling me back the way she came.

"Um, nice to meet you, sir," I said to what I assumed was her father as she led me further back than I thought the house went and then down steps into a basement. There were three hallways, two with open doors. She pulled me into the closed one on the far left before closing it back before me.

Glancing around, I saw more light pink than I think I'd seen in the rest of my life combined. I knew she liked the color, but it was like I walked into a five-year-old's princess dream. Baby pink and white were *everywhere*, baby pink walls with white trim, dark shades of pink on the wall as decoration, a picture of white ballet slippers hung on the walls. It was nothing like the Lianne I'd met at school; her room was decorated like she was the innocent family princess.

"They have a complex," she said with a grumble. "Don't ask."

Judging by her irritation, I knew that wasn't a secret press to talk about this: she really did mean that she'd rip my head off if I said a word.

"He seems... nice?" I had no clue what to say. Sia snickered, and I wished it wouldn't be obvious to glare. I needed Sia on good behavior for the next eighteen hours because for once, I almost had no chance I'd be able to snap back at her. It was the first time that'd been a thing, at least for this amount of time.

The moment was disorienting, like I was some impostor for the life I'd always had until last March. Maybe I was now.

She snorted. "Pain in the ass, more like. Ever since Mom died, it's always 'my little girl' like I'm still six and shit just happened. And the step-bitch isn't better, always pretending we're actual family just because she's been here like a decade." I'd ask how she really felt about her parents, but my empathy assured she felt exactly as she said. For once, the unnerved feeling around her was overshadowed by the awkwardness I felt at how much she disliked her parents. Her dad had seemed nice enough — no one in the house had particularly noteworthy emotions. *Luckily* for me, I could confirm fairly standard emotions for their neighbors as well. Empathy still sucked, but at least their yards were much larger than my town-home's nonexistent one so people weren't as close together. Better only two houses than the seven that frequently happened at home now.

Lianne took my backpack from me as she dropped it on the carpet before pulling me to her bed. "Your parents are the same, right? Won't let you grow up? Your mom wouldn't drive off."

I didn't exactly appreciate her throwing my bag to the floor, but I let it go, especially under the intensity of her gaze, all her focus on me. It was the first time we'd really ever talked outside of school, small conversation here and there before or after class. "She didn't used to be like this. She's just... worried." I knew why. And I loved my mom. I just needed more space instead of her clamping down, her protectiveness suffocating me.

"Wait." Lianne's light gray eyes widened; the color was striking, not like any other persons' eyes I'd ever seen. I didn't want to mention it, something about her that just didn't sit well with me even though she'd never done anything to me. "You're *her*, aren't you?"

"Um?"

She grabbed my right hand, running her fingers over my wrist scars. "That girl, the one that went missing for like a day.

It didn't click that was *you*." Her voice had shifted from its perpetual boredom to excitement, like some chase.

I pulled my hand from her, laying my left hand over the stinging skin of my right wrist. I didn't think any public report had been made since no one else had connected the two. "I don't remember much, sorry." I moved my eyes to the beige carpet. Why couldn't everyone else have my empathy so they'd get the hint to not ask questions? I didn't ask her questions, and I didn't want her to ask me to relive that time more than I already did.

Lianne's mood quickly nosedived, irritated I'd not wanted to talk about her new fascination. "Fine, then what about that weird kid you've always been with? What's his story?"

Blinking, I tilted my head, still not making eye contact. "'Weird kid'?"

"Yeah, what's-his-name. Until Hot-ass transferred in," Lianne said. "Hot-ass" is how she referred to Richard, and the name made me no more comfortable hearing now than any other time she identified him by that name. Lianne didn't worship the ground he walked on despite them entirely too aggressively kissing by the school entrance one morning, seemed to discard him as fast as he discarded her. "Never saw him talk to anyone but you. Thought he was mute for awhile."

"You mean Jordan?"

She shrugged. "Oh, yeah, that's his name. That's your type then, the silent loners? How long've you been together?"

My cheeks flushed. "We're not together." I might've said that a bit fast, but I was tired of the accusation; we'd been accused of being together most of our lives. Sia and Rota had not, in any way, helped with my defense either. "Just old friends, been that way since like third grade."

"Really?" She didn't believe me and made no pretense of hiding it in her tone; I didn't need empathy blaring her disbelief louder than her tone already did. "Nothing more than 'old friends'? But you walk home with him like *every day*. I see you rushing out of class like it's the best thing all day."

Of course I did. It was the one time I didn't feel alone, one time when I could be myself. Maybe it really *was* the best time all day for me since Jordan was the only one who understood what had happened, what I was going through. How it felt to have another voice inside him, watching his every movement, constantly observing every action. How it felt for the past just over half a year to be like a completely different life than the one we'd known entering tenth grade. "Yeah, he's one of my best friends. We haven't had many chances to hang out besides those walks, so it's just nice to catch up with him."

"Four days a week? *Every week*?" Still didn't want empathy, yet again. I wished Sia would suppress it while here so I wasn't overwhelmed, but had no non-obvious way of asking for help.

I still nodded. "Yeah, it's just something we've always done." I searched around, wanting *something* to get me out of this conversation. "We should get started on that project." It wasn't the most graceful topic change, but it also was a fact: we only had this evening to get this part of the project that was due soon finished up.

"Forget you honors types actually care about that shit." She waved her hand to dismiss me, as if she didn't care at all. Actually, it wasn't "as if," she truly didn't, and my grade in bio had suffered so far because of it, much to Mom's — and therefore, my — annoyance. "Things've been so weird since last spring," she said, and I was completely sure I wasn't supposed to hear it.

"'Last spring'?" But as much as she hadn't caught onto hints I'd given, I was returning the favor by not catching her hints anymore. She could be the one on the defensive.

"Just weird shit. Whatever. Father's happy enough, and that got him off my ass at least." I felt her eyes back on me, even as I picked my backpack up and pulled out a binder to start taking project notes down. "Your dad overbearing after you come back from whatever secret place you don't wanna talk about?"

I shook my head. "I've never met him. It's just Mom and me." It was mostly the truth: he left before I was born, but he was apparently someone important in Congress or something. He was on tv sometimes, and Mom had pointed him out once or twice over the years. But those few tv viewings were all I had, and I'd be lying if I said it hadn't stung growing up to not be good enough, or that I'd see other kids with both parents and wonder why I didn't have that. But it was just a fact of life now. It'd always been just Mom and me, so it was all I knew.

Almost like whiplash, her mood shifted to the negative. "Just say you don't want to talk about it. Quit lying to me like I'm some idiot."

"I-I wasn't..." I didn't know what to say or how to react, how to handle her mood suddenly tanking and becoming so aggressive.

"Whatever," she snapped. "Just get on with the damn assignment." With little other choice, I nodded, but suddenly training with Sia and maybe even doing the whole project on my own no longer sounded like such a terrible idea. If nothing else, it sounded far less hostile than the current frigid climate I had on my hands. Even that stupid lock picking I'd finally gotten down had been more pleasant to work with.

Unfortunately, I was a normal high school girl instead right then, and that meant I had the normal high school problem of dreading group projects.

Chapter Seventeen

right now

Siani | December 9
Training House

Rota's aura was already in the training house; I pulled the door open, stepping in and closing it back softly. Almost immediately, I felt a temperature difference inside, a slight warmth that couldn't exclusively be explained by the lack of crisp breeze. Stepping closer, the faint heat gradually increased the closer I was to Rota. "Mm, nice and toasty in here."

"Shush, you're the one saying to meet in damn middle of the night during fuckin' winter."

I snickered, patting his arm. Downside with using alt forms was our clothes were the combat outfits, and those were admittedly not great for the cooler weather; he wasn't wrong in that a jacket would've been great about now. "We're in South Georgia, it doesn't *get* cold here, but nice try."

"Bullshit."

He'd always been like this, preferring heat to cold. Guess it made him a good fit for Opal Pines given it got far hotter than cold. I pulled his arm over, moving him closer to me. "You said you're cold, right?" Really, I just missed him so damn much: talking to him, holding him, him holding me.

"Pssh, you just came in, you're not better." I wanted to kiss him so much, but I wouldn't. It wasn't the time or place. Since he didn't move, I repositioned, placing myself between his legs where my back was against his chest. Despite his complaining and that he'd been in here heating this corner of the training house, I was already warmer than he was. "'Scuse you, don't remember inviting you over here."

I leaned my head back, seeing him staring down at me. "Since when do I need an invite?" These four hours a week just weren't enough. I couldn't take the limited time Kylie had with Jordan; she needed that outlet like I needed this one. So I sat in near solitary confinement, an observer of the world that no one else knew of. Rota was the same, I didn't even need to ask — Jordan wasn't a better conversation partner to him than Kylie was to me; our younger selves couldn't provide the companionship we each needed. If I was truthful, we both needed more than each other even, but this was just all we had right then.

He repositioned, arms hugging me from behind as his legs moved closer to mine. I felt his warm breath on my neck, his steady heartbeat against my shoulder blade. "Life sucks," he mumbled, forehead against my shoulder and neck.

"Things going great, hm?" Not that I really needed to ask; even without empathy, I wouldn't have thought his only interaction being with his younger self would go well. With empathy, well. I'm pretty sure they fought with each other more often than ever agreed on anything.

"Y'know how when we first came, and it was kinda culture shock seeing how much we'd changed when interacting with them?"

"Mm." I knew exactly where this conversation was about to lead, but I let him get there at his own pace. This time was hard on us both in different ways, his guilt and my fear. No... I couldn't afford fear, but his guilt certainly wasn't going away any time soon. He'd always been someone who beat himself up entirely too much.

"It's been so motherfuckin' hard not to take control and slap that dumbass on the damn head. Like, goddammit. Emotional maturity of a three year old."

Chuckling, I brought my fingers to his forearm, tracing mindless patterns against his skin. "No comment." Actually, I had a lot of comments, but none he hadn't heard before... and probably would still hear again, in due time.

We both knew things now that were so obvious but we didn't get at all as Kylie and Jordan: Richard really did value Jordan and genuinely thought he was helping. But he didn't know how to share because he'd never had to before. He didn't know how to be a friend, and this transition period was *so much* rougher to watch when I couldn't just write him off as Kylie had.

"I swear, I didn't feel like such a spineless bitch when I was Jordan." The frustration was so apparent in his voice, the slight rumble of his throat from his otherwise near-whisper.

And as usual, he acted like everything was his — Jordan's — fault. "He has a lot going on, and it's all new to him. You know that." Jordan didn't know how to handle Kylie and Richard, but that was okay. He would learn in time, just not at the pace Rota wanted. And even if I told Rota to be kind, to be patient, he wouldn't: he was too consumed in self-hatred and guilt to be remotely objective for this period of our lives. He saw Kylie in pain and his brain immediately honed in on that, which was as innocent and sweet as ever. But it wasn't right — to himself, to any of them really.

"Yeah, between his bitching and being such a bitch, books his schedule right up." His arms tightened around me. "How's she holding up?"

"She'll be fine." I kissed his arm, resting my cheek against his forearm as I closed my eyes, taking in the moment. His cool skin, the scar on his right forearm I'm pretty sure I had caused during one sparring match. We each had more than a handful of those to be fair. "I am, after all."

He snorted. "That's debatable as fuck."

I rolled my eyes, bringing my fingertips against his arm as I traced mindless patterns once more. "All this is making me miss home more than normal, though. It's spring, isn't it? When...?"

He nodded. "May 17th."

That's even less time than I thought. We had just over five months left. Yet... these last five months were the worst by far. I held onto him tighter. This wasn't enough: I missed home, the family I had gained. I didn't want to see what laid ahead, didn't want to know the future this time. I wanted to be unaware, blissfully thinking the future was promising instead of bleak. I wanted the naivety to believe that things got better, that the sun wasn't just now setting to dusk, dawn far off. "It's so soon, yet so far." He kissed my neck, just once, so softly, his somewhat chapped lips obviously wanting to linger but not doing so. I placed my hand into his, not feeling skin through the gloves he had on. "I think it's getting to me, being alone all the time. More time with my thoughts than I should honestly get."

"You're telling me." He scoffed, his forehead against the back of my right shoulder. "At least your younger self ain't such an idiot."

I playfully popped his hand. "Stop that, I happen to be rather fond of who that idiot becomes." I didn't want to talk about our younger selves anymore. I wanted to just be *Kylie* and him *Jordan* for this brief moment, even if those were names we couldn't claim in this time anymore. "I wonder what's she's doing right now?"

"Like, now-now, or...?"

He didn't need to ask who I was talking about. It was a feeling of home I appreciated right then: context that didn't need explaining, a reminder of those waiting for us back home. "In our time now. I have a good idea of this time's now, and I don't really want to think about it too much. And I wonder how long we've been away for. I'm not going to be amused if we go back and it's been like fifty years." It wouldn't matter, of course, since I had no control over that either way, but I dreaded the thought regardless.

He snickered, me shaking from his laughter since he held onto me for support. "'Cause we get a lot of choice in the matter."

"I know that. But still. Or will it have been like ten minutes? Of all the things the spell was unclear on, time passage was more up there than I really appreciated."

"May, huh?" he said. "I can't tell if I can't wait or am dreading it."

I kissed his cheek and almost lingered but caught myself before I did. "I vote for both."

Chapter Eighteen

victory

I took a deep breath. After months of work, I frequently tied Dani when we sparred. She'd been none too happy about it too. While she said she was proud of the progress I'd made in such a *short* period of time, as she frequently reminded me, my empathy gave away her actual feelings on the matter. I couldn't stop, couldn't spare her ego on this. I *had* to get better: just being at her level wasn't good enough. I had to be *better* than her.

As good as Sia.

That said, I really wished she'd just accept my empathy instead of ignoring it still because it'd become grating for her to snap at me that nothing was wrong. I'd given up with that fight because ultimately, I just needed to focus on improving, but it still made me want to snap back more often than I'd like to admit. It also didn't help that I always felt claustrophobic with the stupid "sparring gear" we wore *for safety*. I had a helmet, shoulder pads, gloves, shin guards, and these weird padded "foot guards" as Dani had called it. I felt like I was covered in the middle of a giant marshmallow, hated it as much as the first time it'd been shoved on me. I didn't care if I got bruised up.

Dani refused to listen to me as she kept stressing *safety*, as if I'd have that in an actual fight.

Amalia sat on the side bench where our water bottles were, chin resting on her knuckles as her eyes went back and forth between us. She had no interest in learning, just liked watching and then healing Dani; she refused to touch me at all after Sia had snapped that one time. That didn't matter: if something needed healing, I could do it myself.

I brought one hand over my heart, other hovering in front of me. Dani made the first move, throwing a punch at me; I dodged to the left. As if she moved in slow motion, I calculated her turning to her right, toward where I dodged. Instinct urging me to sweep my leg out, I knocked her off balance. She recovered before she fell but certainly wasn't amused.

Steadying my eyes, I again estimated her trajectory. As she rushed forward, toward me, I adjusted not a third of an inch to the side as I kicked her chest, knocking the breath out of her. I followed up with a punch to her lower stomach, which knocked her to her knees. I almost swung again before realizing she was panting on the foam pads.

I won: a victory in sparring. Maybe she'd try to say she could keep going or that it didn't count or whatever — she'd pulled that more than once before — , but outside of natural reflexes, there was no way I used any type of magic in that. I'd defeated her in a spar, and I was barely winded at all.

She didn't take my outstretched hand to help her up, moving her eyes away from me as she forced air through her lungs while resting on the mat. "You've improved." It was quiet praise, but praise all the same. It was the first time since I'd started practicing — even before the June incident — that she had genuinely praised me, astonishment but not spite for once.

Whether she meant it to be or not, her statement confirmed she had nothing further to teach me. But I was still nowhere near Sia's level: I couldn't be content with just being able to pin Dani. I needed to practice actual combat, with Sia, with Rota and Jordan, like we'd started in early June and I hadn't been able to do since. I needed out of this marshmallow protection setup, where I struggled with perception and speed.

Ultimately, I needed back in that training house. "I need a favor."

Her eyes on me, she asked, "What? I already told you, the protective gear is necessary. We're not removing it."

No, it wasn't. That's the whole point of healing magic in the first place. I didn't argue again though, instead tightening my fists through the gloves as much as I could. "Cover for me — just a few hours, saying I get here at normal time instead of later."

"You're ready then," Sia said, as if she knew the realization I'd come to. She likely did.

"What? But both of our moms will *kill us* if..." If we were caught, both our moms would be furious. Neither would've tolerated us sneaking around and lying about my location. Who knew how long we'd be grounded for if they found out. But...

I brought my eyes to Dani, meeting her gaze. This was my best shot. Only shot. I couldn't back down, couldn't be a *good girl* because that'd just leave me dead. "I *need* to get magic practice in, more than what this can cover. And I'll still be here on Fridays. Just let us practice more Saturday morning instead of right after school." Mrs. Alana wasn't ever home until six or seven at night — as long as I made it here before then, only Dani and Amalia would realize I wasn't coming straight from school. Even Dani's dad wasn't home before six thirty, having an hour commute into and from the office. But Dani had to back me up on this, because if she said there was a gap, I'd be instantly caught.

Her bottom lip opened, but no words came. She was scared, lonely: feelings I knew all too well lately. I hated I caused them, but I had to do this, no matter the cost.

She nodded. "A-all right. But be careful. And don't be late, 'cause we'll both be grounded for life if we're caught."

It was the chance I'd been waiting on since the end of June.

Chapter Nineteen

feathers of silk

It'd been b'fore the kidnapping since I'd last been here with Kylie. Was still too soon, but instead of being hot as fuck, was freezing as fuck, which ain't at all an improvement. We'd walked together here from after school; Siani apparently had an idea of what we'd do, and it didn't require other clothes, or that'd been what Kylie said. Had me suspicious that it'd be another damn theory lesson 'cause I doubted they'd actually give us a valuable heads up on anything. Couldn't ever be assed to ever do something useful like that.

Kylie's eyes glazed over, as if lost to another world. Wondered what Siani's talking 'bout to get that kind of reaction from her when she'd almost sounded excited for this hell-activity on the way here.

Her left hand reached for her absorption device, gripping it softly from where it'd been hiding under her t-shirt. "I'm not relaying all that."

That's a goddamn wonderful start. The fuck lecture I just missed and apparently ain't gonna get the pleasure of continuing to do so?

I saw her eyes stare straight at me, no longer the timidness of moments prior. Had Siani taken over as Kylie'd indirectly asked then? "So we're going to work on large mana draws. Should've done it earlier, but is what it is. The goals are to summon glyphs and then wings. I just want you both to get familiar with how to control both and dissipate the mana out." My thoughts drifted back to that day, in that castle: the last time I'd seen a "glyph," the first time I'd ever seen or felt humanoid wings, and they'd been attached to my goddamn back like it's natural and not a freak mistake. How soft Kylie's feathers had been against my arm, like I'd always imagined silk to feel.

But she's meant to be special, spectacular. I ain't.

Her eyes stared straight at me, calm and precise. It's like she read my every thought, every increase of my heart rate at the idea of dealing with any of this shit. "I, uh. I ain't no good at..."

She shook her head. "You'll need to go into your alt form — Rota's simulated form. From there, Rota should be able to help you while I'm helping Kylie." Not only's she ignoring I just said I didn't wanna, but now she's wanting me to work with Rotanu. Fuckin' great. And Siani didn't really take "no" well, as I'd heard Kylie complain numerous times.

Her body language softened, so I assumed Kylie had control again. She took a deep breath, soft words coming from her lips, "Riyati, obey your mistress's command, activate withdrawal." The Kylie I knew, wearing a zipped up jacket and jeans and sneakers, was no longer there. Siani's there instead, or at least her body was, the same appearance I'd seen back in March when all this shit started. Kylie nodded at me as her fingers brushed against the gloves on her hands, as if testing the leather. She shivered, rubbing her gloved hands against her bare upper arms.

I didn't wanna assume Rotanu's form. Hated it, hated he looked at all like me, hated I even could have his form instead of being in my body. "It's okay," she said, as if she had any idea why the idea scared me shitless. I understood what Rotanu meant by emotions didn't indicate thoughts and hated I agreed with him. That even if she had empathy, she didn't understand a goddamn thing 'bout how terrifying this shit was to me.

They're all waiting on me; my throat felt dry's fuck as I

mumbled the phrase to assume Rotanu's form: "Ice and fire, merge into one, release." Immediately noticed as I'm even taller than her, as my arms're bare and I have gloves on and pants and boots and longer hair tied back. As I looked like Rotanu did in the subcon, except with fancier clothes. I kept my eyes to the concrete as I nodded. Didn't wanna be here, didn't wanna be dealing with this shit.

"Sia said one at a time, so we can spot each other. I'll, um. I'll try first." I nodded again, didn't wanna bring my eyes up to her but didn't wanna get bitched at either so I hesitantly did so. Kylie held her gloved palm out, eyes focused on her hand. Her lips twisted into a frown as she stared at her hand even more intently. Nothing happened. She huffed. "Well, your 'assistance' sucks." If she struggled with Siani, I had no shot in hell of doing whatever Siani wanted me to do with Rotanu. She rolled her eyes, brushing bangs from her face b'fore taking in a deep breath and nodding. Closing her eyes, her fists tightened; a slight gasp of air escaped her lips. I tensed from the reaction — was she in pain from this shit? Had magic fucked her again?

A glyph opened, her hair swaying from the gusts of wind, lines of water wrapping around the symbols etched into the glyph, colored to her aura. Her feet left the concrete as the wind held her. Her eyes opened back, dazed and unfocused. I saw characters I faintly recognized as Riyatian but ain't able to translate, never having heard their English equivalents, circle around, as if etched into layers and sub-layers of that glyph, with her at the center.

"You okay?" I stepped closer but didn't know if I should reach my hand out to her — that glyph's still opened, her suspended within it. Would it hurt me? Could she even leave it? I knew jack shit 'bout any of this.

"Mm," she said, eyes focusing more as they moved to me. "It's... comforting, actually. Like an absorption device's warmth, but all around me."

That sounded terrifying's fuck, not comforting.

She nodded, I guess to Siani. Tightening her left fist, the glyph disappeared, as if it'd never been there. As she's back with her feet on the concrete like b'fore.

"Guess it's our turn, joy." Rotanu sounded as amused to work with me as I was with any of this shit.

I didn't argue though; something 'bout how intently Kylie watched me, like my success affected her somehow. Didn't know much 'bout magic, but knew enough that focusing on my hand ain't actually the important part, just's an arbitrary anchor of the focus.

But what if Rotanu sabotaged me again? What if I couldn't do this thing they expected? I'd look like a complete dumbass in front of them all. I swallowed, balling my fist, unused to the leather gloves or any gloves, really. Focused on pulling mana from my absorption device, as I'd done that one time in the castle, when that bastard'd made me see that shit I still remembered entirely too well. Flames obscured my vision, ice shards around my limbs, mostly similar Riyatian characters again in layers and sub-layers, colored in my aura. I whimpered from the sight, my heart racing and shallow breaths from my lungs: sure, I succeeded in summoning the glyph, but this'd scared the shit outta me, unsure what to do with any of this. Of the flames being warm but not burning, of the ice refreshing instead of biting. It expanded larger, a sharp gasp from my lungs as my body suddenly stung.

"Shit, sec." Rotanu took partial control as the glyph died down. I dropped to my knees, panting.

A soft hand rested on my shoulder — was it Siani? Seemed too direct for Kylie. "Bit too much mana forced in at the end there, but that's the idea." Definitely Siani. She chuckled, offering her hand out to help me stand. I took it, winded breaths and unsteady legs, like I'd just ran a PE final. "Catch your breath while I work with Kylie on wings next."

This's the easy part, and I already felt like shit. I didn't want those goddamn things back; the few minutes I'd had them back at the castle'd been a mistake as it was.

She stepped back from me, must've swapped with Kylie since I heard a few soft mumbles of agreement. Her fists balled, and then she huffed. Another glyph from her, but it quickly disappeared. How'd she already master doing that? Even if I wanted, ain't sure I could do it again so easily, consistently.

102

Feathers stretched out, clouded-blue and teal, wings attached to her as they'd been that day. Her cheeks darkened, and I couldn't pull my eyes away from how adorable the expression on her face was, a shyness I'd never really seen given how apathetic she'd always been 'bout her appearance. Her left hand pulled her absorption device from where it'd been hidden under the vest, fidgeting with it as I watched her wings twitch and fidget, adjust with every breath and movement of her other limbs. "It's, um. It's a bit strange." I didn't know if she's saying that to me or Siani. She turned around so her back was to me, grabbing her braid forward. "Um. What's it look like? Like, um. They're actually not heavy somehow despite being so *big*, but it's like... I feel sensations from them, like I would on my arm or leg or something."

"Uh." I didn't know how to answer. Was like she'd always had 'em, part of her body, seamlessly extended from her shoulder-blades, her vest tapered in so the fabric didn't interfere at all. Was fuckin' terrifying considering they hadn't been there five minutes prior. "Trying to look at your shoulder blades. Is it okay to, uh." I ain't sure why, but there's something 'bout the idea of touching them that had my heart racing, my cheeks flushed.

Nodding, she pulled the braid even more forward. My heart raced even more as I removed the glove from my right hand and felt the silky feathers against my calloused fingertips. I saw her left wing twitch, pressing against my fingertips. Wait, she said she *felt* from them. I had too, that one time. Swallowing, I pushed feathers aside as I inspected closer to her shoulder blades as she'd requested. As my fingers touched about an inch and a half from where I could see human skin, she shuddered, a rapid inhale as her posture stiffened. I yanked my hand away. "Shit, I didn't — did that hurt? I'm so sorry, I didn't..."

Rotanu snickered, and I would've argued 'bout *what* was so damn funny if I hadn't been more concerned for Kylie at the moment.

She shook her head. "It was just... intense. Not bad, just wasn't expecting it, sorry. I'm expecting it this time." Yet I noticed her cheeks're flushed and so're mine. She continued standing there, waiting, so back into this terrible idea I went.

I moved my fingers back to where they'd been, watching as

her posture yet again tensed. Something 'bout this whole thing's hot, and that made it even worse — was it 'cause she's asking me to touch her back? I didn't know, just tried to push my thoughts away 'til later if ever again. My fingers brushed through feathers that dropped to the concrete and then disappeared 'til I finally felt a connection to her shoulder blade muscle, bone underneath. But the wing's connected through that muscle or bone, ain't sure which, like it'd always been there. I heard her gasp once more, the sound causing my cheeks to darken even more. Felt my ears burning, likely as pink as my face. "It's, uh. It's like they're permanently attached, right at your shoulder blade." I pulled my hand away, memories of her feathers replaying across my fingertips despite no longer touching her at all.

Shuddering, she nodded as she pushed the braid back and turned to face me. "Now Sia's going to help me *get rid of them*. Right?"

But if Kylie's done, if she got rid of them, then... it'd be my turn to look like that. To *feel* from those damn things. I stepped back further. It ain't like I had a choice. I knew it: between Rotanu and Siani, they'd make me, gave no damn 'bout my feelings in this. Still ain't comfortable with my symbol, freaked the fuck outta me and these things're so much more drastic of a change to my body.

Kylie tightened her eyes, and her wings disappeared, as if they'd not been there seconds prior. She smiled at me as her eyes opened back up. "It's not that bad, promise." It was though. Yet another confirmation I ain't human, am a freak.

Rotanu sounded bored as he said, *"Do like you did for the glyph, but push it a bit more. I'll spot so won't overextend mana and make a vacuum this time."*

While it's *nice* of him to say he's doing his damn job for once, that didn't actually comfort me. I felt my heart race, panic set in. Kylie reached her hand out, her gloved hands touching — almost holding — my bare one. "It's okay. You did it once before, it'll be all right."

It ain't all right. I pushed mana to get Rotanu to shuddup but in doing so, burned her, her hands jerking away as she yelped. My eyes widened as I saw burn marks across her fingertips — some purple from frost burns, others charred flesh.

I hurt her.

Siani must've taken over as her eyes no longer watered, instead her left hand laying over her right, then in reverse, the burns disappearing b'fore my eyes.

"I-I can't." I didn't want Rotanu's body. Didn't want to hurt her. Didn't want to be here at all. All of this's so goddamn wrong. "I can't do it. Sorry."

A soft smile pulled at Siani's lips as her eyes rested on me. It's the same expression she'd had that day she healed me in class and said she wouldn't tell Kylie. Like she knew everything I'd ever thought. "Another time, then."

Even if I nodded, I hoped that time'd never come.

Chapter Twenty

two for one

Sia directed most training sessions, but there was one subject in particular Rota *always* took the lead on: Riyatian language lessons. It was the one time his knowledge and enthusiasm *far* exceeded Sia's; she just mentioned that it could be helpful understanding the "why" on parts of spell theory and for working with existing spells, but she seemed otherwise pretty uninterested. And it wasn't that Jordan secretly wanted to learn Riyatian and hadn't ever mentioned it: he was just as bored as I was, his boredom a stark contrast to Rota's enthusiasm as far as empathic reads. They were the only two I could pick up in the training house, so they made it really easy to decipher things for once.

"So English, we indicate singular tense on nouns with an 's' typically. Riyatira handles it differently." Another thing he did during these lessons was switch Riyatian and English words mid-sentence randomly. Sia said it wasn't intentional, he just had a level of fluency that unless we pointed it out, he wouldn't notice he'd switched; it wasn't a problem when just speaking one of them, but apparently it'd been a recurring problem when he worked with both at once. That was another of those

107

instances, with Riyatira being "Riyatian," in this case referring to the language. "Tense and number can be gotten from prefixes and suffixes added to the base word. So like, in this case, Riyatira is Riyati, with the 're' adding in possession, and's how the language itself's referred, even though the actual correct translation'd be closer to Sir Riyatira."

I'd always gotten to skip foreign language classes in high school, and now I wished I'd skipped this one too. If it wasn't for Sia's reputation on prioritizing practical application and not fighting Rota like she had Kisate back almost a year prior, I would've — well, nothing probably, given that I doubted Sia would've let me just bail on him and I needed Jordan as a partner in all this. But still. I hated these abstract grammar concepts almost as much as the raw memorization work he wanted from me.

"Remember this for when he goes off on me for magic theory lectures." I hated I understood what she meant: Rota frequently teased over Sia not being concise, but he wasn't really any better when it came to language lessons.

"So you'll end up with prefixes and suffixes on the same word sometimes. Makes things a pain in the ass at first, but once you get used to it, actually's super helpful 'cause it's almost always consistent compared to like, English, where it breaks its own damn rules all the time."

I pushed my tongue to the roof of my mouth, doing my best to fight back a yawn. After being at school all day and the onslaught of emotions from everyone in said school, the relative peace of just Rota and Jordan's emotions while sitting and listening to Rota lecture was really making me drowsy. Even if I knew I needed to focus — Sia wouldn't have let him talk this long if there wasn't anything important in what he said — , I still really needed to move around soon.

Unfortunately, I also knew it wasn't optional to learn whatever I could from Sia and Rota. It was the only chance I had at survival, no matter how mundane the current lesson was.

"Can I?"

Nodding, I felt myself be pulled from control a moment later. "Can we change it up? Only have about an hour left."

"Oh, uh, sure. Sorry, lost track of time." Rota rubbed the back of his neck, a sheepish chuckle. The friendly expression faded almost instantly to a more neutral one. He must've pushed Jordan in control.

"I figured." Sia seemed more amused than mad, unlike when she'd fussed at Kisate for essentially the exact same thing. "We're going to start with mild sparring. Right now, the goal is to just get used to the concept, though you'll both need alt form just for the sake of not ending up with bloody clothes."

Jordan's anxiety spiked at the word "blood," though I can't say mine was much better.

It didn't matter though. I had to do this. I *would* do this. There was no alternative if I didn't want to be kidnapped and almost die again. The women that attacked that day didn't seem to want to kidnap me based on the ambush. Instead...

They wanted us dead. Me dead.

"How's that even work?" Even if Sia planning on injuries didn't kill some of my resolve, I barely knew how to swing Isare without hurting myself. What if I gave Jordan a concussion? Or what if I accidentally released Isare's blades and severely cut him? It wasn't rare for me to slip on the blade release without meaning to.

"We'll walk you through it," Sia said, pushing me back in control. Guess that's all the explanation we're getting. Maybe Rota was going to be more forthcoming, but I didn't have much hope since this seemed to be Sia's part of the lesson. It was more immediately practical, but also more terrifying.

Taking a deep breath, I felt the air move through my lungs. The words I'd practiced so much in my room. They easily came to me: "Riyati, obey your mistress's command, activate withdrawal." My aura spiked, my body replaced with Sia's form — my "alt form." Jordan was still in his own form, so I tilted my head to the side.

"I'm just gonna work like this." He shifted his weight, eyes away from me.

"But what if you get hurt?" The whole point of us using alt forms was to not damage our clothes or hurt ourselves, something much more likely in our own forms. Wouldn't him coming home with blood all over his jacket be a problem? Mom would've had a fit, asked questions I had no way to give a great answer for.

He shook his head once more. He'd been on edge since the discussion about wings the other week.

"It's fine," Sia said. *"If it's what he wants, we'll work off it."* If that'd been me, there's no way she would've let it slide. But whatever. *"Summon Isare. Once he summons Nateka, we can start the next phase."*

"Aren't we going to have padding or...?" At Dani's, I had that stupid "sparring gear," but right here's far more of where I wanted it. Even more so as I saw Jordan grumble but cast the spell for Nateka, the sword forming in his right hand. His eyes were downcast, to the concrete, but his heart raced as much as mine — probably made mine race even harder because empathy was great like that.

"This is where the healing magic comes in, not whatever Amalia's doing. Better to get the experience in healing more advanced injuries now anyways, so really is a two for one." While I couldn't deny her logic and knowing more advanced healing magic was beneficial, there was a bit too much pep in her tone at me getting potentially banged up from this.

"Isare, head your mistress's call, summon forth." I braced for Isare's presence, preparing to grip the staff with both hands — that lesson had only taken once.

"Grip for striking."

It felt surreal and awkward and wrong, preparing to strike at Jordan. His left hand moved to his right, holding onto Nateka's handle. Preparing for testing a strike, I swung, not intending to hit him even though the swing was in his general direction. His heart raced as he whimpered, bracing for impact, clamming up while awaiting pain but not raising Nateka in any type of blocking position. I hadn't ever seen such a reaction from him before. "Oh, um, sorry. I was just testing my grip."

"O-oh." His voice shook, gripping Nateka to the point his knuckles and fingers were pale. I couldn't place the emotion — some type of terror, but I didn't understand why.

I set Isare down, laying my left hand over his shaking hands.

"Hey, you okay?" Something stabbed into my lower back, painful, piercing. My eyes widened before I clenched them shut.

Another one. These sensory premonitions had become even more frequent lately — I wasn't sure how much Sia blocked now or if she didn't block anything from the premonitions anymore. I winced, hands rushing to where there's *nothing*.

He dropped Nateka, clanking sound echoing through my ears and stinging. His hands went to my shoulders. "Kylie? W-what's wrong?" My heart raced, and it actually was because of myself — or rather, a reaction to this premonition. I lowered my forehead to his shoulder, allowing the pain to pass. I felt a punch to my cheek but I didn't need to look to know it wasn't swollen. "Kylie?"

"Sia, can we...?" Sometimes Sia took control of my body during these premonitions since she could stomach the pain better.

"Mm. Just until it dies down though. Need to continue practicing after." I wasn't thrilled about that given these typically left me exhausted, but whatever, I'd take anything that wasn't me dealing with the full effects of the premonition right then. I nodded.

She shook over, bringing a full breath through my lungs.

"Kylie?"

"She's mentioned before that she has two abilities." Jordan nodded, though even with reduced sensory feedback from both my body and empathy, I felt him jump and gain a sense of uneasiness as he realized Sia had control over my body. "This is the other. Sensory precognition, where we feel the future. It'll pass in a few minutes, just a minor attack."

I didn't want to know what a "not minor" attack was when these were the minor ones.

"Should, uh, should he...?"

Sia chuckled as she closed her eyes. "It's fine. Just give us a few minutes."

He nodded, but his grip tightened as I felt him step closer. "Quit being so damn stubborn." That must've been Rota. He shifted her, hugging her. The uniform pressure helped block out the throbbing across my cheek and lower back.

"Psh. Worrywart."

"One of us has to be."

Chapter Twenty-One

useful

Jordan | January 20
Boyle Residence

I wanted to institute a new family rule: everyone's stuck taking their own damn laundry down to the wash and dealing with it themselves. Tired of finding Thomas's shit in my loads just 'cause when Elaine or Jewel took all the laundry down, couldn't tell the difference between our shit. They'd barely been even dealing with laundry to begin with, me constantly getting stuck with it 'cause they're *too busy*.

As if I ain't busy too. Yet the one time this month they'd handled it, yet again had Thomas's damn shirt in my clean clothes again.

Rubbing my aching right wrist, I bit back a grumble. Damn sword'd made my arm feel like jelly again — was one thing when it's swings against air, a whole other against someone else pushing back I had the *joy* of learning the previous day. Hated the confused glances from Kylie every time I braced from impact, the words she didn't know how to ask.

Guess I'm just lucky she didn't put things together.

"Once I'm finished with laundry, gonna be your turn," I

whispered. Rotanu'd better get on healing this — I knew he had to feel it too.

"Ain't nothing to heal. You're not injured."

"Bullshit." Technically he might've been right, but my damn wrist and calves and upper arms hurt like fuck again. This'd been like the summer but worse somehow, with them three against me. They kept pushing for those damn sessions, and they just kept going and pretending like that time I cut into her shoulder ain't terrifying's fuck. I'd never heard her wince like that b'fore. They wanted us to repeat it again.

Kylie wanted these damn sessions now too. As if they did something 'sides make our bodies ache and waste time and freeze our asses off.

Found another of Thomas's socks, so I threw it on his mattress. Didn't care what he did with it from there; ain't my problem.

"That's 'cause you worked the muscle, not 'cause something's injured. Try again."

I rolled my eyes, folding more clothes and placing them against the wall by my mattress — we'd been here long enough I bothered to stack things properly, but still didn't change the fact that even if we had a dresser, ain't room in here for it. So I did as I'd always done and just folded clothes onto organized piles on the floor. Thomas, in comparison, just had a sea of clothes around his mattress that we both tripped on every damn day, even worse if I needed to piss during the night. Is how half the time, I ended up shoving his clothes into a garbage bag and moving it outta the fuckin' way but also he's fourteen and should be able to put up his own damn clothes at this point.

Clothes all folded, I then straightened blankets from where they'd been messed up by clothes on top. "What's even the point of you being here?"

"Sounded fun at the time."

At least Siani's competent. Whatever Rotanu was, it ain't useful.

I heard banging at the front door, so I sighed and walked over, opening the door. Jewel helped Elaine carry back groceries this time — must've been the monthly trip to restock on cleaning shit and nonperishables. Jewel threw two bags at me that I barely managed to catch, arm muscles pissed at being pushed yet again. Wanted to snap 'bout how a warning or at least please would've been great, but didn't bother — she'd just bitch at me if I did.

Elaine closed the door with her foot as she dropped the bags onto the brown carpet. "Need a shower. Brought it all back, so enjoy." She always bailed first damn minute she got.

I put the milk into the fridge; saw Jewel put eggs on the counter so put them up too while I was over there. As I glanced through the bags, I searched for anything else that needed to go into the mini freezer or fridge. There's another bang at the door, but something's off with the rhythm of it.

"You get it," Jewel said. There's a tremble to her voice, and I hated it 'cause I knew why and didn't want to get the door either.

Another bang. She didn't move. I heard screaming, "Open th'damn door," slurred from the other side.

"We can't get another noise complaint," Jewel said to me, a hissed whisper, as if that explained why *I* had to be one to deal with this.

I lowered my head and nodded. She ain't wrong in that the longer I waited, the worse it'd be. That at least if it's me, Rotanu could take care of it without hospital bills we couldn't afford. Balling my right fist — my wrist still tingling from yesterday — , I walked over, each step heavier than the last as the banging grew louder. I opened the door as Father's fist went to swing into the wood again; I made out the trajectory with my eyes as I instinctively leaned back, him stumbling into the doorway instead.

"Why'd you take so long, useless piece of shit," Father slurred as his fist swung at my collarbone. Again, I instinctively leaned back, much like Siani'd been instructing me to do when Kylie swung at me with Isare. My heart raced as it braced for pain that hadn't come. I tripped over the grocery bags Elaine'd left on the floor, wincing and cursing under my breath as plastic dug into my back kidney. He grabbed me by the shirt collar and yanked me from where I'd fallen, slugging me across the cheek. He then dropped me, and I slammed into the god fuckin' damn groceries again.

My chest heaved as my eyes tightened. One thing — sharp,

firm plastic, maybe like a box or plastic knives — stabbed into me but didn't break skin. "Fuck," I said as I bit back another wince. He walked past me, dropping onto the couch.

"Guess it'll be my problem soon enough," Rotanu said, as if he was amused. Damn ass. He *knew*, had hypermnesia, and couldn't ever be assed to give a heads up. At least he'd never really fought on healing me, though prob'bly just 'cause he felt it too, no matter how removed. I stumbled to my feet, feeling my cheek and back continue throbbing, limping a bit from where I think I'd twisted my ankle.

Elaine's in the shower so instead I went to my and Thomas's room, glancing around to make sure it's empty b'fore shutting then locking the door. Could already hear Father snoring through the walls, and Jewel could deal with putting the rest of shit up. But so help me if she woke him up, I'm *not* saving her ass again.

Rotanu swapped places with me without a word, sliding my shirt off and then laying fingers across my still throbbing cheek. From the corner of his gaze, I made out my aura, first heal spell finishing. He repeated the gestures a few times on my back b'fore lowering his hands to my left ankle, sliding my sock off as he yet again healed me and then put the sock back on. "Should be it," he said, pushing me back in control.

My wrist still ached, and I felt a windedness to me I hadn't b'fore, but otherwise, was fine outside of my heart racing. A breath escaped my lungs as my eyes closed, memories of the past few minutes playing out as if they're happening again. Almost always happened after getting my ass beat, where I lived the event over again more than once. Ain't a part of hypermnesia I 'specially loved, but at least it's just memories and not the actual damn thing all over again. At least the throbbing's fading out already, even if the memories kept playing out b'fore my eyes.

One useful thing in my otherwise cosmic joke of a life.

Chapter Twenty-Two

secret date

Rotanu | January 26
Opal Pines Streets

Well, this's 'bout to be a shit show. On one hand, I knew how this'd play out. On the other hand, I wondered how the ever loving fuck I thought it'd possibly turn out *fine* when I was Jordan back then.

It'd been over a month since Kylie and Jordan'd started practicing again. Jordan kept bitching 'bout going 'til I mentioned if he wanted heals, he better get his damn ass in there. From there, Kyle worked their asses and dragged me into it as needed, mostly as backup or for Riyatian lessons. Wished I could've snuck some history in there too, but ain't the time, and I knew it. Kylie only had two hours a week, didn't have time for anything nonessential. Only reason Riyatian got through's 'cause it'd help with modifying spells by understanding their original translation and Riyatian-specific spell modifiers; I ain't seen another language with spell stabilizers and modifiers built into the character set, though there could've been another language out there that I hadn't encountered that did so — far from knew every language ever.

This particular Friday's *special* though: Jordan had a *guest* coming to practice. Namely Richard, who'd just figured out recently that Jordan met with Kylie on Fridays for more than their half an hour walk near to her town-home, and he's now determined to stop said meetings. In hindsight, I think he thought he'd be interrupting a secret date, which made the truth only more hilarious.

"What are we doing *over here*?" Richard said, as if the presence of dirt offended his very existence; it prob'bly did, actually, which's even more hilarious. Made me wanna throw dirt piles on him just to fuck with him. Guess he didn't support the idea of a secretive nature-themed date.

"Uhm, I mean, if you wanna go home, def don't feel like you gotta come."

"Or you could, I dunno, grow a damn spine and tell him to fuck off."

I got ignored, as expected, though Jordan did roll his eyes.

But like seriously, Jordan's taking Richard to the training house, where he and Kylie practiced magic and weapon mastery. How in the ever loving fuck's this *s'posed* to work? It couldn't. Like god damn, Richard just needed to hear some damn "no's" for once in his life; would've been great for him to learn some boundaries.

Speaking of, Richard continued his comments as Jordan might've well burrowed under ground — some of the offended remarks're directed at places we'd lived and hadn't even been the worst of them. Then again, as far as west side went, there're few places I *hadn't* lived. Instability's the biggest stability of my childhood.

Also to be completely fair to where the training house was, it ain't in the most run-down section as much as just completely abandoned; I think there'd been lead poisoning or something in the past. Never really looked that deep into it. But something'd caused the area to be vacated on a permanent basis. Worked great for our needs, given mana essentially negated the health effects while providing the privacy.

"So *much* walking." Richard's quite effective at bitching. Was a master at it in fact, should spend some time diversifying his skill set into being less of a sexist dumbass since he definitely needed some attention on that front. Learning how to be a not-toxic-as-fuck friend would've been an awesome skill to invest in as well.

"It's, uh, not much farther..." Jordan said. That's also a bullshit lie: there'd be another ten minutes of walking easily, fifteen if Richard kept stopping every time he bitched. At least bitch and walk, would speed things up a hell'va lot.

Richard huffed, as if he's doing the world a great community service by not minding his own damn business. I knew where he's coming from, that he didn't *get* how Jordan could possibly actually care 'bout Kylie. That Richard'd never heard no or to *share* in his life, thought he always knew best 'bout everything and for everyone and that Jordan's fuckin' himself over by caring 'bout someone else, let alone a woman.

...Also in Richard's bitching defense, pretty sure those shoes he had on're easily half a grand and were most certainly *not* built for rural terrain. That just made his bitching all more hilarious though.

As expected, the training house came in view closer to the fifteen-minute mark than the ten-minute mark. Jordan stepped up to the front door, fingers hovering above the rusted doorknob.

"*This* is where you wanted to come? This junk heap is barely even standing. Useless."

"Y-yeah, see? Nothing interesting, so no need to trouble yourself further." What, Jordan wanted to have a backbone *now*? Was too late now. Couldn't just show the random-ass location and expect someone to drop it.

Scoffing, Richard pushed past Jordan, roughly attempting to shove the door open b'fore having to put even more weight into it to get the damn thing to actually move. Another hilarious incident in this comedy hour, as Richard certainly didn't wanna look *weak* in front of Jordan, had to show off and be the big role model but ain't able to open the damn door that always got stuck. Dirt got on his suede jacket; couldn't wait 'til he noticed that one and had another bitch-fit.

Jordan stepped in behind Richard; Kylie's lips're pressed together as she sat toward the back of the house, duffel bag and backpack beside her. She glanced from Richard to Jordan and back. Like anyone'd be, prob'bly trying to figure out why the fuckin' hell'd Jordan bring a friend here.

"I knew it," Richard said. He stomped up to Kylie, who pressed her back against the wall to get the fractions of an inch more space away from him. His emotions shouldn't've been overly loud like mine and Jordan's, but he's also like right on her ass and on some crusade so prob'bly still ain't pleasant. "It's always *you*."

"Um." She once again glanced to Jordan, clearly unsure how to handle any of this shit. What's she s'posed to say? How'd he *think* this'd go?

Jordan moved his eyes away, staring at a broken line in the flooring's concrete. "Sorry." As if that explained or fixed any of the shit show going on.

Right on schedule, Kylie's head dashed to the side — likely had been working on auras to some degree and caught something. She pushed Richard backward as she fell forward, a lance through her shoulder. She gasped, rapid breaths coming from her.

Nimaka's there, to the right of where Kylie'd been. Kylie's suspended above air, lance through her shoulder — only reason she hadn't fallen and ripped the whole muscle out with gravity's 'cause've Kyle, I guessed.

I didn't ask permission as I took over Jordan's body; the time for letting him fuck up his relationships ain't right then, not with the pain Kylie's in. I shortcast Nateka, repaying the gesture by repeating the same thing to Nimaka as I thrust Nateka through her right collarbone. "If you're alone, guessing your friends're still fucked. Don't push me or your luck. Ain't gonna end well." We'd already let them live once, and if she pissed me off too much, I'd rectify that, even knowing the consequences.

Kyle'd took over as she telekinetically yanked the spear from Kylie's shoulder, telekinetically throwing it against the other side of the house, where Richard'd scampered off to. Nimaka rushed her, and she kicked Nimaka in the jaw, a nice cracking sound from Nimaka at the action. Even with blood dripping down her shoulder, Kyle stood straight, eyes locked onto Nimaka. "You sure you fancy your chances alone? Ambush's over now, and it'd be both of us against you. Your friends didn't come out to play with you today, alas."

I hated letting her damn walk again. It ain't time, and I damn well knew why, and I still fuckin' hated it.

Nimaka turned like she's gonna attack Kyle again, but she left her back open to me. I stabbed Nateka through her hip, but didn't follow up on the opening after. I tightened my fist around Nateka, not finishing the job as she teleported away mid-fight again. She had a nasty as fuck incision to heal up, 'specially if none of them specialized in restorative magic like Kyle did. But unless they knew no healing magic, she'd live. And given they'd made it the previous time, someone knew how to heal.

Removing the blood-soaked t-shirt Kylie had on, Kyle stood in a sports bra, not bothering for privacy despite Richard and even myself and Jordan still being there. I didn't blame her given the amount of blood flowing from the stab wound. I saw her faintly sway — light headed from blood loss almost certainly.

I placed one hand on her uninjured arm. "Let me," I said. She tightened her eyes as she nodded, at least not fighting me on this for once — was a miracle in and of itself, really; I laid a hand over the incision, biting back a grimace as I felt warm blood coat my palm and fingers.

"Wait, wait, you didn't just fuckin'—"

"Yeah?" I asked.

"Richard's right there. You can't just — he's seeing all this."

"Should've thought 'bout that b'fore you brought him into the lion's den, huh?" Funny thing about actions — and actions resulting from lack of spines — was that they had consequences; it's something Jordan just didn't seem to goddamn understand.

Speaking of Richard, he walked over — well, stumbled more like. There's no way he'd admit that Kylie saved him from the injury I healed right then. Should've been him fucked instead of her. Was an adorable earnest act on Kylie's behalf, given she ain't comfortable around him for rather obvious reasons. His eyes switched between where Kylie'd been stabbed and my —

well, Jordan's — bloody hand, 'specially as my aura covered the injury and mended it.

"W-who's that bitch?" he asked. I didn't answer. His voice grew even quieter as he said, "All this... it means that day at the forest. It really *was* you, wasn't it?" The day we'd met, him being the only one around right after Act, as I — as Jordan — ran into the forest, elemental control not, well, *controlled,* to say the least. Richard hadn't connected the dots, but had found someone who didn't know who he was. Jordan still didn't know who he was, never bothered to ask.

Heal finished, I gave control back to Jordan without providing any answer: his fuck up, his bullshit to deal with. "I, uh..." Jordan's eyes moved to his hand as he withdrew it from Kylie's shoulder, glancing toward and then rapidly away from his bloodied right hand. Kyle still had control of Kylie's body, using the otherwise destroyed t-shirt and water manipulation to wipe off the blood stains on her front torso.

"Can you get the back?" she said, handing the half blood soaked, half water soaked ruined t-shirt to Jordan.

"Uh, uhm..."

Oh, *now* he registered she only had a bra and no t-shirt on. Dumbass. I took control back as I nodded; Kyle turned around, letting me remove the blood from her shoulder and back.

"What just...?" Richard's clearly in a state of shock. Not completely unreasonable, me wanting to grief him aside.

"You almost got skewered is what. Make the trip worth it?" Kyle asked.

He intently stared at her, scowl on his features. She's not at all helping his disdain toward Kylie, but I ain't getting in the middle. She's a grown-ass woman, could handle herself. "How dare you talk to me like that."

Kyle's tone was amused at worst as she said, "Oh, you *want* to be skewered next time? I can arrange that, isn't hard." He's effectively a toy for her. She saw through him like she saw through everyone, and he'd be raising hell if he knew how aware she was — how aware we both were, really.

"What just happened? *Tell me.*" His attention turned to me, well, to Jordan, in his perspective. Didn't wanna deal with Kyle:

she had far more bite than Kylie ever had toward him, that bitchiness Kylie just hadn't quite refined yet.

Jordan didn't fight for control back. I ain't sure how Kylie felt, but doubted she's particularly thrilled. They didn't know the consequences of public magic usage yet, but neither're comfortable with magic in the first place. The only outsider who really knew's Dani, and it seemed Kylie already regretted that as it was. Jordan didn't even wanna know himself, wanted to bury his head in the motherfuckin' sand to ignore the obvious. Was mortified, I remembered.

"I just did," Kyle said. "You almost died. She saved you. End of the story."

His head turned between me and Kyle, patience very clearly waning. "That explains jack shit. And who the fuck is 'she'?"

Kyle shrugged, toying with her prey for sure. I sighed, knowing this's where I had to draw the line. He's too easy of a read for her, and he didn't know enough 'bout what's going on to let her at him. "Calm your ass down. Just a bit of dirt, ain't gonna kill you."

His attention turned to me, eyes widening momentarily. Understandable, given it's a tone Jordan'd never used with him. With anyone outside of family and myself, really. Too damn timid to actually speak up, and that's how shitshows like today happened in the first place. "You've been hiding this the whole time. Why didn't you tell me? Is this why you're always sneaking off with her?"

Could've given control back to Jordan and let this be his problem. I didn't want to though, not yet. Had been holding my tongue a hell'va lot lately and's a *prime* time to catch up. "*Jordan*'s hiding in a corner right now. He'll be back soon, but in the meantime, I'm Rotanu. To your question, yeah, he's been hiding it. Your pretentious ass didn't catch jack shit. Might just be a sign you don't know everything, who knows."

Chapter Twenty-Three

restriction

Kylie | January 26
Caloso Residence

"Wow," Amalia said. Her fingers ran over the faint scar I had on my back shoulder from the attack earlier. "This is healed beautifully — I've never seen something so severe almost disappear from a healing spell." My cheeks flushed, glancing away from her. The long-sleeved shirt I had on while waiting had been ruined; we left it in the training house and I had to wear the shirt I'd planned to wear tomorrow while heading over here. Had gym clothes on now where my back was more exposed, and I wish it hadn't been. Even if I knew she was just admiring the handiwork of the spell, I still wasn't exactly comfortable with her running her fingers along the scar.

Dani came over, focusing in on it, which made me feel even more self-conscious; she was frustrated and uncomfortable, and I was right there with her, wishing Amalia's attention was on something else than the hyper-focus of where Rota'd healed me earlier. "Barely see anything," Dani said, tone bored and flat.

"Exactly! But if you examine — like, right here," she pointed to the skin next to the scarring. "You can see that there's absolutely no bruising beside it at all. Who'd you say did this? It wasn't you, right?"

I shook my head. I didn't want to talk about earlier today. About another attack on my life. On *that person* coming with Jordan and finding out and me having to trust that he wouldn't ruin my whole life when he couldn't even hold a civil conversation with me. He already made every time I met with Jordan after school a nightmare.

What had I ever done to him?

"It was *him*, then," Dani grumbled.

"'Him'?" Amalia asked. Dani hadn't ever mentioned Jordan, I guess, and that didn't really surprise me. She didn't handle me being a better mage than her, and she certainly didn't like knowing he was better or that she wouldn't have been able to heal me as well as Rota had. "There's someone else you know? Why doesn't he come too then?"

A less than flattering trait I'd learned about Amalia was that she must've been the most air-headed person I'd ever met. Or at least, the most air-headed I ever had to frequently interact with; there were probably more air-headed people in school, but they weren't my problem. She couldn't read the room at all, didn't notice neither Dani or myself wanted this conversation, kept pushing for more and more information that neither of us wanted to provide. "Hey Dani, can we get started?"

Dani nodded. Never took much to get her off a topic when it involved Jordan, and for once, that actually worked in my favor. "Yeah, good idea." It helped her birthday had been two days ago, and I'd already given her a gift card to that hipster clothing store she'd always loved. She was in a good mood and wanted to keep it that way, welcoming the diversion.

I put the marshmallow-suit back on; I hated this thing even more now that I practiced with Jordan and we didn't have giant puffy foam strapped to us. I didn't bother to fight with Dani over it anymore: I was here mostly to keep my alibi for Friday training with Jordan, to keep Dani happy enough that she covered for me. I often won now, actively worked to try new ways of sparring against Dani or different restrictions against myself. Like today, where I'd decided I'd only take her down with kicks. It would definitely be a challenge, but that would help me learn how to evade better as well as improve my legwork. I needed something out of these sessions, and she was just *too slow* if I didn't add extra difficulties in. "I'm good," I said.

Readying myself, I charged first this time, kicking with my left foot. Dani blocked with her arm, but that gave me time to put weight on my wrists before sliding my other foot against her ankle, tripping her to the padding. She coughed before checking her wrist. Judging by the throbbing, felt like a sprain. "I thought you'd be more sore," she said with a grumble. Pretty sure that was just an excuse, but maybe she really had thought that.

"Oh, um, sorry. It completely healed." Nothing in what I thought were her emotions suggested irritation or jealousy as so frequently happened now. Amalia saying how thorough Rota's heals were should've established I was fine, but Dani was also the worst mage out of us, by a sizable margin. I didn't practice magic with her at all anymore; instead, Amalia and her practiced whatever magic Amalia knew on Friday late afternoons while I practiced with Jordan. It was more efficient and infinitely less frustrating that way.

Amalia came closer, running her fingers over Dani's wrist. "Oh, I think I can heal this!"

Still that same fascination, one she didn't display toward me after Sia's snap, instead putting even more emphasis on healing Dani. As usual, Dani's heart rate increased as she nodded. Felt Dani's racing heart contrast with Amalia's excitement at her yellow aura manifesting and circling Dani's wrist.

I glanced away, felt like a third wheel; it didn't help that I caused said injury without intending. I did a similar technique to Jordan the other week, and he just got right back up. Was it a difference between them, or something to do with mana differences in our bodies? I couldn't tell anymore, and that was frustrating in and of itself. I was forgetting how not being a mage felt, my life previous to last year even more distance than ever before.

"Th-thanks," Dani said, moving her wrist to check it.

"Of course!"

Going forward, I had to be more careful with Dani. I never

wanted to hurt her, hadn't meant to at all. I needed to understand how much power I put into each swing better so this didn't happen again — another restriction on top of the ones I already implemented for myself with her. Jordan wasn't more muscular, didn't have any of Dani's training, didn't even have the stupid marshmallow sparring gear. I lowered my gaze to my fingers, still covered by the sparring gloves. It'd been so easy not even a year ago, just needed to defer to Dani for anything dangerous.

I'd really changed, hadn't I?

Chapter Twenty-Four

not him

Jordan | February 10
Opal Pines Park

It'd been two weeks since Richard found out, and he'd been enthralled ever since — wished he'd go back to flaunting chicks comparatively. Wouldn't get off my ass 'bout magic this or magic that, like I knew anything 'bout that shit. I wished I could give the whole package to him, let it be his problem instead since he's so fond of it. My idea of a fun Saturday ain't waiting in the damn cold at the park, on this bench where we usually met up. Same one I'd always met up with Kylie at. I zipped my jacket up more — damn thing wasn't thick enough, had to be in the 40s.

"Yo," Richard said. He had on a long black coat that was buttoned. Looked hell'va lot warmer than what I had on.

We should've went to the training house, but I'm sick of the damn place. Was already there the previous day, Siani lecturing as she bitched how my form's wrong and *of course* Rotanu agreed with her. I didn't wanna know a damn form. Only time I saw Kylie now's the 20 minute walks Monday through Thursday — 'cause we'd been walking faster now after these damn trainings so didn't even take the full half hour anymore

—, then the two hours of hell in that damn house on Friday. My longtime friend's all but gone: in her place, a girl that's exhausted to the point of collapse 'cause she's working on damn magic all the time. Even the conversations after school rarely're 'bout routine things anymore, always how she had more to do, a fight with her mom, something Siani taught her. I actually missed hearing her bitch 'bout homework or a test. Was like the furthest thing from her concerns now, only a shallow attempt to appease her mother. It meant that Richard'd been the only time I got to just be a teenager and get away from all the magic shit, and now even that's fucked 'cause of that damn training session he invited himself to.

Even right then, he ain't with a chick 'cause he wanted me to be some entertainer and didn't believe I really didn't know that much. Didn't believe Rotanu existed at all, thought that incident'd been *me*, as if *I'd* said that shit that day instead of Rotanu.

As fuckin' if. The more I'm stuck with that ass, the more I realized there's no way he's some future me. All those lectures about *Riyatira*, as if I had the time or capacity to give a damn.

I half waved back, still hoping I could convince him maybe *this time* to not try to make me do some "trick." All I could really do's make a little fire or ice ball in my hand. Rest's like mana transfer or I guess basic shit with Nateka. "'Sup?"

He gestured toward me as he walked in the direction of the forest, not waiting on me to get up. Fuck, there went that hope. What'd he want back there? Ain't exactly the funnest place in existence.

Jogging, at least the damn nonsense in the training house meant my stamina'd increased; I wasn't at all out of breath despite him having been ahead.

"You said your memory's improved." I nodded, though he ain't exactly asking me a question there. I didn't like that my memory'd changed, but wasn't something I could win I'd come to realize: memories so easily recallable, like I lived them again and again with no trouble. Had made school more tolerable in exchange of all the other shit, I guess. "Show me where we met that day."

Like it's some test. I knew where it was, of course, but felt annoyed that he's basically calling me a liar for something I wished I'm lying 'bout. "Uh, but why?"

His gaze intensified, eyes cutting at me. "I want to go there. That isn't a problem, I assume."

Weird-ass request, but whatever. I started walking that path I'd haphazardly taken months ago, the day after my *Act*. The day I'd met Richard and barely missed being walked in on while burning down the damn forest 'cause Rotanu yet again didn't have his shit together.

Richard struggled to walk in the forest's terrain, unsurprising given the uneven footing and not at all tennis shoes he wore. He didn't comment on it though, as if observing me; was so different to that day we went to the training house and he bitched the whole way. It all made me even more self-conscious 'bout this whole damn thing.

Why didn't Rotanu just let Kylie and Siani handle it that day and stay outta the way? There's no need to get involved, could've let them handle it and kept Richard off my ass — Siani's more than strong enough to handle whatever came up. Maybe they'd even get along better, could talk 'bout this shit between the three of them and free me from it all.

The more I retraced these steps, the scarier as fuck it became that I knew exactly where to go; it's so clear to me, each step like a live replay despite it being almost half a year later. Half a year since I became even weirder and more of a freak than I'd ever thought possible. Half a year since whoever this imposter that claimed to be a "future me" invaded my head, never left me to a moment of privacy.

I saw the trees and grass I'd once burned through frost and fire manipulation. Was barely any sign left now, but had more dead trees and some dirt piles instead of grass and leaves. "Wow," Richard said under his breath. Guess he really did think I'm bullshitting him for whatever reason. Wish I was. His gloved finger traced along some of the bark. "This really is the spot."

"Y-yeah." I lowered my eyes away from him. Felt like a damn animal on display, preforming tricks for praise even if I didn't wanna do any of this shit.

"You deserve better," he said. I glanced up to him, not sure what to make of the words. I'd never heard 'em 'fore, not directed at me. "Quit waiting on that bitch. You have *power.*"

I didn't know what to say, what to even attempt to articulate. "It's not that..." I didn't want power. I wanted to hide, for no one to notice me, to just pass through one day to another and it not get even motherfuckin' worse as'd been the case since last March.

"He keeps goin' after Kylie like any of this's her fault."

Kylie's the one who ran into this forest that day. She knew better, we all did. Dani and me just tried to chase after her, confused as hell at what she'd been thinking. Siani's the reason we lived, but what would've happened if she never chased after that red-haired brat that tried to murder us all?

"How long do you plan on waiting? Forever? What, do you want to die a virgin?"

Virgin? I'd never even kissed someone, forget making out or outright fuckin'. Wasn't something I dared to even pretend would happen to someone like me. He and Kylie must've been the only people at school who didn't notice the looks I got. Kylie'd grown up with me getting them, but I didn't know how the fuck Richard missed them.

"Not like you've got much of a choice." Rotanu's tone's sober yet amused. A weird combination that just pissed me off. Choice? What, 'cause've him and Siani?

He ain't me. I wouldn't've withheld all the shit he did, let Kylie get hurt as he had. Wouldn't've wasted my time learning 'bout damn magic and its failed kingdom. Wouldn't've —

"You spaced out again." Richard's annoyed, his tone certainly ripping me outta my thoughts. I could hardly blame him though: it'd been annoying when I was in his position too, where I never knew the other side of the conversation.

I rubbed my neck, immediately regretting the action given how cold my fingers were against my moderately warmer neck. Wished my hair's a bit longer so that it'd fully cover my neck, something I'd never considered b'fore being in Rotanu's form and it not being a problem for the first time in my life. "Uh, sorry. Just's...loud." Thank whatever gods there were that I didn't have all four of them as long as Kylie did; the barely one month'd been hell enough. And having one still's annoying as shit, given it's what'd distracted me to begin with.

"How so?" Richard asked.

I lowered my gaze further, to the burned grass. "It's like I said. There's this other person in my head, since all this started. And he doesn't take a goddamn hint on when to shut up."

A smirk pulled to Richard's lips. "Oh right. *Him.*" There's an anger to his tone, far past the annoyance of seconds prior. Similar but not as severe as the expression he got any time Kylie got brought up.

"Y-yeah?" It almost sounded like he *finally* believed me, that Rotanu existed, that I hadn't been the one to say that shit to him.

"You said that *other person*'s attached to that bitch right?" I'd never explicitly said it, but Rotanu'd been cozy as ever with Siani that day, as he always was around her. I nodded nonetheless though 'cause pissing Rotanu off sounded like a damn joyride. "I know a *perfect* starter girlfriend for you."

The phrase made me recoil; like the women he knew're nothing more than objects to use and dispose of. But... they liked it, didn't they? That's why he had the entire school's female population fighting to get his attention. He knew what he's doing, more than myself at least.

And it'd show once and for all, I'm not *him*.

Chapter Twenty-Five

liar

Siani | February 12
North Opal Pines High

Kylie rushed through the halls as normal. Yet again, class had run late. I don't know why they expected any different at this point. I f anything, I wondered if he did it to other periods, and the non-honors track students just didn't care. Unfortunately, he was discovering that even the honors track students had their patience thresholds, and he was running through them rather rapidly.

She reached the door, the speed she'd been working on enabling her to fully leave Lianne behind half across the hall, sliding in and out and between the crowd. I wondered how much of a change she realized it was; I didn't remember noticing anything, not yet. But it was a while ago now, and it definitely was significantly easier to observe as someone not in the middle of everything. Kylie snuck out between two of the football players talking as they held a door open for themselves. Her eyes searched for Jordan, seeing him there, Richard beside him.

And beside Richard was a girl around Jordan's height, dark black hair to her forearm. Maybe I was biased, but she had way too much makeup on, like it was matted to her face, dark black lipstick clashing with the pink blush. She had on a pink turtleneck and a skirt I wasn't sure how she hadn't been called into the office over given they complained about dress code nonstop. Fishnet stockings and some admittedly cute knee-high fake leather boots. Richard noticed Kylie, and the smug satisfaction he had made me want to gag. Rota braced for the next few minutes, and it'd been a lie to say I didn't do the same. Jordan's eyes moved to Kylie, and panic filled him further than it'd already been.

Kylie had no idea; she was the only one who didn't.

I had been a damn idiot when I was this age.

"Hey, sorry, I swear he's getting later each day," Kylie said. Richard turned toward Jordan and raised his eyebrow. Kylie reached for her absorption device, gripping it in her hand as she glanced between the two. She could sense something unsaid between them but didn't know what. She didn't see the writing on the wall at all. "Is everything all right?"

Jordan moved his gaze to the dead grass. Richard huffed, crossing his arms over his chest. "He's not going with you. He has a *girlfriend* now, isn't that right?" Jordan nodded, doubt and insecurity and fear rushing him. He kept his eyes away from Kylie; Rota tensed, no body required. He wasn't intervening, but his resolve had shaken, wasn't going to hold out past this event. He knew the risks of trying to change our past, how we'd both risk losing people we considered family, with deviations. But he'd always been soft, loving. And above all else, he wanted me safe, wanted Kylie safe. He'd impulsively take the risk soon; he'd been entirely too close to doing it right then. I was the one — Kylie was the one — most hurt by the next events, and they were scars I was willingly choosing: our pasts made us who we were then, and this pain was part of our past. "This is Emily, his *girlfriend*," Richard said, pushing her toward Jordan.

"Yeah, you're so cute," Emily said as she kissed Jordan's cheek. Kylie didn't notice, but I did: he recoiled, cheeks red. He wasn't comfortable with her touch, and it would be awhile before either of them realized he'd never been that way toward me or Kylie.

"O-oh, I see," Kylie said, her voice soft. She was hurt, but she wouldn't admit it, not to Richard, Jordan, or most of all, to herself. What did she expect, him to wait around forever? How was that fair to either of them? "Congrats."

Richard spoke up again, intervening further. He wasn't even honest with himself about why Jordan needed a girlfriend: he said it's for Jordan, but it wasn't. It was clearly for his own pride, still wounded from my words, Rota's words, from Kylie's rejection at the beginning of the year. He wasn't nearly as complex as he thought he was, but arrogance wasn't anything new for him. He did genuinely care about Jordan, and even I couldn't deny that, but this instance wasn't misplaced guidance; it was passive malice. Yet... he also wasn't wrong to point out Jordan shouldn't wait around forever. "He won't be walking home with you anymore. He has his girlfriend now and is *busy*."

Kylie watched Jordan, his insecurity so loud for us both right then. But he didn't debate Richard, didn't deny his words. He just kept his eyes on the grass, effectively paralyzed. Kylie didn't know how to take his reaction, his emotions, his silence. "I'll just head on, then," she said, trying to sound neutral, but it was a poor attempt, even without empathy.

Jordan said nothing; I couldn't see his face, only feel those around. Richard's smug satisfaction, Rota's anger, and Jordan's insecurity and anxiety. I didn't remember how Kylie separated who was who, or if she even did.

Instead, she walked quicker than normal, taking a deep breath as she exited the school grounds.

"Something you wanted to say?" I knew she didn't want to acknowledge it. She was a liar, most of all to herself: she would say it was fine when it wasn't. If I just sat her down, explained to her how Jordan's emotions and Richard's interplayed in, how Jordan never argued with people, how obviously uncomfortable he was, it could be resolved.

But I wouldn't. I wouldn't intervene because this needed to happen.

"It's just been a long day. I wouldn't have rushed out like that if I'd known," she said. She didn't ask why I never said anything, how it contradicted my relationship with Rota. She didn't want to know.

She didn't want to acknowledge this upset her at all in the first place; she was, after all, a liar.

Chapter Twenty-Six

too much

Jordan | February 12
Regional Thorpe Library

Standing closer to the bookshelf, I pretended to scan through the pages of some economics book. Didn't give a damn 'bout whatever I had open, but gave me an excuse to be in the public library, and more importantly, the public library's heat. Prob'bly could remember the damn thing later anyways, just reference back to this memory. Had been that way for school books and anything else I experienced. *Hypermnesia*. Only remotely decent thing to come outta this whole shit show, and even then, ain't completely fine since there's some memories I don't want that fuckin' vivid.

Turning the page, there's pure silence, only my thoughts. Rotanu hadn't said a word the entire time since I'd left school.

I turned another page I pretended to read. I wasn't him. Didn't matter if he liked Siani or if I'd had a crush on Kylie for years. Nothing'd come of it. All she ever talked about's magic this or magic that now. Not even Richard's good enough for her. He's right: I needed to just cut my losses and move on. Besides, Emily seemed nice enough. Was friendly, significantly more, uh, hands on than Kylie'd ever been. Even as kids, she'd always liked space.

Then again, so had I, too often having bruises on me. Only reason I didn't have them now's 'cause've Rotanu, but even then, it's how he *made* me go to those Friday hell sessions: he wouldn't heal my injuries, would have to wait for Siani to do so, and fuck knew next time I'd have a chance to see her with how things'd been, 'specially if I didn't go on Fridays.

...'specially now that I wasn't walking home with Kylie anymore.

Flipping another page, I saw someone walking toward me: Ms. Carslie. I grumbled, knowing why she's heading my way: closing time, so no more easy heat. She nodded at me — I'd done this for years during the worst of the summers and once it got cold in winter. Maybe it's how Thomas started his dictionary kick given he came here with me when we were younger. Maybe even now, just not when I'm around. Wasn't sure if she knew I'm just here 'cause of the heat or if she thought I'm really that interested; never asked. I nodded back, checking the page I theoretically left off on, if it could be called that, b'fore putting it back on the shelf, in its spot. I tightened the jacket I'd never taken off as I left, cold air immediately invading my lungs as it stung.

"You don't even like her," Rotanu said.

There went the damn peace. "You can go back to your bitch corner, don't wanna hear it." It's hard as ever keeping my voice to a mumble, made me self-conscious 'cause I'm in the middle of the sidewalk. Wished my voice's softer so I could've whispered better.

"You really think it's fine? You know *you and her both're just getting used by him to fuck with Kylie."*

He's acting like some goddamn protector after all the bullshit he'd let happen to Kylie? The kidnapping, the attacks from those bitches, never an ounce of a motherfuckin' warning. "What d'you care? It's fine when she gets kidnapped and tortured, but me getting a *girlfriend's* your line? What fuckin' gives?"

Rotanu scoffed. *"Maybe if she remotely got you hot. You don't though, just having a damn bitch-fest."*

Emily's cute, didn't matter what he said. And I didn't have

to justify who I wanted to date, not to him of all people. Didn't matter what I said, he's gonna bitch 'cause it ain't what he wanted, showed the differences between us.

At least this apartment's closer to the library, lets these night walks be shorter to get outta the direct cold. Who knew how much longer'd we be here though; had already been enough months I'm surprised there ain't a notice, usually was around now.

Unlocking the door, I pushed it open, hearing a squeak in it that'd gotten me beat more than once already 'cause of it waking Father up. Missed the fresh air immediately when I stepped in, alcohol stench long since taking over the apartment. Father ain't on the couch, so must've still been out somewhere. Jewel's in the kitchen, washing a plastic cup. "The hell've you been?" she asked, already on the offensive and pissed. Great. "It's your turn for dinner."

"Forgot." Had been distracted, didn't wanna come back to this shitstorm when I had enough on my mind.

"Yeah, well, it's about time you start actually pulling your own weight." She put her hand on her hip as she blew hair from her face. "You should've been applying back in March, but you keep dragging your feet."

First I'd heard I should've been doing anything outside of the chores I'd always had, like fixing dinner as I'd admittedly sneaked out on. "Huh?"

She rolled her eyes. "Elaine'n I did it at 16. What, think you're too good?" I raised my eyebrow at her, not sure the fuck she's getting at. I just wanted to go to bed, throw five blankets over my face to get some warmth. Fuck, could I hide making a small flame, just to get some heat under the blankets? Prob'bly too risky but still hell'va tempting. "A job, lazy ass. Especially since you can't be bothered to do anything else helpful 'round here."

I saw what'd happened with Jewel and Elaine all the time, where Father stole money from them for booze. Whether I worked or not wouldn't make a damn difference 'cause he'd just steal that too and get even more wasted, prob'bly beat my ass more than he did already. I'm barely balancing shit as it was. With everything that'd happened since March, since May, since — "I'm going to bed, night." I turned, walked off, couldn't deal with her bitching on top of Rotanu chewing my ass out the whole walk home and Richard telling me what to do and Kylie forcing magic on me and...

It's just too much. I'm fuckin' sick and tired of everyone making every damn decision for me.

Chapter Twenty-Seven

hints

This's one of those times I wished I could've just knocked my ass out cold. Not pretend, as I'd done back in June when the others're here. Truly just wanted to clock out. I'd lived through this shit show once already; watching it while knowing the outcome ain't better. Memories overlaid, me as him. He tugged on the hem of his jacket, self-conscious.

"First date" nerves, and on Valentine's Day no less, even though that hadn't remotely clicked in his dense-ass brain yet. Whole thing's a special kind of hell. They walked from the school grounds here, me freezing by virtue of sharing a body with his idiotic ass that's out in this cold for no damn reason. Part of why I wanted to clock out, didn't wanna see the shit show again, and I wanted to freeze through it the second time even less.

"What'd you wanna get?" Jordan asked.

"Hmm." Emily grabbed onto his left arm, wrapping her arms and then pressing her boobs into his arm. His cheeks flushed as he glanced away, to the strip mall. "Let's go into that one," she said, pulling him to some women's clothing store.

Jordan nodded, allowing himself to be tugged; the smell of whatever perfume they used at the door made me want to gag even with the reduced senses I had from not controlling his body, and Jordan did cough, trying to hide it under his breath. Poorly. "Sorry, cold air's still in my throat."

She rolled her eyes while letting go of his arm, wandering through the incoming spring shirts that must've just come out. She held a white ruffled blouse over her torso. "What do you think?"

"It, uh, looks nice?"

I wanted to bang my head into a wall. Dumbass.

She shoved the shirt at him, walking to another with a huff under her breath. A lime green tank top this time, same back and forth with her clearly wanting him to give praise and instead he could barely look her in the eye.

It repeated a few more times, Jordan a pseudo-cart for her. "Thanks for all this," she said, reaching up to kiss him on the cheek.

More than I wanted, I remembered that moment, why he jerked away: the flash in his mind that took him away from right then in that store to the memory of Kylie tied up at Asuza's, of his mind replacing her over Emily. An event he'd deny like fuck if I confronted him on it, so I didn't bother. He acted like I *didn't know*; he'd already figured out he can't forget a damn thing, so why'd he think I'm different? Why'd he think I ain't aware this's just some passive aggressive bullshit to spite me, damn whoever got caught up in the crossfire?

"Uh, sure, but I ain't done anything really." And that's 'bout to be the *problem*.

She made her eyes large as she pursed her lips together, pushing this innocent look that she in no way actually pulled off. "You're getting these for me, since you said they looked good, right?" There it was.

Wasn't a shot in frigid hell that'd happen; with what money? That sinking pit in his stomach at knowing the reality of what he'd have to say. "I, uh, sorry." He moved his eyes around the store, anywhere but meeting her gaze. "Don't have any cash on me." It's a shitty lie, implied there'd ever any cash he had on hand. Maybe if he did as Jewel said and actually worked, wouldn't've been a problem. That's a whole other shit show for not right then though.

"What?" Her tone's flat, the sugar sweet softness there a moment prior completely gone. "Then why are we even here?" At least he's smart enough to not say what he thought, 'bout how's he s'posed to know when she wanted to come here in the first place, not him. She shoved the shirts at him as she left. He awkwardly hung them on the closest rack — even though like none of them belonged there — b'fore rushing out to reach her. As soon as he reached her, she turned around, glaring at him. "What, *now* you're interested?"

"I, uh, sorry, I didn't..."

"*Richard* would've bought them, not just led me on." Not wrong, but he'd prob'ly buy the whole damn store on a coin toss. "You don't wanna be touched, you won't buy anything. What's even the point?"

There wasn't really one. Just trying to spite the world and failing miserably. "I'm sorry, I just. I'm still learning how this works." As if he ain't aware on some level that she's just using him to be around Richard. Was so damn obvious in hindsight, but he's really that dense, I guess. Another thing I wanted to yell at him, at Emily even, 'bout all this shit, dumbass teenager nonsense. Didn't matter, he wouldn't listen to a word I said. For all the shit I gave Kyle over the years, I'm realizing I'm more stubborn than I'd ever known.

But whatever. Maybe it's my punishment to have to sit through this shit. The benefits and detriments of hypermnesia. Kyle wasn't wrong that some mistakes needed to be made, even if it's goddamn hell watching now. There's just one fuckup I couldn't let happen, I'd realized. Everything else ain't worth the risk of changing things, but that one moment... That's the only time I realized I just couldn't let things go.

"Whatever, I'm going home."

He didn't catch the hint to walk with her, instead saying, "Uh, all right, I'll see you tomorrow then."

He didn't catch a lot of hints, actually.

Chapter Twenty-Eight
counterbalance

Kylie | February 17
Rae Residence

I bit into a chocolate chip cookie as I sat at my desk. "Mmkay," I said between nibbles. "What now?"

"Memory work on non-spell theory."

Oh joy, like my least favorite thing. I liked things I could directly apply or that kept me safe. I couldn't exactly work with Isare in my room, but I could've worked on more efficient healing spells, or further aura tracking, or... something. Sia took over, finishing my cookie off. Rude, I wanted the last bite.

She brushed the crumbs off from the page and my fingers as she got a notebook out and laid it beside the spell book on my desk I'd been flipping through. I couldn't understand most of it, but that didn't stop me from trying. "So remember our good friend magic levels?"

I was in trouble if she started quizzing me on the distinctions between them again. While I knew enough magic to understand the importance of them, like how I could adapt to my situation by knowing each level's rules, I still didn't have them down perfectly, not like she wanted. *"Yeah."*

"There's an additional cutoff that applies." *Of course* there was. She wrote down "AE- 88+" on the page. I was assuming the "88+" referred to magipoten, likely max given how difficult it was to get that high as a theoretical max, let alone current sustaining amount. I was just in the 30's as it was, and Jordan was below me. Dani and even Amalia were nowhere near their teens in current magipoten. I had no idea what "AE" stood for though. "That 88 max threshold necessitates a natural counterbalance. I don't know why it's that way." It was one of the few times I got a read on Sia's emotions, not from actual empathy but from her tone. Frustration and even helplessness. But why? "A 'counter existence,' or more direct translation of the actual Riyatian, 'nekase kiseki dekoudi' — 'anti existence.' They're a person, but their magic is tied to their respective 'original existence,' as theory calls it, as terrible as the phrasing is."

"Wait, but..." My estimated max magipoten was 90. That meant I fell under this somehow.

"Mm." Sia set the pencil down, hand resting against the cool fake hardwood of my desk. "You're the 'original existence' in this case. There's someone out there whose mana is tied to yours. I don't know why 88 mandates a counterbalance, but from my understanding, it wasn't something Riyati did. They weren't fans, given it took power away from the throne."

I ignored the rare history lesson from Sia, too many other thoughts about this racing through my mind; I didn't know what to ask or how I felt about it. Cheated, almost. Sia let me sit in silence until I asked, *"How can someone's mana be tied to mine? What's that even mean?"* My mana was something naturally generated, like blood or a muscle that I kept pushing, working more and more. Someone else just naturally had *more* because of the effort I put in? Didn't ever need to do anything themselves?

"The amount of mana they have must equal the amount you have. The only exception is when you use my form, since it doesn't 'exist' right now."

It really was like they benefited from all the suffering I'd done. A group project that I was stuck doing alone. *"Do they have air and water elemental alignment too then?"* Like some twin I'd never met, never heard of.

148

Sia shook her — my — head. "No. Their magic doesn't match to an element, because they're not an 'original.'" Now I was even more confused: all magic traced to an element, tables I'd seared into my brain. "Think of it like its own element, one only they can use. Except where 'normal' magic creates from mana, theirs destroys from mana, hence why 'anti' was the prefix chosen back in Riyati, well, the translation for it at least." Sia still hadn't written any more on the page. What was the point of even bringing all this up? Some random person I didn't know somewhere in the world got to live life peacefully in exchange for me being constantly hunted and having to work nonstop. "It's not just their mana tied to yours. Or rather, it's the logical conclusion of their mana pool tied to yours."

"What do you mean?"

Sia's eyes moved back over the single line she'd written. "Mana composes the body for them, just as it does for you, even if it's a different type of mana. But... the only reason they exist is to counterbalance. If it's not needed anymore — if you're not alive — , then their mana disappears."

This really was unfair, knowledge I wish she'd never mentioned. Someone else got all the fun and none of the work, and they weren't even dependent on mana, apparently. *"So their body isn't dependent like mine either?"*

She shook her head. "It is." That didn't make sense though. Because if their mana was tied to mine...

"But wait, then..." Then their life was effectively tied to mine. If I died, this person somewhere in the world that had to *counter* my mana would die too. And I'd already almost died far more than once this past year.

Once again, Sia nodded, her voice soft yet without much inflection, a mixture of objective fact and something I couldn't discern. "That's correct. They'd essentially get what could be called aggressive 'magic cancer,' and it'd likely shut their body down within a day of your death. As soon as you had Act, they were forced into Act with no context. Comparatively, the reverse isn't true, the... privilege, I guess you'd call it, of being the 'original.' If they die, another one is born somewhere to continue countering, the original unaware anything had changed."

"But they're a person, like anyone else? Not an item or a plant or something? They have a family and friends and... do they even know?"

That same tone, calm but not really, factual but yet wasn't. "Nothing innate, if that's what you're asking."

If I died, they died too, not knowing why, not having any context. That was somehow even worse than myself because they didn't even know to be scared, how at risk they were. *"Is it someone I know? Someone close, like Jordan was?"* I don't know why I asked. Sia wouldn't answer, not about something future-related. She was always tight-lipped there, only bits and pieces about Rota slipping out on the rare occasion. Sia said nothing, further confirming I wasn't getting an answer. II wasn't going to push — there wasn't any point in doing so — , but before I could even drop the topic, I noticed Dani's aura approaching my front door, further distracting me; her emotions were frantic, panicked, near hysterics. *"What's she...?"* I reached for control as Sia taught me, was able to swap with her for control of my body. I walked down the stairs, reaching the front door right as Dani rang the doorbell.

Dani never randomly came over anymore, was with Amalia usually. I didn't really blame her since Amalia was an admittedly much more patient magic mentor than me or Sia. I opened the front door, Dani's hands shaking as she pushed herself inside. "We need to—. Your room," she said.

"Mom's at work." It was like she didn't hear me, still walking to my room. I closed the door and locked it back. I walked back up the stairs and into my room. Dani kept looking at my door, like someone was listening in, despite me being home alone. I sighed and shut the door. I would just have to track auras more closely to make sure no one came by since it was hard to hear our doorbell with my door shut. "What's going on?"

That hysteria increased, her mouth moving but no sound coming.

I didn't understand, tried to hone into her emotions more, but panic and fear — my heart racing, breathing shallow, terror and paranoia... they grew louder and louder. I winced, swallowing down the new lump in my throat. I couldn't tell if her reaction did cause some amount of fear in me or if it was just all my empathy.

"Amalia's gone."

"What?"

Her balled fist slammed down on my mattress, again and again. "These... these adult men. They just ambushed us and grabbed her, said something about getting another 'mage.' We were downtown, were fixing to get dinner and... and... I didn't know what to do, ran here. Doesn't matter how good Mom is, she doesn't — can't — . Not when magic's involved. We already saw that with you, so then..."

People other than me were attacked because of magic? Is that why there'd been nothing since that attack when Richard was there? I lowered my gaze from Dani to ask Sia, "It was them?"

"No, the group that's attacked you and had their lives artificially extended by Asuza are all women." A brief pause before Sia continued, "This *is why you don't use magic publicly."* A far softer tone than I normally heard from Sia as she added, *"Like I'd tried to tell her."* Sia had always been snappier than normal every time Amalia used magic. She had told Amalia to stop, over and over.

"What?" My tone was flat, soft. Dani looked to me, sniffling. I couldn't focus on her between her emotions making me panic and Sia's words making my own anxiety consume whatever was left of me trying to stay rational.

"There's an organization out there that kidnaps mages. Experiments and tortures on them until they die out from either lack of mana or from the conditions. Most likely, she..."

I couldn't tell Dani that. Last June, I'd almost died from a lack of mana. I remembered how it felt to be tied up, how my body increasingly rebelled. My wrists ached recalling the memories, the scars still there even now. "Do you know where?" I didn't want to finish that sentence, not with Dani looking at me so expectantly, like I'd be able to save the day. Like I had any control at all with magic-related things and wasn't subject to whatever Sia deemed appropriate for me to experience.

"No. I've never seen her since." It wasn't a lie. Sia would've

changed the topic or been vague or something that wasn't a direct denial. If Sia didn't know, couldn't help, then what did that mean for Amalia? Was she even still alive?

What had my life become, where fear was all I knew?

"Kylie? What's she — where's Amalia?"

I shook my head. I didn't want to say it. I didn't want to acknowledge what Sia had just said, share the news with Dani. Because if I acknowledged Sia's words, then that meant Dani was at risk too. And Jordan. Rota had to know, right? Sia would've at least told him. But what if she hadn't? Was Jordan also at risk?

There was another threat to our lives we'd never even considered.

My voice wavered as my head throbbed from panic — mine and Dani's intermixing into one encompassing blur. "I don't know." If I wasn't killed by those women that worked for Asuza, I'd be tortured to death by people who experimented on mages. That's why I'd never met anyone else until Amalia. That's why Sia had always been so quiet in public about magic, even to Rota, why she'd told Amalia to be more subtle.

That's why I had another reason to live in fear.

Chapter Twenty-Nine

sins

Siani | March 3
Training House

I'd never had Rota's recall — I couldn't remotely compete there; hypermnesia wasn't exactly something I'd be able to practice and obtain. For years now, I'd relied on his memory where mine failed. The only reason I knew the exact date this would all end was because of his memory even. But... he wasn't the passive child like the Jordan of this time anymore. He'd always been more cautious and indecisive than me, but he'd learned to speak up, take the action he thought best. And the moment had come where our priorities diverged: thus far, he'd been caught between his love and someone effectively family to him. It'd ripped at his heart to see Kylie walk away from them that school afternoon when she met Emily. I felt his inner resolve solidify, willing to risk the future if it spared her pain. He'd lost sight of pain's necessity, but I'd follow through. For them, for him, even.

After all, if he said he wanted to change the past for Kylie, then no one was more justified than myself in rejecting that change, knowing what that meant. I knew better than anyone the tears that would come. I knew the hopelessness and sorrow and isolation, the desperation and despair and desire. While he may have just reached his answer, I knew mine from the moment we'd arrived here.

I wouldn't falter, even when it meant betraying him.

And really, I knew all along this would be the point that divided us. He still held too much regret and it clouded his perception. That was why, as soon as I could, I had us start meeting in secret. I had established a pattern, creating an environment for him to lower his guard long before I needed him to do so. He'd suspect nothing now, just another weekly meetup. But... it was time for us to hand over control, prepare for that day we left: May 17th. Just over two months away now.

As usual, Kylie was asleep, and judging by surrounding emotions, only Rota was awake inside the training house as usual. I was a few feet away from the door, here at our regularly scheduled time in a shortcast of Kylie's alt form, my form. I shortcast Isare with a modification into a knife as I held it while running my pointer finger along the center of my palm, felt for a vein. There was no fair way to keep Rota from interfering, which meant I couldn't use fair methods: like Kisate and Takite, I needed blood magic. I needed a stronger potency of mana than a normal cast would provide, a seal for my sin. I used Isare to slice skin open, the familiar bubbling sting flashing through my brain. At least I was the empath instead of Rota; if he knew this happened, he would've had questions I didn't want to supply an answer to. I knew the incision would naturally heal quickly, so I had to be fast: I had minutes at best, even at Kylie's magipoten, so I dismissed Isare and opened the door, seeing some blood drip on the handle. It was the only clue I'd give him, one no one else would notice.

As I stepped in, closing the door back behind me, I noticed that he had a small flame out in his palm, no lamp on. I wasn't sure if he just didn't want the lamps on or was cold — both could've been accurate given his mental state right then.

"Hey," I said, keeping my voice soft. I stepped close to him but didn't sit down beside him like I normally did.

He shifted his right hand away to the side as he opened his left arm, indicating he wanted to hold on to me. I took a deep breath, nodding as I sat between his legs instead, my back against his chest. He thought nothing of it, dismissing the flame as his arms wrapped around my shoulders, hugging me from behind. "This ain't right. I hate it." He'd been crying, having perception on how much this hurt Kylie in a way he hadn't had years ago as Jordan. "Thinks he's just showing his ass off to me, not getting how much it's fuckin' with her in the process. It's the next time now. I can't do it. I just... I can't." As much as I often envied his hypermnesia, I'd never considered how maybe it prevented him from ever moving on, wounds never able to be obscured. He remembered everything like it'd happened seconds prior: every regret couldn't scab over. Maybe it was cruel to still push forward knowing that, but...

It was my sin to bear. "Can... can we not talk about it, for right now?" I let my voice falter, a tremble to it. I knew comforting me would take priority to him, especially for the coming events. I felt more like a bitch for this than when I severed Kylie's absorption device back in June to lure Asuza.

"Sorry," he mumbled, grip against me tightening. As ever, his emotions threatened to overpower me, but I embraced that for once. A tear dripped down my cheek, dropped onto his arm. "Dammit." He mistook my tears for my own distress instead of as a response to his emotions. Maybe he wasn't completely wrong and some of the tears were mine though: I hated manipulating him like this and never wanted this particular night to end.

But the sun would rise; our time would be over four hours from now. I turned around, pushing the front of my body against his chest as I took my arms behind my back, rested my head against his collarbone. My left pointer finger ran across the barely bleeding incision I'd made, almost completely healed already. Had to push to force more blood through the remaining incision, blood wet and warm against my fingertip. Careful to keep the blood on that finger, I intermixed it with focused mana as I adjusted my position to Rota, my right arm hugging onto his back. "Just for a minute, okay?" I kept the tremble in my tone, a faux weakness.

"Kyle..." His arms wrapped back around me. I brought my

left fingers, baring my pointer finger, against his side, reaching under his vest and slacks and even the edge of his boxers. "H-hey, I'm pissed too, but that's prob'bly…" My pinky brushed against his symbol; he shuddered from the sensation, like a pleasant electric pulse through his body that I also experienced thanks to my empathy. I laid my index finger over where my pinky had been, covering his symbol in my blood, in the spell that now just awaited finalization.

I sniffled, redirecting his attention so predictably. My hand was buried under his slacks and his head was turned away, so he didn't see my aura for the brief second it was visible to normal vision, and he'd never learned to read auras properly to have any insight beyond what was directly visible. "I love you, Jordan." It was the first time I'd called him his name since we'd been in this time period, a divide I'd been insistent on even when we're alone. We weren't Kylie and Jordan, we were Siani and Rotanu because this time already had a Kylie and Jordan. We were visitors at best. Yet right then, I wasn't sure if he even recognized it'd been the first time, his posture relaxing into my touch more than any time I'd addressed him as "Rota" during an intimate moment here.

His fingers stroked through my hair, kissing the top of my head. "I know… I know you do." He kissed me again, this time on my forehead. "I love you too, Kyle."

I'd always been the one more willing to make the dangerous bets, the one who believed the ends justified the means. And for them, for him, I would gladly bear these sins: after all, he was my love, and I wouldn't let him spare my feelings for their existence, his existence.

Chapter Thirty

silence

Rotanu | March 6
Opal Pines West District

It's the day I never wanted to come. Still didn't have a perfect answer or solution. But I couldn't let the past happen. Couldn't go through with it, not after seeing all this shit play out again, not knowing how it hurt Kyle — would hurt Kylie. It's a gamble though, that I wouldn't lose some of the most important people to me and Kyle. But I just couldn't stand by and let her get hurt. Had already stood by when I knew Asuza'd kidnap her, when I knew his bitches'd attack us. When I let them walk multiple times now. I knew why. I thought I'd come up with some perfect solution where she wouldn't get hurt and they'd still be okay if I had just a bit more time to think 'bout it.

I guess I'd failed, and maybe even failed them all with how far the light was from Kylie's eyes of late.

So that Richard wouldn't interfere, training'd been swapped to Tuesday afternoon during spring break. Jordan's pissed as ever that he had to come, and yet again running late while blaming it on every damn person but himself. Didn't get the importance of training, to himself or to giving Kylie *something* to latch onto. She trusted him, and he'd treated her no better than he'd always hated being treated. Didn't have a damn spine to tell Richard no, to tell him that his bitch-fit with Kylie's unacceptable. As Jordan, it'd made me uncertain, unsure what's right or what to say or how to balance things. I'd been a complete ass: the answer's obvious, and it's telling Richard to fuckin' grow up and back the fuck off. I knew he meant well. I knew he thought he's looking out for Jordan. But Richard wasn't the god he thought he was. And 'specially here, his way ain't the right way.

They're both egocentric dumbasses, leaving Kylie alone and abandoned. I just couldn't let it go further. Not today.

Jordan reached for the doorknob; I noticed a drop of blood on it — that hadn't been there Saturday night when I'd entered b'fore Kyle. Had someone else been here in between? Not like it mattered, but still weird. Had more important things to focus on: there's no way Kyle'd mix Jordan and me, but I could fool Kylie if I tried. And I didn't need to deceive Kyle, only Kylie. Well, I guess deciding to change shit's kinda a form of deception since it hadn't been something we agreed on, but whatever.

He opened the door, Kylie in the center of the loft-house and already in alt form with Isare as she practiced building speed by spinning Isare between her hands. She lowered the staff as she noticed Jordan there. "Hey." It's so obvious that something's wrong, her tone softer than normal, hands tightening onto Isare's grip. Timidness even for the Kylie of late.

"What's up?" he asked.

"Before we start." She held Isare against her, like it'd protect her from the knowledge she felt ethically compelled to share. "There's something I need to tell you."

"Huh? 'Sup?"

All I needed to do's soften the initial reaction. If it refocused his anger on me, whatever; he could have his bitch-fit with me later if it meant the next few minutes never happened, tonight never happened, tomorrow didn't need to happen. I pulled Jordan from his body, pushing myself in. Or I should've, but nothing happened. The fuck? I hadn't struggled with this since like week one I'd been stuck in this hell. I tried again, focusing.

Felt mana manifest from Jordan's symbol, something I hadn't noticed as Jordan, something that shouldn't've happened at all.

"The other day, Dani... she came by." Kylie's eyes lowered. "I don't think I mentioned her too much, but that other mage, Amalia. She's gone."

I felt Jordan's heart race at the word "gone," both of our minds flashing back to Kylie tied up almost dead in Asuza's excuse of a castle. Again trying to take control, I felt more mana surge from his symbol, heart rate increasing both from Kylie's words and as a biological reaction to the mana being summoned. Tried to control auras, and was overwhelmed with them briefly — how'd that still work, but I couldn't take control? How the fuck couldn't I take control? The entire spell's based on Kyle's initial cast —

My metaphorical heart stopped.

"'Gone'?" Jordan's confused, wondered why Asuza's bitch-army'd go after a random mage. "But those like.... psycho-bitches, didn't Rotanu and Siani scare them off?"

Kylie's lower lip trembled as her knuckles went white from how tightly she gripped Isare. Her eyes're downcast, prob'ly trying not to freeze up more than she already had. Trying to deal with my emotions and Jordan's on top of her own. "Sia finally told me why you don't use magic in public." Her voice had a softness to it, defeated and exhausted and terrified. "It's not just us — there's other mages. But this... this group. They find mages. And they take them. Even she doesn't know where, just that she believes they torture and kill, and... just..."

Jordan stepped back. As much as I'd ever tried, I pushed for control. Just this one reaction. It's all I needed to temper, all I needed to prevent. Blocking my access's impossible; even Kyle couldn't disrupt shared consciousness under normal means.

But something abnormal'd happened, that I couldn't deny. And there's only one person who could've pulled something like this off, something normally impossible. Someone who knew rules and technicalities and loopholes better than I'd ever to dream knowing: Kyle.

Jordan stumbled, and I'd thought as Jordan I'd stumbled from her words, them replaying back in my ears more than once. But it ain't: it's from Jordan's symbol, and a seal over it. The doorknob that'd had blood... that whole time, her getting uncharacteristically handsy and going for my symbol and I thought's just distress but's her fuckin' anticipating I'd do this and I should've goddamn seen it coming. She'd know I got weak, would've more than accounted for this moment, and always took every damn thing on herself.

"Wait, just... just *having* this damn... it's enough for...?" I remembered his — then my — mind shuffling between Kylie at Asuza's Castle and the beatings from my asswipe of a father. Imagining that there's no school, no Richard or Kylie to break up the punches and slaps and kicks.

If I had a body, I would've cried from frustration. I wanted to be pissed as fuck at her, but god motherfuckin' dammit. She's shouldering every damn thing herself, fuckin' herself, to protect them. To protect me.

The reason she hadn't wanted to leave early Sunday morning, just wanted a few minutes longer than usual, was that she'd been saying goodbye. Couldn't trust me 'cause she knew I'd buckle so took it on herself and I wanted to block my ears from the next bit. She didn't deserve this, Kylie didn't deserve this.

"Don't use magic in public. That's the safest way." Kylie's voice was a forced neutral, trying to hide how much she wanted to break down crying. I wanted to run to her, comfort her. Tell her it'd be okay, as I had so many times since we'd been here.

Only Jordan could now. And he wouldn't, too stuck up his ass.

"You think I do now?" It's the first time he'd — I'd — ever snapped on her. Been minor snips over the years or sarcastic jabs, but Jordan's voice was lower, angry at the world and taking it out on her. Like she'd decided any of this shit. She rapidly shook her head as she gripped Isare tighter.

I wanted to cuss his ass out, but he'd ignore me. Prob'bly'd just spur him into even more aggression, lashing out at her instead of me. I wished it'd be reversed, that he'd chew my ass out. Not hers, not when she's innocent.

"I just... it wasn't fair you didn't know. Wanted you to know." She's being considerate, trying to give him a heads up. Wanted him to know what's going on, have some degree of agency.

Jordan scoffed, glaring at her. "So what, we're out here literal sitting ducks in this damn building? No one'd notice us getting kidnapped here — has that been the damn plan all along?"

Kylie shook her head, eyes still to her feet. "I think it's why we practice here, since it's so abandoned. Less likely to be seen." Kylie's voice'd been barely above a whisper, her doing her damnest to bite back tears at what had to be his suffocating emotions. Our suffocating emotions.

"Fuck that." Jordan balled his fists, raised his voice even louder. I winced, though he didn't notice; knew how each syllable sliced straight into Kylie, knew how Kyle wasn't helping her or comforting her or trying to put things into perspective at all, would just observe quietly. Like I'm doing, now nothing more than a spectator. Might've even been part of the cost of the blood magic she'd used on me; like hell'd I know the exact spell or technicalities of how she pulled it off to know anything for sure. "I never wanted any of this shit, and now I'm getting set up to be kidnapped like you did? No, I'm done. Fuck it all." She said nothing, so he continued this shitstorm of a bitching. "I hate magic. Goddamn hate how much of a freak I've become from it, all the shit that's happened since last March. I just wanna be a damn normal high schooler, why's that so fuckin' much to ask?"

"I — ." I saw her lip tremble, redness around her cheeks. She tried to hide her tears, and he didn't even notice. "I-I'm sorry. I just thought..."

My emotions got the best of me — I couldn't reach out to soothe her, but I wanted his goddamn mouth sealed shut: *"Shut the ever loving fuck up. She's innocent in all this, bitch at me if you gotta bitch at someone."*

It's like I said nothing, or maybe I angered him even more, fuel to the fire. "I hate my fucked up life, and you going into that damn forest that day might as well ruined any shot I had for something decent." He turned around, walking out. Leaving without any other word, no apology, no admittance that he'd crossed several lines. And she didn't call out for him: not to cuss his ass out as she should've, not from Kyle wanting to tell me something. Silence.

As much as I could, I retreated from the world around me. I wanted to scream at and maybe even punch Jordan. I wanted to cry and cuss Kyle's ass out. I wanted to hug Kylie and tell her everything'd be all right.

I wasn't as selfless as her: I wanted this whole shit show avoided, even knowing how much of our pasts depended off it. Didn't want it as a permanent stain of regret on my consciousness. She took my agency so I wouldn't have to bear the weight of tonight, of just now, of tomorrow. If I told Jordan what'd happened, even if he ignored me, I could prob'bly create a time paradox or something and get around her, and yet...

I'd be silent, trust in her judgment. She wouldn't have done this lightly, and no matter how pissed I was, I knew her motive's honestly so much purer than mine.

Yet, now May 17th felt so far away, and I already missed her like hell.

Chapter Thirty-One

only solution

Kylie | March 6
Rae Residence

I'd just wanted to do the right thing. Over and over, I had just tried to do the right thing. I didn't argue with Mom about how unreasonable it was that she wanted me on constant house arrest like I was a child even now, like eight months after I'd been kidnapped. I'd tried to work with Dani, tried to get to know Amalia, tried to tell Jordan so he knew and didn't find out like Dani and Amalia had.

It was the first time I'd ever heard him raise his voice. He screamed at me. I felt his panic, fear. He was scared. I got it.

Bringing my knees to my chest, I tightened my grip as I fought to prevent more tears. It was already dark out. I'd been crying on my bed for hours, I'd finally been calming down, but...

He didn't want to be kidnapped *like me*. Like I'm defective. Like it's fine if my life's in danger, but now that something might affect him, it's a problem. That fear was something I'd lived with for months now. It started before Asuza kidnapped me and had only gotten worse since then. How did he think it felt knowing people wanted me dead, had tried to murder me more than once?

No. I couldn't keep thinking about all this. I rubbed my eyes, softly smacking my face. Mom would be home soon, and I couldn't be crying when she got home. She would ask questions I couldn't answer. Sia was resting, so I had an actual moment alone for once. Being alone meant I had to fully control my empathy and auras, but I was getting better at it. Better enough that I honed in on Mom's faint aura pulling into the garage before the door opened. But she was not in good humor, was furious. What'd happened?

Going into my bathroom, I splashed some water over my face and then wiped it off. I had bags from where I hadn't slept well past few nights since I got the news about Amalia, but I looked about as good as it was getting all things considered. I forced a smile in the bathroom, and none of the light made it up to my eyes.

I felt so alone.

Taking a deep breath, I walked down the steps as I heard Mom open the garage door and come in. "Welcome back."

She said nothing, anger festering more. How was that the wrong thing to say? I watched as she softly sat her bag down on the dining room table, back to me. "Alana called me today." I didn't know what to say, so I stayed quiet while I waited for her to continue. "That girl Dani's been with lately. She's gone missing."

"What?" I had to pretend I didn't already know. I wouldn't have known if Dani hadn't run over, trying to make the same connections Mrs. Alana and probably Mom wanted. It wasn't the same, though. Not at all.

"She's wondering if it's connected to your case."

I moved my eyes away. "I-I see. I don't know anything, I'm sorry." I hated lying. I hated I knew this would cause more wasted resources and time and no one could help Amalia if even Sia didn't know where she was.

She turned around, her arms across her chest. "Yet you've been sneaking out *somewhere*, because you weren't going directly to the Caloso's on Fridays." Biting down on my tongue, I did my best to keep my eyes from going wide at being caught. "*And* you've been hiding grades from me. That's two

C's this past month alone. Thank god it wasn't on your midterms at least."

What could I say? The truth? The truth was something she'd call me a bigger liar on, and if I showed I wasn't lying, I'd... How would I even have that conversation? Try to say that I used magic, but people wanted me dead because I didn't let them kill me last summer? That another group of people thought I was a human pincushion in waiting, and that's where Amalia likely was, if she was even still alive? "I..." I wanted to be held, told everything would be all right.

But Jordan had yelled and left, Rota said absolutely nothing, and Mom was so furious my hands threatened to shake from the intensity of her rage.

"No. No more lies. *He* finally got to you, not helped by that so-called lab partner." She huffed. I didn't bother to defend Jordan or Lianne, couldn't against the force of her anger. She pulled a stack of papers from her bag and tossed it on the counter. "You're grounded for a month. Straight to and from school, nothing else, and rest of break, you're not to leave this house. If I find out otherwise, I'm putting in a transfer application to another high school."

I'd been in this district my whole life. If I transferred, I'd know no one. I only had around two and a half months of this year and my senior year left in high school; all the friends I'd made growing up from elementary — the passive acquaintances, the hallways I'd grown to know so well — would be gone. "Yes, ma'am." I had nothing else to say. It felt like oceans slamming into all sides of me, dragging me under.

She wouldn't even look at me, held her forehead with her hand as her head throbbed. I'd caused that, hadn't I? I'd further stressed her out without meaning to. "I can't believe I'm even having this conversation with you. Just go to your room."

"Yes, ma'am." I had no fight left.

I went back upstairs, softly closing my bedroom door. Sia still wasn't awake. It was just me.

My heart raced as I leaned my back against the door, the wood cool against my skin. What did Mom want from me? She couldn't handle the truth. School just wasn't my priority when

I wasn't sure I'd be alive a week from now. I still had scarring on my wrists and ankles. Every time I tried to pretend I was normal, those scars snapped me back to reality all too quickly: I could be back in that position if not worse within minutes.

Jordan said I'd ruined his life. Amalia was missing, and all resources to find her attempted to connect my case to hers, to the attacker of mine that was no longer on the world but I couldn't tell anyone that, even more so now that I knew people actively wanted to experiment on me if they realized I was a mage. Mom was right: I'd been a failure of a student, making lower grades than ever before in my life. I couldn't connect with Dani anymore, like she lived a life I could only dream of. I envied other students in my high school who only cared about dances and mixers and homework, like I once had and couldn't now.

Everyone would be better off if I was dead. I couldn't ruin their lives if I wasn't around. Those women would be happy, their creepy undead leader avenged if I was gone, no reason to go after Jordan if I wasn't around.

I walked to the bathroom, flipped the light on and looked in the mirror. There was no light in my features, my eyes; I looked half dead, bags and pale skin, hair needing brushing. My head turned to the pictures in my room, most had been there so long, they might as well been part of the wall. Three of Dani, us through the years in poses scattered around. Mom said pictures were gateways to the people close to us, yet Dani might as well have been in a different country for all we understood each other. I had two of me and Mom, one in some summer camp I didn't even remember as I held the completion certificate up. The other was when I went to class with her one day four or five years ago during summer break and one of her students took a picture of us together in her office.

There were two of Jordan and me — the first when we'd first met, before Mom hated him. We were working on the class project in our classroom, were so focused on it we hadn't even noticed Mom taking the picture. The other was more recent, one I'd taken around my 16th birthday with Jordan, holding a peace sign as he shyly smiled, his gaze awkward but soft.

That one hurt the most right now, memories of us no longer

walking to school together because he walked with his girlfriend instead. Of only seeing each other for training. Of him yelling at me, of it being my fault both of our lives were at risk.

It was true. It was all my fault.

"Isare," I said. "Head your mistress's call, summon forth." The staff materialized in my hands. "Form shift— knife form." The weapon behaved as expected, shifting from its default bladed staff form to a knife. Isare was comforting to hold, just like holding onto my absorption device: a bond with materials composed of or containing my mana. I tightened my eyes as I brought the knife against my throat.

Why'd I even make it out in June? Maybe it would've been better if I died like Chloé and Leah had. I wasn't meant to be alive anymore; it somehow made so much sense, why everything had only gotten worse since that day.

The knife's edge was sharp, could feel it nick my throat as I swallowed, cold blade against my flesh. I just had to pull my hand back. End it. Make everyone happy.

I tightened my grip around the hilt. Felt water rush to my eyes.

Why was this my only solution? Why couldn't I be happy? I dropped the knife to the tile, hearing it clank before disappearing as I dismissed it.

I couldn't even die right, too much of a coward. Stumbling to my bed, I collapsed back. My lamp by the window was on, and I couldn't be bothered to turn it off. I just didn't want to be in pain. Why was that so much to ask?

Why was it so much to ask for me to just not feel pain and terror and sadness anymore?

A blur faded into my vision, ebbing consciousness from me. A momentary relief that couldn't come soon enough, and maybe I'd wake up with the past year as some long nightmare.

Chapter Thirty-Two

arbiter

Jordan | March 7
Opal Pines East District Streets

I fucked up. It ain't her fault. I'm scared shitless still, but there's no way she isn't as well. Was damn Rotanu and Siani's faults for hiding shit again. Like motherfuckin' usual.

She deserved an apology, and as she'd been so often since last June, I assumed she's at home, likely in her room. I turned the corner, seeing her town-home in view. A few houses down, I noticed Lianne, her arms crossed and leaning on her left hip. Was standing on one of the driveways even though I never'd seen her in this subdivision b'fore despite how many times I'd been over throughout the years. Maybe just moved? Neither of us waved, hadn't really ever talked despite the classes we'd shared more than once. She'd always given me the creeps, this bad feeling in my stomach. And it didn't really matter to begin with since I'm here to apologize to Kylie.

I walked up, ringing the doorbell. Could usually hear either her or Mrs. Rae moving when they got close to the door, but heard nothing even after a minute or two. A light was on in Kylie's bedroom, which was weird since it's early afternoon — no way she needed it on, 'specially with her blinds open as they were. Also meant she's home since she never left her blinds open if she ain't. So why isn't she answering the door?

It's yet another goddamn thing withheld, ain't it? "Anything I should know?" I asked under my breath. Rotanu's awake, but he gave jack shit of a reply.

So something *was* wrong.

I walked over to the garage keypad, flicking the cover off. Years ago, Kylie'd given me the keypad number. Didn't even remember why at this point. I keyed in *1-8-1-5* before hitting *Enter*, watching as the door lifted. I closed the door back once I'm at the control pad by the interior doorway. Why's my heart racing? No... that's a dumb question. It's 'cause I didn't know what he neglected to mention *this time*: was she kidnapped again? Was it by by those psycho-bitches or those people she scared the shit outta me 'bout yesterday? What didn't Siani bother telling her?

Why's the last thing I said's biting her damn head off for something not her fault? Why didn't Rotanu just take over like he'd done any other time? Usually's overprotective of Kylie, but he just sat there.

The house's silent. There's no way she hadn't heard the doorbell with her door open as it was, and she had to have heard me opening the door from the garage too. But it didn't sound like she'd moved at all. I walked up the stairs, into her room, looking around for signs of a struggle, of —

She's on the bed, asleep. How? Even b'fore all this, she wouldn't have slept that hard; had complained over the years 'bout people ringing the doorbell and waking her up during the weekend way more than once.

"H-hey," I said as I knocked on the door frame. Didn't really know what to do since of all the possibilities I'd braced for, her sleeping like a damn rock ain't one of them. Felt awkward to go into her room with her unconscious, like I'm stalking or peeping at her or some other shit that made me uncomfortable's fuck.

She didn't acknowledge me: her eyes didn't open, just a steady rise and fall of her chest. She ain't dead, was breathing, but... Hell's going on?

I walked over to her, shaking her shoulder. "Hey, you okay?" Her eyes shot open. There's something so wrong though: were focused on me, but there's no warmth to her face. Didn't even seem pissed, as she kinda had a right to be. Just blank, a neutral I didn't think possible, hadn't seen from her b'fore.

"State intention." Her voice's monotone, as emotionless as her face.

The fuck? How was I s'posed to respond to *that*? "Uh?"

"Repeat, state intention. Failure to do so will result in identification as 'threat.'" There ain't a tease, no hint of this being some elaborate joke to get back at me for yesterday. Her face's completely neutral, voice had no inflection at all.

I didn't know what to say, how to take this. Had come to apologize, but that seemed so far away now compared to whatever the fuckin' hell's going on with her, with trying to make sure she's all right when she obviously ain't. "I, uh, wanted to check on you? Everything okay?"

"Motive discerned. Physical state acceptable." Her eyes're that same blankness, not even watching me. Just staring straight up to the white popcorn bedroom ceiling.

"She's not there."

I wanted to ask how she couldn't "be there" when she's literally in front of me, yet I couldn't disagree with him. This ain't Kylie, there's no warmth, no smile. His own voice'd been serious, restrained even. Even when admitting he'd let her get kidnapped, he'd not sounded as upset.

"Additional assistance is not required at this time. Engaging standby until additional inquiries are requested." Her eyes closed back.

"The fuck?" Her eyes didn't open back at my words; her only sign of life's her even breaths.

"It won't work." He still had that solemn tone that surpassed when she'd been *kidnapped*. How the fuck's this *worse* than that? What didn't I know, didn't I say? *"This's... she finally broke from it all. Hindsight, amazing it took this long."*

Like she's some machine that ain't had proper care. A toy discarded. Wanted to cuss his ass over it, but that seriousness in his tone stopped me. "'Broke'?"

"One of the modifications Riyati did's a fail-safe threshold. Anyone above 85 max magipoten — basically wings —, there's a shitty-ass design implemented." Another thing 'bout us he and Siani'd neglected to mention. What a goddamn joy. *"If emotions overwhelm a mage that high, there's a fail-safe that triggers in them, severing their personality from their body."*

The reason it seemed like she "wasn't there" was 'cause it's the truth, assuming he didn't lie right then. But what he described's exactly how she looked right then: a body with no soul, like some machine impersonating a human. "This's..." It couldn't be how she lived the rest of her life. It ain't fair, right. "Siani ain't like this."

"Yeah. There's a way to reconnect the two, provisionally."

Then why ain't he doing it? Why's he leaving her like this? Was it to fuck with me? Leave her outta this shit, was bad enough he couldn't be assed to stop yesterday. "Okay?"

I hated how she didn't acknowledge anything I said to Rotanu. Just continued laying there, as if she understood nothing. Heard nothing.

"You did this to her. You get that right?" Rotanu's tone'd lowered, a danger to it I'd never heard b'fore. Didn't know I could sound like that, an anger I'd never had, even at him and Siani for all the bullshit they'd put us through. *"You're off blaming me and Kyle, but you ain't stopped to think how you keep adding shit onto her. How do you think she felt when you cussed her out?"* Terrible, that's why I came here to apologize in the first place, and I felt even guiltier as fuck and also kinda pissed they'd yet again not bothered to warn us 'bout shit. *"Fuck, when you couldn't even be assed to tell her to her face 'bout Emily, whole goddamn shit show that is. You let Richard do it, you spineless ass."*

"Yeah, I fucked up. It's why I headed over here to apologize. But you're acting like it's all my fault when you and Siani keep hiding every goddamn thing, can't be assed to even let us know how fucked we are." More rules we never knew 'bout. More secrets they continuously let us walk right into. Same bullshit, different day. "What's wrong with letting us at least *pretend* to be normal? Why's that such a damn sin?"

172

He still had that low tone, it having a danger I'd never felt from him b'fore. *"Your 'normal life' put her in NEO. Congrats."*

I rolled my eyes. Yet again, he avoided any responsibility in how he'd just let all this shit happen. "Just fix this. It's awkward's fuck being here with her unconscious."

"Would've shut your ass up earlier if I could've, trust me."

This whole shit show didn't add up: he'd always been protective over Kylie and Siani, even when keeping all these damn secrets. It wasn't like him to not yank me outta control and immediately go to her. But he wasn't. Why?

Whatever. Would cuss his ass out later, and he'd better have a damn good reason if he's not gonna help with shit while freeloading in my head. "So I can do something where she's herself again?" He didn't immediately speak. The silence made the situation even more awkward; wasn't sure if he's debating something or just fucking with me, and standing over an effectively unconscious Kylie in her room alone made me feel sketch as fuck, like some creep. "Well?"

"Only an 'Arbiter' can issue commands to a mage that's triggered NEO. Every mage with NEO must have at least one person they'd accept, but there's no guarantee it's you for her with as much of a ass as you've been." The anger's gone from his tone, but that other tone'd grown even stronger — as if he's sad, solemn.

There's a snowball in hell's chance Rotanu wasn't Siani's "Arbiter" and we both knew it. "Humor me." I somehow always kept getting roped into these damn magic things, and this time ain't any different.

"It's for her I'm telling you this." I rolled my eyes. *"Say, 'Initiate Arbiter override protocol.'"*

Just like her words, it's so mechanical, like some program a hacker'd say on a TV show or something. "'Initiate Arbiter override protocol.'"

Her eyes opened back up, still that emotionless blank stare at the ceiling. "Protocol established. Request for Arbiter candidate's confirmation."

"Say your full name, nothing else."

This made no fuckin' sense, but he's getting more

conversation outta her than I had, so whatever. Best shot I had right then. "Jordan Caleb Boyle."

Her response's instant, no hesitation after I finished saying my name: "Evaluation process for Arbiter candidate initiated. Please wait."

"Stay quiet, any word'll either just confuse NEO or lead it to think you're attempting to harm it."

"It"? Not her? What even was this "NEO" thing? As pissed as I wanted to get at Rotanu, it'd been a deliberate word choice and not one he would've made lightly. I knew that much 'bout him if nothing else. Even if it pissed me off how he flaunted it, he loved Siani. I knew he did.

"Candidate 'Jordan Caleb Boyle' accepted with Arbiter designation. Please seal contract."

Contract? She ain't moving to get a piece of paper and pen though. Wasn't moving at all for that matter, and what'd she want me to sign for to begin with? "Uh."

"It takes blood and a mana transfer to finish the process for establishing Arbiter."

Fuckin' hell was this? "Wait, *blood*?" Why'd Riyati had damn blood signature shit? Ain't that dangerous or like...

"Yours, to be precise. And on her symbol." While there's a hint of amusement in his reaction, it ain't nearly as much as the situation'd normally have for him.

I'd never seen her symbol, but then again, we didn't exactly have show and tell over all this shit. "Where's that exactly?" He knew, I'm sure. Just seemed like something he and Siani would've shared with each other at one point or another with all the other secrets they hid.

"Upper right thigh."

She's fuckin' unconscious, and he wanted me to put blood *where*? "You're fuckin' with me."

"See for yourself."

I bit back a grumble. This's sketchy as all fuckin' goddamn hell, but I couldn't leave her like this — whatever "this" was. My cheeks flushed as I pushed her shorts up on her right leg. I didn't see a damn thing, despite the shorts pushed up a good inch higher, my ears burning from blood bypassing my cheeks and turning my ears red too, as'd always happened when I got embarrassed as fuck. Right as I'm 'bout to cuss Rotanu's ass out more than I'd ever done b'fore, I saw it, same size as my own, this small little dot that had her aura color overlaid on it, right at the line of where her shorts rested, as Rotanu'd said.

Fuck, he's really goddamn serious 'bout all this then. I inhaled through my nose, hating that I felt more attracted at her damn thigh than I had at any point toward my own girlfriend. Fuck's wrong with me? Emily's cute, spent way more time on her appearance than Kylie ever had. Was openly affectionate, wanted contact I couldn't even dream of Kylie wanting with me.

Dammit. Not the point right then, nor remotely appropriate.

I took a deep breath. "You're not joking 'bout the blood either, are you?"

"What d'you think?"

I didn't need to ask how to get myself to bleed. But I depended on him to heal me, and if he ain't taking control now, prob'ly wouldn't for that either. Likely wanted me to *naturally* heal so I'd suffer. Ass. "Nateka, manifest into reality." The sword formed in my right hand. I tensed as I brought the blade against my left pointer finger, all too easily feeling the sting of blood rising, bubbling to the top of my skin. I dismissed the sword, placing that drop of blood on her symbol. I watched as her symbol absorbed it somehow, disappearing, only a bit of a smear where some'd gotten on her thigh. I brought my finger to my mouth, hoping to staunch the bleeding from my saliva. Tasted like disgusting iron, just like every other time I'd tasted blood, but it ain't as if I had a ton of options here. "Now what?" He'd said something 'bout a mana transfer. I'd only ever done that once though, and surely he didn't mean...

"I already told you: you need to transfer mana through her symbol to finalize the process."

As if I didn't remember what he'd said the first time. He knew I did, and I'm asking 'cause it makes jack shit sense what he wants from me. The only time I'd done a mana transfer, it'd been through physical contact; all too easily, my lips against her skin playing through my vision, the memory of the other time I'd transferred mana to her. "Yeah, but like. I only did that once, and that time..."

"That's how mana transfers work: lip contact from the host to the receiver."

He still ain't playful at all, not fuckin' with me. He meant it, and hadn't been bullshitting me so far which prob'bly meant he still ain't. My cheeks lit up even further.

Her eyes still stared up, at the ceiling. Even right then, hadn't turned to face me. She wasn't there. It's awkward's fuck and suspicious's hell, and I didn't like I got even mildly turned on 'cause it ain't right, and...

If she got pissed, I'm completely blaming Rotanu for this shit show.

"Sorry," I said as I kneeled down, my lips on her symbol, pushing mana as I'd done that one time.

I'd only pushed the slightest amount when she said with that same monotone voice, "Contract established. Input current orders, Arbiter."

I nearly jumped back, heart racing, cheeks red. "Ah, uh." I stood back up straight, checking over her. Seeing if she's pissed as fuck. But she ain't. Only change'd been that her eyes moved from the ceiling to me for the first time. Made it even more clear something's wrong though, that she wasn't really there. Eyes following me without any tint of emotion, face completely neutral.

"That did it." Rotanu didn't even sound smug, not even angry anymore. Just wistful, almost melancholy. *"Tell her 'Restart with personality layer initiated.'"*

Personality layer? Like some quirk that was optional, unnecessary. What'd happened to her to cause this? Rotanu'd said I did it, but how? How's me getting scared and being bitchy at her something that'd cause *this* to happen?

"'Restart with personality layer initiated.'"

"Order acknowledged." Order? I shouldn't've been giving *anyone* orders, much less her. Yet her eyes immediately softened as she said, "What's...?" She sat up, only then noticing I'm there. "Jordan? What's going on? Why're you...?"

What could I say? I didn't know shit 'bout what just

happened, couldn't explain it to her if I tried. And the parts I did know, I didn't wanna even attempt to explain, justify. "I, uh, I was gonna stop by, but got worried when you didn't answer." My cheeks're still red, heart racing. And her damn empathy had to pick up on it given her own cheeks're similar.

"You're hurt," she said, reaching for my left hand. She laid her fingers over the one bleeding, healing it.

"Oh, uh, thanks. Was a, uh, accident. Hadn't..."

"Mm." Her eyes lowered, away from me. "Sorry to have worried you." Her hands stayed an extra moment before going back to her lap.

"It's, uh. I just..." I tightened my right fist — if nothing else, I had to apologize, whole reason I came over here to begin with. "I'm sorry. For ripping your head off yesterday. It's Siani and Rotanu hiding fuckin' shit again, and it's just. I'm tired of it. But it ain't your fault."

She nodded, eyes on her bed and not at me. "I understand. It's made your life a lot harder than it should've been." Her voice's soft, understanding. Meek, even. I wanted her to yell at me as Rotanu had, understood how to cope with yelling, but this. She didn't blame me, and I wished she did. Didn't know what to do in a situation like this. Rotanu'd been the one to handle this type of shit, not me.

"Y-yeah. It's been hell lately. I think I need a break, from training and shit. Just... figure stuff out."

"All right." Her expression wavered for a minute as her eyes gained a glassy tint. "I'm sorry to have worried you, but you should probably leave before Mom gets home."

Oh fuck, that'd be the icing on the damn cake to this whole weird-ass thing. Ms. Rae'd eat my ass alive if I'm up here alone with Kylie and... fuck. "R-right. I'll see you at school next week."

"Of course."

Chapter Thirty-Three

no emotion output

Kylie | March 7
Rae Residence

What's wrong with me? I knew Jordan had been concerned about me. He had this sigh of relief when I asked why he was in my room — which I still didn't get *why he was in my room* — , and empathy meant I knew he really *was* relieved when he saw me wake up. I knew he genuinely felt bad about yesterday, completely meant his apology and came all the way here instead of waiting for whenever he saw me next. I knew all this, and yet... I didn't feel better. Not really.

Even ignoring that yesterday was still too fresh in my mind, I had been so asleep that didn't hear Jordan come into my house. He would've rung the doorbell first — how did I sleep through that? How'd I miss him walking up the steps and into my room in the first place? What if it hadn't been him? What if it'd been one of the women that had tried to kill me? What if it'd been one of the people that hated mages and kidnapped them as they did Amalia? I couldn't be that asleep, and the fact that I had been terrified me.

And he shouldn't be around me anyways. Mom would've hit the roof after yesterday. His girlfriend probably wouldn't have been happy he was with me instead of her. Maybe it would've caused a fight between them, where I would've ruined his life more than I already had, would've made things more complicated than they already were. At least he'd left pretty quickly, but his emotions felt louder than usual, blaring into my head enough that I wanted a painkiller even if I knew they didn't really work for me anymore.

I wasn't sure how far I could detect his emotions now, but it'd taken entirely too long before they became only the faint pulse they currently were. I was finally able to start observing surrounding auras instead of blocking them to deal with the empathic over-stimulation. But... there were bright auras nearby — too bright for anyone that lived in this neighborhood for sure, and that ignored that I knew both auras, or at least auras very similar to them: one was a similar gray to Lianne's and the other like one of those women that tried to kill me. They weren't approaching though, just stationary. Were these mages visiting someone? They had to be mages; the auras were too bright for someone that wasn't a mage. They couldn't have been Lianne or one of those women that wanted me dead though... wouldn't have made sense for them to be together, to be just sitting nearby. Doubt that woman — Nimaka — would've gone over to one of my neighbors for afternoon snacks randomly. They likely were just people with similar auras visiting, and I misinterpreted something again. I fell back against my pillow, seeing my fan spin in a cycle. "What am I even doing?"

"Hm?"

Oh, Sia was awake again. Guess I should've expected that since I seemed to sleep through the night and half the morning with it. I glanced to my desk clock and saw it was already past two in the afternoon. Hadn't slept this late in a while. "Were you talking with Jordan and Rota while I was sleeping?" That'd make more sense for why I hadn't heard anything; if Sia had control, then everything would've been muted, might've intentionally made things even quieter so I could sleep in. She could've sensed their aura — or emotions for that matter —

and taken control before they'd even rang the doorbell in the first place.

Her voice was strangely soft as she said, *"No. I can't get control anymore."*

What did she mean by that? How could she not get control? The entire near-year she'd been with me, she could control my body — even override me and Kisate if she wanted. "Wait, but why? Was it something I did?" Was there a way I could accidentally prevent her from getting control? It was probably something else I screwed up and needed to fix, like so much of my life lately.

"It's not you. It'll make sense eventually, but ultimately boils down to, I can't get control now, just help with auras, empathy, and sensory precog."

It wasn't my fault, but it also wasn't something she'd give me a straight answer on. She'd already generally been handing more and more aura and empathic reads to me, had been blocking out sensory precognition attacks less and less. She said I'd improved, could handle them more now, or that my mana had grown enough that she couldn't completely mask the sensory precognition attacks from me like she could last year.

Why did it feel like she was preparing to leave me too? What if those women attacked again? How would I survive without Sia taking control? I couldn't fight them — I could barely release Isare's blades without fumbling with the release mechanism. The thought terrified me even more, this hole in my stomach I wanted gone. "Do you know why Jordan and Rota were here?" He'd never come into my room while I was sleeping like that. He said it was to apologize and check on me, and I didn't want to say he lied but he'd been too nervous around me, skittish and shy.

"Jordan's not exactly known to be a great liar."

So she did know then, and my suspicion that something else went on was correct. Why'd he lie then? Did that mean his apology was fake too, no matter sincere his emotions had felt? "Yeah, and he was super awkward while standing in my bedroom staring at me. Something's off."

"Mm."

I'd gotten the memo that she didn't want to tell me, but I had to keep pushing. What happened while I was asleep? Why couldn't get she control? Were Jordan and Rota involved somehow? Rota wouldn't have hurt Sia, I knew that, but... Things didn't make sense. "Sia, please. Really not in the mood."

"I know." Her voice was soft, reflective. I felt emotions of neighbors beside and across and houses down, blended into this hum constantly at the back of my mind. But I'd never been able to get any consistent empathic reads from Sia. It wasn't because of us body sharing — I'd had no problem with the others, even the ones that'd been in Jordan. Even Rota now. I assumed it had to do with how she helped control and block empathic reads, and I doubted it was accidental that I couldn't read her emotions. She wanted her feelings private, a respect I'm sure she didn't return. *"I know."* This second time was even quieter. *"I don't know why Jordan came over. Honestly don't. I don't think he lied about it being to apologize though."*

It was something. She rarely outright lied, instead giving half-truths or omitting details she didn't want to say. "How long was he here? Was it when you got up?"

There was this hesitance, an uncharacteristic pause that wasn't her ignoring me, but still wasn't an immediate answer. *"I was awake before they got here. Couldn't see everything since your eyes were closed for parts, but had empathic and aura reads along with hearing things as normal."*

So she'd been unable to take control before they got here. What could've caused it then?

I seemed to get more consistent answers about whatever happened with Jordan and Rota, so I didn't press further about her ability to take control. Maybe later, when she was in more of a *sharing* mood. And at least if she had empathy and aura reads along with being able to hear things, she might've caught some of the conversation between them. "Did they say anything about why they're here? Or like, was it even Jordan the whole time?" Jordan rarely came over, especially now. The visit felt more like something Rota would've done; maybe he'd wanted to see Sia. Jordan couldn't have wanted to see me even if he had wanted to apologize, not with yesterday, not with how his life was in danger because of me.

Even that theory didn't make sense though: it was hard to fully separate out Jordan and Rota, but between the two, there'd been anxious, nervousness, relief, sadness, resignation... Even as two separate people, the emotions conflicted with each other, and I wasn't sure which was which to any consistent pattern.

"Riyati had a lot of skeletons. Something spooked them — not a historian, don't know what — , and they started pushing genetic alterations to extremely high magipoten mages, essentially wings tiers." Why was I suddenly getting a Riyati history lesson? If it'd been Rota, I probably would've outright interrupted — I wasn't in the mood to be lectured. I just wanted answers that she seemed to be avoiding. But... Sia was precise and pragmatic. If it wasn't something immediately practical, it would be eventually. This wasn't a random topic change: it would be important somehow, if not right now. *"The alteration was meant as a fail-safe for the most powerful mages: if one of those mages experiences enough distress to cause potential threat to the kingdom's well-being, the connection between consciousness and the body gets severed."*

I knew I could summon wings; I'd done it at Asuza's Castle and in training. They were surreal in their own right, but that was something thoroughly established. Dani couldn't summon them, and I doubted Amalia could've. But I knew Jordan could as well, since he'd done it at the castle too. That meant this "fail-safe" thing I should fall under, Jordan should fall under. "Okay?"

"One of the specifications with this alteration is that if it triggers, there must be at least one eligible person as a handler of sorts. The Riyatian word is Awawo Someite. Who knows when, but there was an additional alteration to accept the English word 'Arbiter' in place of Awawo Someite, which is what Rota and I tend to use." That meant the awa-some whatever wasn't a literal translation then, and she wasn't wasting time on explaining the differences between the literal and non-literal translation as Rota had done so many times. *"There can only be one Arbiter designated at a time for that alteration state."* She paused, as if she had hesitations or doubts or something that sounded

decidedly un-Sia-like. *"If that 'Arbiter Candidate' is accepted by the altered state, that 'Arbiter' essentially gains full control over the altered person."* Why was she telling me this? What did it have to do with anything? It felt more and more like some random tangent she'd decided to use as a distraction, and I rapidly lost patience with whatever explanation this was. I would've rather her outright lied or just said no than lead me on some history lesson I wasn't in the mood for. *"That altered state, you triggered it last night: Miido Saawawo Ikusuetatu, or very loosely translated, No Emotion Output. Rota and I call it NEO."* Her voice softened to barely a whisper in my head, strangely affectionate somehow. *"The only reason you're conscious right now is because your NEO state accepted Jordan as Arbiter, and he gave the reconnection command between your body and consciousness."*

"What?" She had to be lying. I was me. Here and awake and just had slept hard after yesterday sucked so much. There was no way something like this NEO-thing existed. No way I was conscious right then because Jordan *wanted* it. I doubted he even wanted me around since he barely spoke at all to me anymore, blamed me for everything, and — *"Whatever his reasons for coming were, we're fortunate he did. Only he and maybe Mom could've been accepted by NEO, and even Mom's pushing it."* Nothing about this was "fortunate." And it couldn't have been true, a moment where she lied outright to me. *"If you want proof, there's something called the Arbiter Seal around your symbol now."*

It had to be a lie. It *had* to be. Pushing my shorts up higher than the right side already was, there was smeared dried blood near my symbol, something that hadn't been there last night. Glancing even closer, I saw a hairline circle outlining my symbol, a blur of dark red and navy. Jordan's aura, branded onto my body like I was some merchandise. "What about Dani?" At least Dani hadn't yelled at me for ruining her life, even if I did deserve it.

"I don't know for certain since it's not something that we could readily test. But, Jordan's the most probable candidate. There isn't much choice on that." Choice? She said it was just from

people around me, and I felt frustrated with Dani, but... Sia almost had a growl toward the end of her sentence, an anger I hadn't heard from her since Kisate had left.

Did I really want to ask why she sounded so angry? Did I even want to know? What else was there to take? How else could I be kicked? She hadn't been lying about NEO: I'd been branded just like she said. Yet her voice had been soft describing NEO and Arbiter; whatever she meant with a lack of choice, it had her furious. I didn't want to know. But I had to, didn't I? I'd be in an even worse position if I was oblivious. "Just say it."

She sounded neither surprised nor hesitant as she said, *"It's Kisate. Kisate and Takite. They used blood magic right before Chloé was kidnapped by Asuza, altering future incarnations. Those alterations started with yourself and Jordan. Was a reckless plan that wouldn't ever have worked to begin with."*

I didn't know what I expected to hear, didn't know how I felt that I'd been altered to be different from Chloé or Leah or Kisate. I felt almost numb as I asked, "What kind of alterations?" Blood magic used a high concentration of mana that could only be obtained by a blood sacrifice. The stronger the spell, the more mana and blood required. So anything that had Sia this pissed and needed blood magic to begin with certainly wasn't going to be pleasant for me.

Another pause from Sia. *"Your feelings, particularly toward Jordan. She altered berserk state to have an innate docility toward him. At an instinctual level, you'll trust him. It's why I say he's the primary candidate for Arbiter, because those instinctual alterations means he'll always be someone close to your heart at an unconscious level. There's more changes, like magipoten being two higher than the previous incarnations, but that's at least beneficial. The altered berserk state is why he and Rota are always so loud emotionally. Like a direct signal to your unconsciousness that overrides everyone else around."*

This was why Sia got along with Chloé and Leah, but every chance she had, she sniped at Kisate. She *knew* and didn't tell me so I could get along with them, not deal with the knowledge when I shared a body with someone who took another choice from me before I'd even been born.

185

Shaking my head, I pushed my consciousness from my body. Retreated to my subcon, the blackness all around me. It was empty compared to how it'd been before I was kidnapped. But Sia was there still, and I rushed to her. She was warm, even though I wasn't sure how since we were just consciousnesses right then. She returned the hug, running her fingers over my back in a soothing arc. I felt my eyes water, hiccups filling the fake lungs I possessed within the subcon. First I had sniffles, then gasps for breath as I sobbed. I wasn't even sure why, but the tears didn't stop. I was tired: tired of fighting, of suffering, of people hurting me and not understanding me and wanting me gone. Sia didn't ask, just let me cry while repeating the back strokes, as if she was calming a baby. "It'd been better if I didn't make it out in June, wouldn't it?"

She brought me closer. "You have to decide that."

Decide what? I didn't get to decide anything, that's all I'd learned since then.

A year ago, I just wanted to get into a college out of Opal Pines. Keep Mom off my back by getting good grades and hang out with people I cared about. Mom not liking Jordan was the worst of my problems. When I got a C on something, it felt like my life was in danger.

All I could do now was just survive. Not run, not even walk. Just crawling on the metaphorical floor, waiting for the mercy kill. "Probably already been decided by someone else."

"It's your life, not theirs. You're the one that makes the call in the end."

I wished that was even remotely the truth.

Chapter Thirty-Four
related incidents

Kylie no longer watched the clock intently during final period, no longer rushed out ahead of other students. There was no point, no person waiting on her. She and Jordan hadn't said a word to each other since she woke up after he'd become her NEO-state's Arbiter. I honestly didn't know what Rota had said about NEO and his role as Arbiter, but the sight of Kylie's NEO state had clearly gotten to him: it'd been clear from the few words Jordan had said and Rota's emotions that day. I didn't focus in as Kylie walked out with Lianne, talking about something relating to the upcoming final bio project. Just saw that Kylie's eyes momentarily drifted to where Jordan stood on the school grounds grass, the same place he'd waited for her most of this year. Emily held his arm as Richard leaned back against the support pillar; Richard and Emily talked to each other while Jordan nodded, obviously distracted. His eyes met Kylie's for a second before both glanced away.

It was funny how similar their emotions of embarrassment and awkwardness were. Kylie read his emotions but didn't want to deal with the situation, didn't pick up on how he recoiled every time Emily touched him. I'm not sure he really picked up on that either, though I was sure Rota did. It was a time of my life I was happy to not be directly reliving — observing from the side had been bad enough.

Kylie walked past them without a word, her head lowered. She'd claim that it was that her natural stride had gotten faster and that's why she moved past them so quickly, but it'd been another poor lie.

Three weeks had passed with this routine. Three weeks, and they'd yet to say more than mumbled passing greetings and even that had been disappearing, refusing to speak to each other; for the first time in years, Kylie hadn't given him a birthday gift, unsure if it was overstepping a boundary with his girlfriend. The closest I'd come to talking to Rota was honing in on his emotions during school periods, and I knew that was still way more of a check in than he could do for me.

I wasn't lonely: lonely meant I regretted my actions. Kylie and Jordan didn't speak while Rota and I couldn't speak. There was no more sneaking out, and it'd been stopped by my own hand. I refused to regret my choice. Rota could feel lonely; he had no other way of communicating to anyone but Jordan and maybe comments through Jordan to Richard. This hasn't been his choice.

But not me. I knew the risks and drawbacks, and I refused to be lonely.

Kylie was off the school grounds but there were still other students on the surrounding sidewalk. A few were people she had known for years. Instead of trying to talk to them, she lowered her head and mumbled, "When can we work more on empathy?"

"You can do it passively any time, but there's more important stuff for our actual sessions." I ignored the huff she gave, clearly not happy with the answer. We needed to make the most of the time left, but that was something I couldn't tell her directly.

"What's today?"

"Endurance, since that doesn't matter if Mom's around."

Mom wasn't demanding texts with Kylie at the door

anymore, but she wasn't far from it either. "Oh right, she's home early tonight. Great..."

She said nothing else the rest of the walk back: there wasn't much to catch up on when you shared a body with someone. Kylie opened the front door, putting her keys in the key holder near the front door as she locked the door back. She then went straight up the stairs to her bedroom, closing the door as she dropped her backpack by her desk. Grabbing gym clothes, she went into the bathroom to change into them before coming out.

I didn't really need to tell Kylie how to start for of the physical exercise routines now, but it'd become part of the routine for me to do so anyways. *You know the drill: start with 50 push-ups.* It was like back during the summer, except worse since Kylie only went to and from school; otherwise, she was in her bedroom, it and the training house the only two places she wanted to be now. She had another week or two left of being grounded before she could visit the training house, which made magic practice near to impossible. Rather than focusing on what she couldn't do, we focused on what she could: magic theory and physical conditioning. Unlike Dani, she had no gym equipment, so she relied on bedroom furniture and what could be done with just herself. No equipment was fine enough, just meant we needed to be creative with the exercises — or we would've needed to be creative, if I didn't have these routines rather seared into my brain at this point.

Kylie pulled her hair back into a low ponytail as she nodded. She'd barely been able to do ten push-ups when we started right after she was grounded. Up-down-up-down, again and again. She counted aloud, her breathing only a bit uneven toward the latter half. She glanced to the clock as she moved onto her knees. "Almost under four minutes. Better than last week."

"Crunches now, then move into the stretching positions."

"Mm." Tucking her feet under her bed frame, she laid on the carpet, hands behind her head. I felt her stomach muscles sting from the exercise, but she didn't complain, just kept going. She understood: there was no room for complaints, no room for complacency. "Huh?" Pausing as she rose, Kylie detected Dani's aura. While there was nothing Mom had said

189

about being visited by friends, Dani still hadn't been by since she asked about Amalia's abduction; Dani hadn't really "randomly" dropped by since near to the beginning of the school year.

Kylie moved to her feet, standing as she opened her bedroom door and walked down the steps, arriving just before Dani rang the doorbell. Dani was startled, jumping back from the doorbell she had been reaching to ring. "H-hey, can I come in for a few?"

Hesitantly, Kylie nodded as she stepped to the side for Dani to enter. Like with classmates, Kylie was fairly obviously not in the mood for conversation, but Dani had a more skittish edge to her that was uncharacteristic of the redhead... or at least had been uncharacteristic, once upon a time. "Did something happen?"

"I just..." Dani stood in the entryway, stepping forward so Kylie could close the door. "Are you sure you don't know anything?"

Kylie closed the door behind Dani, sitting on the couch as she wiped sweat from her forehead with her lower arm. "About?"

Dani glanced up to Kylie's bedroom, but Kylie didn't move; unlike the last time Dani was over, Kylie was only willing to entertain a brief visit. There was no friendly invitation for a surprise sleepover or even an evening visit as they'd done so often growing up. When Kylie didn't get up from the couch, Dani sat close to Kylie. "Amalia. Like, have you heard anything else, or does *she* know anything?"

"I already told you everything we know," Kylie said as she shook her head, eyes going to her lap. She didn't even bother checking with me, and no matter what she would've claimed, it was because she didn't want to think about the risks of being a mage, what had happened to Amalia, more than she already did. "Sia said mages that openly use magic like she did... They're often kidnapped, never seen again. That's all we know."

Dani's hands moved to Kylie's shoulders, digging in. "You won't even ask her? Just let me talk to her then."

I couldn't. Kylie knew that as well as myself now. She didn't know I was the one that had done it, but she'd none too subtly tried to force me in control of her body, and it'd failed each time

— with how the blood magic worked for blocking Rota, I'd given up my own ability to gain control as well.

"I'm sorry." Kylie didn't tell Dani I couldn't get control. From what I remembered, she just didn't want to deal with another argument, instead preferring to direct her limited energy elsewhere instead of fighting with Dani. "It has nothing to do with what happened in June, anything with me." Kylie never told her more attacks happened; from what Dani knew, the last time Kylie had anything "abnormal" happen was back in June with Asuza's kidnapping. She'd just wanted to keep learning magic and martial arts because she could, not because she had to for survival. She'd wanted to train with Jordan because it was fun, not because Kylie felt it was her only chance.

"You're both teenage girls that went missing by weird men. They *have* to be related incidents. Even Mom agrees." Dani huffed after Kylie said nothing further. It wasn't the reaction Dani wanted, and it was a reminder to Dani of how little control she actually had over things. She didn't realize it, but it was also an admission of exactly how little she understood too: in a larger town, no one would've blinked twice at the cases being unrelated. "Since you're not helping and just *leaving* Amalia, I had to tell Mom you weren't even with us half the time you said you were. You're not even willing to do the bare minimum to help her, and *I* got grounded for two weeks because of you, and even accused of lying about the magic and disappearance stuff that *did* happen but Mom won't believe because I covered for you. So tell me what's going on already since you obviously know more than you're letting on and this is all your fault."

Pieces suddenly all fit together to Kylie for how Mom found out. Why the timing had been so close to things that went on with Amalia. A flash of anger boiled inside her, at Dani being the one who — intentionally — let it slip that Kylie had been sneaking around, at Dani telling secrets that weren't ever meant to be shared with outsiders. "Wait, you *told* her I was late? Told her about magic?"

Dani's hands recoiled from Kylie at the sharpness of Kylie's tone. "Y-yeah, if you're not going to help Amalia, why should I cover for you? And maybe there's more details Mom would catch that could help. She's right that we're still children, and she's a professional. I went to you first and you didn't even try, so I had to tell her."

It was a moment I'd never forgiven Dani for, not until just then when I experienced it as an outsider. It was the moment as Kylie, I realized we lived in different worlds: if Dani got in over her head, she just needed to go to her mom to make it better. Kylie couldn't go to Mom; even if Mom knew, she couldn't stop an entire organization that experimented on mages. Even if Mom knew, she couldn't protect Kylie from Asuza's little fan club that wanted Kylie's head. It'd just be even more stress on Mom than things were.

Dani had already lost her friend; Mom had already lost her daughter. I didn't — couldn't — understand how it felt to be them when I struggled to survive as me back during this. I now understood how Dani was wrong, but only because Kylie's situation wasn't a normal one.

"There's nothing I can do." Kylie's voice was dry, monotone. "I recommend to not use magic publicly, which shouldn't be a problem since it's just a hobby for you and nothing more."

"That's it? Seriously, that's all you're going to say?" Dani's voice increased as she stood, hands flailing by her side with each word. "Then just take it all back. I don't want to be kidnapped too, don't want whatever happened to you that you're leaving Amalia in."

Kylie didn't even ask me if it was possible: her practice in theory was strong enough to know the answer. "There is no 'taking it back.' Sia warned you, and you said you didn't care. If you're going to tattle about that too, good luck getting anyone to believe you without ending up wherever Amalia is. You saw it yourself: people want mages dead. And you're forever in that bucket because *you asked for it*. If Sia — if *I* — am not strong enough, then you'll never have a shot escaping with how low your magipoten is. Keep that in mind next time you're sharing things to your mom."

Dani's cheeks flushed as her eyes grew glassy. "Maybe *she* really is who you'll become. A monster." She stood up and slammed the door closed as she left. Dani refused to cry in front of Kylie but it really didn't matter given empathy, not that Dani acknowledged that either.

Kylie lowered her eyes to her lap, keeping her head down. "I shouldn't have ever depended on her to begin with. She can't understand what it's like." A moment passed before she said, "Just give me two minutes, and I'll get back to training."

"Mm, sure." She acted as if I had no idea what was wrong, as if I didn't know her emotions and how she wanted to cry and felt so alone. I said nothing of comfort, just giving her time to pick herself up.

She took a deep breath, forcing air into her lungs. As she stood, she noticed Mom's aura coming into view. "Great..." Kylie tightened her eyes and took another breath, walking over to the kitchen and getting a cup of water. The garage opened, and a few minutes later, Mom stepped in. "Welcome back." It was a valiant attempt at pretending nothing was wrong. She genuinely had lied better than even a few weeks ago, but she still needed a lot of work before she'd make an actually passable lie.

"Thanks, Sweetie." Mom was tired enough to not notice though, a big briefcase likely full of papers in her right hand. "How was school?"

"It's all right."

Mom hesitated as she opened the briefcase, noticing Kylie's mood was off. "I'm glad to hear it's going well. Anything exciting coming up?"

"Not really. Going to go back upstairs now." Kylie left, fully intent on continuing training instead of dealing with any of the emotions she pretended weren't ensnaring her.

Chapter Thirty-Five

brighter than others

Kylie | March 31
Rae Residence

I guess at least we got to work on this project in my room instead of having to work on the kitchen table where Mom graded papers. It still was rather miserable that she didn't trust me enough that she'd snuck up more than once to make sure Lianne and I were actually working on the project. To my credit, one of us was.

That was me, by the way.

I had internet articles up on my laptop, both of our biology textbooks laid out to specific pages, and my notebook beside me on the carpet. I kept going back and forth between them as I tried to work on this poster board we had to present in a few weeks. It was a good twenty-five percent of my grade, and all I needed was to do bad and watch Mom go ballistic again after we'd almost been getting on speaking terms again. I wasn't grounded, but Mom was none too subtle that Lianne was *coming over here* instead of the reverse, and it wasn't worth the fight otherwise.

At this point, I just wish Sia had been my partner instead of Lianne, who very obviously didn't care about her grade as she sat on my bed, making flicking gestures as she scrolled through something on her phone. I wasn't even sure why she was here if she had no intention to help. Sia would've at least humored me with help so we could do other things faster, something I also would've preferred. It would've given me more time to write out magic branches, or push myself in exercise — I was able to do push-ups with only my hands and one foot for support now, though couldn't do as many of them as I'd like, admittedly.

Squinting at some of my messily scribbled notes that I'd not wanted to take in the first place, I struggled to make out what I wrote that day. Hoping Sia paid attention, I took my pointer finger and traced a question mark over my notes. Maybe she could figure it out — it was worth the shot at least.

"What, you think I wanted to go through biology again? I totally tune that class out." That was valid, but I also huffed in irritation. *"Something... Latin name? Apex maybe? No clue on the Latin thing after it though."* It was something, so I started flipping through Lianne's copy of our bio book looking for something with "Apex" and "Latin thing" in it.

"Hey, I've always wondered," Lianne said. I didn't like the intensity I felt from her right then, like I was prey during a hunt. Lianne's distrust and anxiousness increased as she focused on me. I braced from her feelings, not liking where she seemed to be heading with this question. "Why're you brighter? Like you and what's his name are the brightest, but you're still brighter than him even."

"Um, like smart? Or like?" Was it a compliment? Weird one, but I'd take what I could get right then, and it wasn't like we were the closest friends to begin with — just stuck together as lab partners all year, and I needed to save my GPA to keep Mom out of my hair.

Her eyes honed in on me. I moved my attention away, even less comfortable with how focused on me she was. "No... That like... teal, and blue. It's so bright." My hand froze flipping through the pages — those were my aura colors. She could see auras? Wouldn't that mean she was a mage too?

The only mage I'd met that wasn't tied up in Riyatian stuff was Amalia.

I couldn't risk association like Dani had. I couldn't go missing again on Mom; she'd not been the same since June, and neither was I. Those women weren't dead — stalled by Sia and Rota, but only they knew for how long. And what would happen now that Sia couldn't get control? I couldn't fight them and win. Would I be kidnapped again? Killed on the spot? "Like my eye color? Guess it's unusual, yeah. Never heard it described that way before though." In my defense, Jordan was probably the closest to my eye color I'd ever met, actually. Well, outside of Kisate, Leah, Chloé, and especially Sia, but they didn't count. I'd always assumed I got my eye color from my father since Mom had dark blue eyes — not quite navy, but definitely on the darker side of blue.

She scoffed, tossing her phone on my bed so she could stare straight at me. "You know that's not what I meant. Why're you lying again?"

Tightening my fists, I shook my head. "I guess I don't know what you mean. I'm sorry."

I wished Dani didn't know now. Jordan was bad enough, hated me because of things. I knew he wasn't reckless with magic, though. And while that jerk he was always with saw it as some party, for some reason he had kept his mouth shut better than Dani since Jordan and him were still at school, weren't kidnapped like Amalia. But... I just couldn't trust anyone anymore. It was too much of a risk, a liability.

"Whatever." Lianne flopped back around on my bed, roughly grabbing her phone. Her anger sank into my stomach and through my chest like a poison.

I wished I trusted her enough to not play dumb, to actually have a friend in magic again. But that was a danger I couldn't afford, to protect me and even her.

197

Chapter Thirty-Six

the trick

Jordan | April 4
Opal Pines West District

Rotanu'd refused to heal me ever since that NEO-thing, and Kylie'd not asked for more of the training shit, content to give me the space I'd asked for. Meant that I thought I was finally free of these damn "training sessions," even if it'd sucked ass not getting healed. But whatever. Had grown up dealing with bruises and cuts, and none of them lasted long as they used to, usually gone in days if not hours. Small blessings in the middle of this magic shitstorm, 'specially since pain meds're less effective by the day due to damn mana killing them b'fore they took effect — took ibuprofen two days ago to get any relief, and it took seven for what two used to do.

What I hadn't counted on's that Richard still drug me around as his magic entertainer. Didn't bitch 'bout coming to the damn training house, just drove to the closest road and left his car locked as we walked the rest — seemed like a shitty-ass idea considering I'm just waiting for the thing to be broken into, but it'd yet to happen. I wasn't in a place to complain 'bout getting free rides around town instead of walking every damn where, so I didn't argue. Felt bad for Emily though, since

Richard told her to walk herself back home, and unlike when I said I couldn't walk with her, she's actually fine with it. Said it's no trouble at all, a normal response of hers to Richard.

I'm running outta shit to show him though. He ain't amused by the basically lighter-size flame or a small ice cube in my hand anymore. Wanted something *more impressive,* he said.

Still's better than what Rotanu and Siani wanted from me: Richard didn't want me to get stabbed in those mock fight things. Didn't ask for me to be an emotion test subject, hurting my oldest friend just being near her. Party tricks're fine. Harmless. And Richard'd really looked out for me in a way that no one else had in a while, Kylie too absorbed with magic now. Richard cared if I did actual teenager things, things I honestly never thought I'd get to experience, like a girlfriend.

"Wish there'd be a more *pleasant* area for this though," Richard said. I didn't disagree, but from what Kylie'd said, being in the middle of nowhere's even more intended than I'd thought. Originally'd assumed it's 'cause we didn't want someone we knew overseeing us looking like freaks but... somehow, even that would've been better than what Kylie had mentioned about open magic usage. Something else Siani and Rotanu neglected to promptly mention despite being fully aware.

I didn't reply since it wasn't the first time he'd grumbled that. Instead, I pushed the door open, throwing my weight behind it as I'd learned to do. Door open, I saw there's already someone here — Kylie, Isare in her hands but pushed against her chest, eyes glancing around. She's in alt form, prob'bly to train with. "Get out of here," she screamed. "Now!"

What? We hadn't spoken in over a month — I didn't know what to say to her after that day with NEO, but that ain't a reason to scream at me.

"Not like you own this place," Richard said, pushing in front of me as he glared at her, arms crossed over his chest. "We can be here all we want."

She shook her head, eyes darting around. "That's not—" A lance stabbed through her right arm; she gasped, eyes wide open b'fore clenching shut. Blood sprayed out in front of us, lance tip completely through to the other side of skin.

200

It wasn't a demand: it's a beg, a warning. One of those bitches's here, and — why hadn't Siani taken control? Why was it Kylie at all?

"It's up to you now."

What in the motherfuckin' goddamn hell did he mean by *that*? Why hadn't Siani taken over? Why's he just letting them get fucked over? It made no goddamn sense. Kylie and me... we're not meant to be involved in this shit. It's all some freak accident. I shouldn't have this power, not over fire and ice, not over her. It ain't right.

"The others were scared of you from how you were before, yet now..." It's the one Rotanu'd identified as Nimaka. She seemed to know Kylie better than the other two. "What happened? Not so confident now, are we?" She plunged the spear through Kylie's arm even more so b'fore yanking it out as she kicked Kylie to the broken concrete floor. There's no way that's Sia. This entire time, I hadn't seen Sia get as much of a scratch on her. This's Kylie, but I didn't get *why*. Why're Rotanu and Siani content to leave us to die suddenly?

I'm useless. Not meant for any of this shit. Didn't know anything except party tricks and didn't wanna know more but there's so much blood. This faint whisper in my mind begged for me to rush in anyways. For the first time, I wanted to stab someone, kill even. I could only stare, my hands trembling, but the fuck could I do?

Nimaka stabbed Kylie through her leg, entirely too close to her symbol — if Nimaka pierced that then... then what?

She'd die, from what Takite and Rotanu'd said. A broken symbol meant no mana circulation, and no mana circulation meant death for those of us stuck with this hell of an existence.

"Help me, dammit," I said to Rotanu — why hadn't he said anything? Why hadn't he taken fuckin' control of my body to save her as he had the other times? What'd changed? Why's he letting her suffer?

He said nothing. Not even a pathetic-ass attempt to justify himself.

I had to do *something*, couldn't just leave her. Something in the back of my mind snapped as Nimaka stepped on Kylie's right arm, a crunch beneath her boot heel as Kylie just whimpered. "Nateka, manifest," I said under my breath, charging her.

It did jack shit: her blocking and then deflecting Nateka out of my grip, lance thrust through my ankle as I screamed and fell to a crouched position, trying to shift weight off that foot. Was blinding, yet every moment was slower as I focused on Kylie, even my own pain distancing as I checked if she's still breathing or not. She coughed, alive and somehow still conscious.

"You as well..." She grabbed my chin, tilting my head up to stare at her face. "What happened, I wonder?" Her nails dug into my jaw. "And who were you talking to there?"

"H-hey, Jordan — stop playing around. Go kick her ass like before," Richard said, but it ain't his normal confidence. For the first time, I heard him nervous, scared even.

Swinging Nateka upward, I tried to attack. She didn't release her grip on my chin as she deflected the strike with her lance, not even a mild distraction for her. I had no plan, pain flashing through me, but I couldn't just leave Kylie right then. "I can't." Further realization we're fucked 'cause Rotanu and Siani're just leaving us to die. "It's like I told you." Her eyes zoomed in at me, licking her lower lip.

"But before, you..." Richard said. I heard movement behind me, what sounded like him tripping on something and landing on his ass. Kylie's eyes're clenched shut in pain, sharp breaths as her fist balled and she attempted to pull herself up despite everything. How? How could she still even move?

The faint whisper increased in intensity, this urge for killing I'd never had. I wanted Nimaka dead, wanted her in pain. I didn't understand — I hated violence, I...

"Kutari," Richard said. But his voice wasn't like b'fore, too calm, amused even. Like he's in control as he'd always been with none of the very reasonable panic of seconds b'fore. "Generate effective immediately."

A spell?

Forcing my head to turn, I saw Richard with some bladed pole arm. "All right, you did your part, Bitch. Now kindly go fuck off to wherever you live, if you wouldn't mind."

Nimaka's eyes widened. "So that's the trick." But she ain't

angry or confused. She's giddy more like, as if she understood the solution to a problem. "I'll be back. Try to stay alive until then, or don't." She kicked Kylie one last time as she disappeared b'fore my eyes.

Richard dismissed the weapon he'd called Kutari as he walked over to Kylie and me. He held a hand against Kylie's shoulder, a lime green aura manifesting around his hand.

"Did you know?" I said under my breath to Rotanu.

"Yeah. Your present's still my past, even now."

Richard had Act, just like Kylie and me had last spring, had another older self seemingly, just as we did. Yet whoever this other self was, he's not only willing to touch Kylie as bloodied as she was, but reached down and healed her. His attention'd immediately directed to her, so different with how Richard barely acknowledged she existed and made it a pain in the ass to talk to her.

Kylie pushed herself up, forcing air down her lungs with deep breaths. She nodded. "I-I can from here. Sia said you can't…"

"If I get this one, you should be able to do the others, right? Less overall mana consumption since I can't collapse for Initial Cycle yet." There'd been strategy behind his willingness to heal Kylie then, but even still, was so uncharacteristic. Richard didn't seem to be awake at all, just like it'd been for Kylie and me when we had Act. Was this how Act always worked, with other selves and passing out? Dani and that Amalia girl didn't seem to have other selves, but everything's so fucked, I didn't know what's normal and what wasn't.

Kylie healed herself b'fore moving closer, her left hand on my ankle, healing magic pushing through where I'd been stabbed; it mended, a faint scar and bloodied sock all that remained. "Thanks," I said, testing my ankle as I stood; she'd healed it perfectly as far as I could tell, just as if Rotanu or Siani'd done it. Was impressive as hell, given that even a few months back, she would've struggled with something that deep.

Heat rose to my cheeks as I saw her symbol from how she kneeled in her alt form's shorts. I couldn't make the red and blue outline out from where I was, but images of that one day — when I'd first heard "Arbiter" and "NEO" — flashed through my mind, memories so fluid as if I'm back there again. I pushed my eyes away from her. I didn't want that type of power, shouldn't have had it over anyone, let alone her. Suddenly didn't know what to say yet again, so I said nothing, just watched as she healed herself over and over.

More missing truths from those that were s'posed to be our future selves, looking out for us.

Chapter Thirty-Seven

enough

Kylie | April 4
Rae Residence

I closed the bathroom door, biting down on my lip as I sat the change of clothes and towel on the counter. I'd made it back without a single tear. That was something, right? It wouldn't much longer — I felt water rising to my eyes — , but I'd made it back. I quickly turned the shower on: I needed to further heal and clean my alt form. I'd thankfully been training when things happened, so my actual clothes and body were fine, but I needed to take care of alt form for next time.

Quickly undressing, I mumbled the alt form transformation phrase. As soon as the spell finished, I felt my muscles sting — the clothes were freshly bloodying again so I took them off and undid the braid before stepping into the shower.

The water stung, humidity filling my lungs like a balloon ready to pop. I saw red mix in with the otherwise clear water but couldn't be bothered to heal myself yet. The water was too hot, leaving my skin flushed, but I just had no energy to turn it down, the sting being something in my life I could control for once. The remaining incisions weren't worth the mana in healing magic anyways; they would probably close before I got out of the shower. And besides...

I wasn't enough.

Until last March, my life had been predictable, peaceful. Mom rode me about school, but that'd been my biggest problem, all I knew. No one wanted to kill me. I wasn't actively ruining the lives of everyone around me. I wasn't even strong enough to just kill myself — the memories of Kisate's desperation at being trapped forever freezing me the one time I might've otherwise gone through with it.

Now I'd triggered NEO and only had any form of consciousness at Jordan's *whim*. His aura was seared around my symbol, like I was branded cattle. How was I supposed to be around him when at any moment, he could decide maybe I'd be better off without my consciousness?

Maybe I would've been. Maybe I owed him that power with how I'd ruined all of our lives. Even Richard's now, somehow, despite not saying a word to him directly in months.

It was another thing Rota and Sia hadn't mentioned but so obviously had known. I didn't ask why she didn't say it. What was the point? Even if she'd never had my best interest completely at heart, she was the only ally I had now.

It hurt, thinking about any time before that day in June. How Sia and Rota joked and I'd get mad because how could she claim to be me yet was with him that way? That calm emotion that Rota had, so different from Jordan, a peace as he bantered with Sia. Or when they'd talk to each other, even if only one of them or even neither had control, somehow *knowing* regardless.

Maybe I'd messed up Sia's past now with everything else. Even if I'd had feelings for Jordan, he didn't feel like Rota did. He wouldn't even look me in the eyes, wouldn't talk to me.

He hated magic, so I guess it made sense. If it wasn't for me, he'd be a lot happier in life, wouldn't have had the numerous mage-related problems in our lives now. Maybe that's why he was fine going to practice or train or whatever they did when he and Richard kept coming to the training house but he wouldn't even look at me anymore. Richard didn't put his life in danger; I did.

I tightened my eyes, wishing these thoughts would just *stop*. I wished my mind quit replaying the banter between Sia and Rota and how Jordan's girlfriend hung over him in a way Sia hadn't ever done with Rota and how angry it made me for absolutely no good reason every time I saw them together.

Balling my fists, I felt more tears slip down my face. Sia was awake, but she didn't say anything. What was there to say? Wasn't like she could take over my body anymore. Wasn't like she could let me rest and try to process and not deal with Mom's anxiousness that kept crowding into my head, as if my own emotions weren't overwhelming enough.

I needed to get it together. First thing, I needed to heal myself because the rest of the incisions hadn't fully done so yet after all. I laid my hand over my left calf, pushing a healing spell, then another, then moved my hand to my arm and healed again as I felt my chest heave from back to back spells. The red in the water trickled out as all the injuries healed. I then washed my alt form's hair, it so much longer than my own. I'd have to braid it back later, something I had practiced after showers like this months ago back when it'd been optional. I hadn't even considered the possibility that I'd not have a choice because Sia wouldn't be able to. There was a sense of irony in that I wished I had less control now, would've been fine just handing things off to Sia.

As I washed blood off my alt form's leg, my eyes rested on my symbol: it had Jordan's Arbiter Seal, just as my own body did. I didn't remember if it'd always been there or only appeared after it'd appeared on my own body. I'd ask Sia, but I didn't trust any answer she'd give for something like this.

I couldn't even blame Sia for lying when I'd lied to Mom and asked Dani to lie for me. I just wanted to get better, to be able to sleep at night without fear. Why was that so wrong?

Why wasn't I enough? Enough for Mom, enough for Sia, enough for Dani.

Enough for Jordan.

Sniffling more, I hurried through the rest of the bathing process, stepping out to redress back in the alt form clothes before releasing the transformation and taking a quick bath. I didn't actually need it, having spent basically the whole time in my alt form, but Mom would be suspicious and ask questions if I spent that much time with the water on and didn't have wet hair or turn on the hairdryer. She'd probably lecture me again about how having wet hair in winter caused colds, as if that was remotely my biggest problem now.

I wished it was. I wished I'd caught a cold instead of the frigidness inside my chest, suffocating air out of my lungs, fatigue running rampant across my limbs, whole body red between the tears and the too hot water that left welts that disappeared as quickly as they rose thanks to my mana. I didn't feel numb, but numb probably would've been an improvement to my own emotions and the emotions ever invading my head of anxiety and pain and elation and —

Even if I knew I couldn't wish for silence — that'd been what caused NEO to begin with — I wanted to. I wondered if I could trigger NEO a second time, just be done with it all.

Tightening my eyes clenched shut and then opening them, I shut the water off, dressing in the clothes I'd left on the counter. Opening the bathroom door, I put the dirty clothes into my hamper as I walked back to the bathroom and then grabbed the hairdryer under the cabinet to dry my hair. I'd have to wait until Mom wasn't here to dry my alt form's hair since it took easily three times as long as my own and she'd notice something like that.

The ongoing noise of the hairdryer somehow made my thoughts even louder. Was he happier now? I guess it'd make sense if he was since he had the ideal high school life now, friends and a girlfriend and busy afternoons doing teenage things. A life like I used to have.

Mom's aura moved, coming up the stairs. What'd I do this time? I wasn't in the mood, but I couldn't say that, couldn't show it. Hopefully my cheeks and eyes weren't still red and puffy; I'd say it's from the shower if she asked. She knocked on the door, and I turned the hairdryer off. As I did, she came in. "You okay, Sweetie?"

I nodded even though I was the opposite of okay. "Yeah, just accidentally let the water get a little too hot."

She didn't believe me. I needed to get better at lying — she would've believed whatever Sia said, no matter how ridiculous. I tried to force a smile, but that only worried her more. Her hand stroked my hair for a few seconds before she laid papers on my desk. "I won't make you, but you really should consider it."

Transferring schools meant running away from all that I knew, had ever known. It'd be a completely new district my senior year, no classmates I'd known for a decade, no Jordan around to even briefly see.

"I'll think about it." It wasn't like before, when not knowing anyone terrified me. I just didn't care anymore.

"I'll have dinner ready in about half an hour," she said, this pity and helplessness increasing as she looked at me. Maybe I just looked that pitiful now. I'd done most of my crying in my alt form but not all of it, so it might've been obvious. Or maybe she'd heard me even though I tried to use the water to mask my shallow breaths.

She left after I nodded, leaving me to resume drying my hair.

"You can talk about it, if you want," Sia said.

I shook my head. What was there to talk about that I hadn't already said? She'd just lie, and I wasn't in the mood to even pretend to believe her.

Chapter Thirty-Eight

suggestions

It's amazing how when I tried to have a conversation, he just ignored the shit outta me, but when *he* wanted to talk, he got pissy as all shit if I didn't answer *fast enough* for him. I didn't even maintain any control over his elements or aura reading anymore, and just honestly wanted to go goddamn home already.

'Specially right then, when I'm stuck listening to his fuckin' bitching *again*.

"You couldn't've said a damn thing?" Jordan's voice's mildly above a whisper but still quiet so that he didn't wake Richard up. I ain't sure why he bothered when he knew the Initial Cycle'd kicked Richard's ass like it had his and Kylie's. Outside of Richard and Sai, we're alone at the apartment — everyone else'd long since left to whatever they're doing this entirely too frigid for April morning. "What's the point of even pretending? Why lie that it'd just been me and Kylie dragged into this shit-fest?"

Of all people, he should've known I'm a shitty liar. Better than when I was younger, but I've always been a damn easy read. *"Never lied, and ain't ever said it's just you two. What we* said's *that the reincarnation spell's* intended *for Kisate and Takite. But even then, I said someone else cast it."*

Jordan paused, searching through his memory of my exact words. Cussed under his breath after a second: confirmation of my exact phrasing. He made the assumption all on his own, and sure, I remembered the misconception, but ain't my problem to correct. "So there's more? And Richard's got a 'future self' or whatever, and 'past selves'? How many more times're we going through this bullshit? Getting really fuckin' tired of these damn games you keep playing." Richard's the reincarnation of the general that cast the reincarnation spell that night; our age order'd maintained, but the gaps themselves're severely condensed compared to things originally — Kisate and Takite're similar in age, but Richard's original incarnation had to be at least thirty years older than them both, maybe more. Was hard to tell from Takite's memories, the few I had.

"Ain't playing a damn game." Refusing to tell him every single thing that happened for the next four years wasn't a game; he didn't deserve special treatment more than he already got. 'Sides, it hurt like fuck to see all this shit again, had sucked to deal with, and ain't like I got a ton of people to talk to now. *"And Richard's only got a future self— no past incarnations."*

"How's that even possible? You said — "

"Means at least one of his prior incarnations had Act and used the dismissal spell, and that none after the dismissal spell died unclean deaths. Dunno when or any of that shit, just's deductive reasoning based on how shit works."

Takite died from the reincarnation spell, and both John and Dmitri committed suicide. Kisate died from the reincarnation spell, and both Chloé and Leah died from Asuza murdering them. But Richard's incarnations hadn't been closely involved past the original death from the reincarnation spell, at least that I had any recollection of.

"Probably lying again." Jordan rolled his eyes.

"Sure, go with that if you want." I just wanted to be home and away from this shit show. I'd done my time: almost everything's lined up now, just waited for the final event to play

out. I'm sure Kyle's the same. Didn't realize how easy Sai —
well, "Saite," the Richard of my time — got it compared to us.

"And I can't believe we brought him *here* of all goddamn
places. Ain't there some super secret hide away?"

*"You think leaving him in the training house where said
attack happened's better?"* Richard slept in Jordan's bed; had
lied to Thomas that Richard's staying over — as if *that'd* ever
happened b'fore. Would've been a hilarious joke if it ain't such
a shitty lie. But there's no way Sai would've made it back to his
house with how the Initial Cycle'd been kicking his ass after
both weapon summoning and using moderate healing magic so
soon after Act. Alt form hadn't been established for him yet,
which meant he's going purely off Richard's mana, and
honestly dunno know how he'd managed even making it here.
And it ain't the first time I'd — Jordan'd — slept on the floor,
so his bitching's useless as ever.

"Why're you so goddamn useless?" Jordan sat on the old
couch, cloth different color than five years ago, let alone
however old the damn thing was. Smelled of alcohol like
everything else in the apartment, had been rained on more than
once when between apartments. Prob'ly had mold in it. Was
half tempted to put that thought in Jordan's head for shits and
giggles to distract him off my ass and onto a cleaning project.

I heard a "The fuck?" from Jordan and Thomas's bedroom.
Definitely's Richard since Sai knew. Jordan's whole postured
stiffened: ain't like bringing friends over's something I — or
Elaine, Jewel, and Thomas — did growing up; only friend b'fore
Richard's Kylie, and well, she'd been oblivious to certain things.

Richard stumbled out of the bedroom, holding his temple
with his left hand as he glanced around. His right hand went to
his nose as he gagged. "Fuck's this?"

Jordan's eyes moved away from Richard to the honestly
filthy carpet. I hated when our apartments had carpet 'cause
they're shitty b'fore we got 'em and ain't better after to say the
least. Was just how things were. At least could pretend and
scrub laminate hardwood with bleach or shit. There's patches
of color across the carpet too — previous tenants' leftover gifts
as stains that never got removed or cleaned. "Rainbow carpet"

as I'd sarcastically referred to this and similar frequently stained carpets like it. Red here, blue there, purple and why's that yellow; it got to a point that I knew better than to think too much 'bout it. "Uh, morning." I felt Jordan rub his neck, still keeping his eyes from Richard.

Richard said nothing a moment, the disgusted tone in his voice reemerging as he said, "Wait, you *live* in this hovel? Where? There's no space." Was 'bout average size for my family's apartments, but Richard wouldn't know that. Richard huffed, pulling his cell phone out of his pocket. "This won't do."

"Don't," Jordan said. He stood, hands reaching toward Richard, frozen right b'fore touching Richard's glove. I remembered my thoughts from then, that anything Richard did would just piss off my asswipe of a father, that Richard'd only make things worse. That I'd be more of a laughingstock and Richard and Emily'd bail if they knew what things're really like.

But that single word wasn't even a demand, only a whispered plead. He didn't have the balls to tell Richard to fuck off on imposing expectations on his life. Richard didn't pause, kept tapping buttons on his phone. Banging started outside the apartment, against the door in heavy swings; it caused Richard's head to shoot up, finger hovering above his phone's screen.

Jordan stepped back as his — my — asswipe of a father stumbled through the door, alcohol on his breath like normal. Must've passed out drunk in an alley or something again and just woke up. Too bad he didn't stay there, would've been an improvement. "Damn police," he said, a slur to his words. He swung at Jordan, who instinctively jerked back. Didn't matter, since the moment Jordan realized he ain't in pain gave an opening for the second fist to slug Jordan across the cheek, stinging and probably bruising. Either dodge everything or dodge nothing, but dodging some just pissed the asswipe off, and Jordan'd learn that well.

I heard shuffling, but it's from outside Jordan's vision. Steps're too steady to be the asswipe though, no way he'd be sober enough to have that steady of a gait. Richard ain't that confident either though, not in a situation like this. Which meant it's Sai.

"Hey," he said. Jordan glanced up, could feel his heart racing through the body we shared, both from being slugged and fear of Richard not knowing what he'd walked into, of the asswipe moving onto Richard instead and someone outside the family getting dragged into this shit. He saw Richard's aura — a light green — manifest around his irises, contrasting his blue eye color. "Good time for a nap, I'd say."

Out of anyone I knew, he's the fuckin' luckiest bastard when it came to abilities: "suggestion," where he'd *suggest* ideas to people, influence them. Had drawbacks and shit, but ain't like Kyle's where she dealt with empathy or precognition, and hypermnesia had its own bullshit.

I watched as the asswipe's drunken steps stumbled to the couch and immediately collapsed, loud snoring bouncing off the walls.

Sai sighed, shaking his head. "Idiot. Not even a fraction of resistance, probably wasn't completely awake to begin with." Could definitely believe it. With as much of a stagger plus slur as he had, surprised he even made it home to begin with. If Jordan hadn't been stunned by the first dodge, even he prob'ly could've dodged both with how sloppy and slow they were.

I wish I could've talked with Sai, but fuck, guess I'd like to talk to damn near anyone that's not my dumbass younger self right now.

"Fuck just...?" Jordan said, his voice barely above a mumble.

Sai chuckled; was funny the difference types of confidence between him and Richard. Sai's prob'ly still the most hotheaded of us, but he's a shit-ton more composed than Richard. "Took care of your problem next few hours. Can't do more than a single heal still though, so you'll have to pick the ones to live with." His eyes hardened as they rested on Jordan. It pissed him off, could clearly see it. But Sai knew, wasn't his first time dealing with my shitty home life. "But nothing else, since that's what you want, isn't it?"

Jordan's eyes widened, a soft nod.

It's a shitty life, but it'd been the only one he knew, and getting outsiders involved's too risky. Too much potential for someone else to get hurt instead of him, and he might've hated being hit, but someone else getting hit instead's even worse, no matter his bitching otherwise.

Chapter Thirty-Nine

not much time left

Siani | April 6
Training House

Today was one of those days I wished I could wake up and not be an empath. Sure, I could suppress the reads down for the most part, but even that wasn't enough for right then: we were in the training house, all six of us, the younger three and us older selves. Kylie in a room with either Jordan or Richard — let alone both at once — was a less than pleasant experience given everything that'd been going on, yet that's exactly how it was.

This one thing had to happen: the younger ones didn't know, but we had just over a month remaining. And even though Sai's an arrogant ass, he's family to Rota. So before we could leave, Richard needed access to the simulation of Sai's form, to alt form as Kylie and Jordan respectively had. But I couldn't do it this time as I had for Rota and myself, and it wasn't like it was something anyone could cast — only Kylie and myself could pull this off due to how the spell was crafted. Maybe even unfortunately for her, Kylie had the training and theoretical knowledge to cast the spell, even if she'd need my assistance to guide her through and wouldn't understand how the spell functioned for years yet. Yet to say she wasn't thrilled to be here, let alone do something she perceived as helping Richard, was both understandable and an understatement. At least unlike Rota and me, Sai still could get control since he wasn't affected by the blood spell I'd used. He had control right then instead of Richard, which was helpful since Sai was easier to work with over Richard given Rota had a leash on Sai.

"Why am *I* here again?" Jordan quietly said, likely to Rota. I'm not sure what Rota would tell him, but he was essentially the peace offering between Kylie and Richard, because if Sai gave control back, we'd get nothing done without Jordan present. Given Jordan grumbled under this breath, he didn't like whatever Rota said, which also was less than surprising considering both were always rather irritable with each other now.

Kylie tightened her grip around her backpack, keeping her eyes from either Jordan or Sai in Richard's form. "What did I need to do?"

She wouldn't train with them around. It had been a fight to get her to walk out here knowing they were here to begin with, and she refused to ride with Richard and Jordan, instead coming by herself. It seemed like the world still gave Richard everything and her nothing, and in some ways, she wasn't wrong. It wasn't a contest though, regardless of what she or Richard thought. But if it was, we'd win. I wasn't much a fan of losing, after all. *"Richard needs access to his alt form. That's something you set up for yourself with my guidance and partial control back at your Act, and then I set up for Jordan when we met after his Act. I can't do it for Richard, though, so I'll walk you through the steps."*

A huff escaped from her lips, clearly unhappy with the idea. She saw it as another way he replaced her, got the "fun" of being a mage without his life being in danger. "Fine, let's get this over with." But she knew she couldn't fight me and win.

"Tell Sai we're ready, and ask what the trigger phrase was."

She swallowed, no words from her throat; she couldn't even look at Sai — well, at Richard's body; Sai's body wasn't there yet, that being the end goal.

"You're ready?" Sai asked. I didn't know what he thought of his younger self's actions now. I also wasn't sure I wanted to —

doubt he regretted them enough to try to change things as Rota had, and knew I'd never heard anything remotely sounding like an apology come out of his mouth, let alone one to me for his admitted less than ideal behavior at this age. He knew enough to at least pretend to be the adult right then... though, that in and of itself was a rarity, granted, despite him being the oldest.

Kylie nodded, still not looking at him. "She wants to know what the trigger phrase was." It was like a relay game, except I heard it all, as did Rota. For once as of late, his emotions were at peace, a sense of nostalgia from watching Kylie and Sai interact.

"'Earth, manifest that which is mine.'"

"You'll have to focus for this next part because the spell is a bit complex." That was an understatement, admittedly; even not knowing the theory, the execution was around her skill limit. She nodded, saying nothing. Silence was her form of protest, and as long as she cast the spell right, she could stonewall me as much as she wanted. *"Switch to alt form."*

She swallowed, hesitating, before she set her backpack down beside her. Another moment passed before she said the transformation phrase: "Riyati, obey your mistress's command, activate withdrawal." As expected, her body and magipoten switched to simulations of my own.

"This spell's going to feel different. Just lean into it. I'll be monitoring for problems and can help adjust mana flow relative to things if needed." She nodded again. Wonder how long I was getting solitary confinement treatment for this one? *"Say 'Riyati, access stored blueprint relative' while focusing on Sai's aura."*

Her eyes finally went to Sai in Richard's form: he had his arms crossed over his chest, blankly staring at something off in the distance. He was probably bored, if I took a guess by his emotions. For whatever grace, he was *quietly* bored for once, but he wasn't nearly as annoyed as I'd expected from his normal lack of patience or social grace.

He probably saw the growth we'd all had since this time yet never stopped to notice until we had no choice but to, same as Rota and myself when we first came back to this time.

"Riyati," Kylie said, testing the word on her lips as she closed her eyes, focusing in on his aura. Mana instantly flowed to her, a caught breath through her lungs. "Access stored blueprint relative." Her heart raced from the mana stimulation, absorption device gained even more warmth as the excess mana filtered into it.

"Bind to aura for continued permission renewal until access revoked."

At least she was easily distracted by this, the fascination over the spell and mana from it fully engaging her attention even if only for a moment. This was a taste at far more complex spells than she'd ever seen, spells she wouldn't know how to manage by herself for a while yet. Richard's aura was more illuminated than before his Act, helping to separate the man in front of her with the subject of so much drama this year. "Bind to aura for continued permission renewal until access revoked."

"Allow direct withdrawal and simulation of specified blueprint based off aura specifications." I wish I had this memorized, but I didn't. I wasn't sure what it said about me and the amount of magic I'd worked with over the years, but I had the pattern and syntax memorized more than any direct speech or spell. It all followed a logic, one that Kylie would learn so well, it'd be as natural as breathing. If only creating spells was this easy, but it never was.

"Allow direct withdrawal and simulation of specified blueprint based off aura specifications." The glyphs finally tripped, as expected: the first was under Kylie, her aura of teal and clouded-blue gray filling the glyph. She didn't notice that this one had no water, no wind, and that there was a reason for it. A second glyph opened under Sai, his aura of green filling out each symbol.

"Phrase set: earth, manifest that which is mine."

She paused, recognizing the phrase as the one Sai said minutes ago. I think that ripped her back to reality, to this moment and away from the fascination of theory and praxis. Her voice shook as she said, "Phrase set: earth, manifest that which is mine."

The glyphs under her and Sai immediately vanished.

"Tell him to try it, I'm monitoring."

Kylie's eyes jerked away from Sai as she held her absorption device. "She said to try it, she's monitoring." I felt more amused than I should've been how monotone and verbatim she'd been there, the bare minimum compliance.

"Right, here goes." He sounded less than excited. We both knew she had to eventually get it right, but that didn't mean the first time. That should've worked though since I measured and directed mana to the same specifications as I'd done months ago when I did this myself for Rota. Also to be fair, Sai generally just didn't like practicing magic with me: he's a spoil-sport on physical injuries when I felt they were just part of the experience and fun. What was the point of sparring if there wasn't some blood loss and blurred vision involved? Nothing a healing spell couldn't fix. Eventually. "Earth, manifest that which is mine." The mana draws and auth's passed thankfully uneventfully, Sai's simulated body and magipoten replacing where Richard had been.

One more thing crossed off the to-do list. There wasn't much time left now, after all.

Chapter Forty

choice

Shit's still so surreal, despite it being in my life over a year now. Ain't nothing they've needed me for so far, and that'd been great, but having Kylie and Richard — or "Sai," the apparent nickname for Saite — in the same room's awkward's fuck. Already pissed Rotanu didn't say shit again and that I'm forced back to this damn house. I wanted nothing to do with any of it, yet kept being roped back in every goddamn other minute.

Compared to Siani and Rotanu with Kylie and me, Saite didn't look that different from Richard — guess it's 'cause Richard's older or something like that; he wasn't any taller, was more muscular but ain't exactly like Richard's scrawny like me to begin with. Hair's choppier and pulled back but still basically same length as Richard's. Had on a dark green coat with lots of silver buttons. Similar slacks to what Rotanu wore and some combat shoes. Black leather gloves, just like Rotanu's form had. There's a style of dress shared between Siani, Rotanu, and Saite: all had gloves, and sure it's all "combat gear," but there's something else beyond just that theme I wasn't able to place. Something faint, familiar. Didn't really matter but still's this itch, like a word right on the tip of my tongue that I couldn't articulate, except's 'bout the similarities between the "alt form" outfits.

"I think that's all I'm needed for," Kylie said, her eyes away from us both. I didn't want her to leave but didn't know how to tell her that. Didn't know if I could, given how she and Richard got along. I didn't wanna be here either, where we'd been attacked by those damn bitches more than once now. Really questioned how this was safer since they seemed drawn here.

Saite said nothing as I watched his eyes steady on Kylie, briefly shifting to me for a moment b'fore the tips of his lips had a smirk, not fully present, but enough that I'm effectively confused as shit 'bout what he found funny. "Thanks, 'preciate it," he said.

I saw less of Saite in Richard than I did Siani in Kylie, 'specially now. Kylie had this edge to her she'd never had prior to this shit. There wasn't the teenage girl I'd grown up with now. She's gone, hadn't been there since the kidnapping last June.

Then again, Richard's basically gone too now, was fuckin' thrilled with everything going on. And I ain't got a good feel on Saite yet — definitely's different from Richard: calmer, confidence somehow so different than Richard's. Saite didn't seem that bothered by Kylie, 'specially with that small smirk he had. Wished I saw him interact with Siani, 'cause ain't sure what it meant if they got along with how little Richard and Kylie did.

Wished even more so I ain't here and knew nothing to begin with.

She swapped from Siani's form back into her own, eyes still away from us. As she adjusted her clothes, I noticed that spot on her thigh: the *Arbiter Seal*, as Rotanu'd called it. The dark red and dark blue outline around her symbol. I swallowed, memories of that day, of my lips — "Goodbye," she said.

My eyes rushed away from her as I nodded. That whole day felt like some surreal dream or nightmare. Ain't sure which. Rotanu couldn't've been literal with her personality being optional though. 'Bout me being the one that got to choose. She's better than me, always'd been.

Yet I couldn't look her in the eyes anymore. Too embarrassed by what'd happened. Didn't know how to process if Rotanu'd been telling the truth and I had this *power* over her I in no way wanted. Rotanu'd been quiet this whole time as it was. Didn't even pressure me to come — that'd been Richard. Small blessing's with all the other shit going on.

She closed the door, herself on the outside.

Saite put his hand on my shoulder, pressing down a moment before releasing and walking past me, to the counter in what'd been a kitchenette, sitting on it. Or I assumed it's Saite at least — Richard hadn't ever done something like that b'fore. Almost felt like he's trying to comfort me, but ain't sure 'bout what. "Reminds me. 'Rota' — was going to generate a spell book, but forgot what's undead, preferably pre-conjugated for genitive?"

Rotanu made an air-blowing sound, which absolutely made shit-all logic considering he had no control of my body to do so. *"Lazy ass."* Yet he sounded almost amused by the question. Something more to it than I got. More than I wanted to get, for that matter. *"Yosomerizokone, assuming he wants singular."*

As much as I wanted to bitch how was I s'posed to repeat *that* back to Saite, damn hypermnesia meant it wasn't a recall problem, but a "how the fuck'd he even say that" one. "It's, uh. Yo-so..." Had to fuckin' mentally slow him speaking so I could poorly break it into syllables. Wished he'd just said the damn thing. "Yo-so-mer-ri-zo-ko-neh."

"Held the r too long and the ne ain't that pronounced. Should've been softer."

"Then *you* say it."

Saite snickered, his hand moving in a dismissive gesture back and forth. "I got it, close enough." He hopped off the counter, then suddenly started dusting his clothes, as if the dust from where he'd been sitting b'fore bothered him now. "Don't know how he could sit there." Was still in the alt form, but I guess they'd swapped. Couldn't read the difference as easily as Kylie and Siani, but I'd known Kylie most've my life and been around Siani a fair bit since she'd been here. "Now, I want to learn more spells, like that fire shit Jordan can do. Will be hilarious showing that off and watching reactions."

I shook my head. He couldn't. That Amalia chick'd gone

missing. I saw fliers up still, the same name Kylie'd mentioned. Nothing. A reminder that even right then, I might be watched and taken away from everything I'd known. Do hell knew what to me. And it wasn't like I'd be reported missing or anything that happened that one evening Kylie'd been kidnapped; no one in my family'd care, only'd notice when they couldn't yell at me to go do shit for them or couldn't blame shit on me.

"Pompous ass, ain't he?" Rotanu said with almost a chuckle.

Richard huffed, rolling his eyes. "Not like Michelle and David'd let them." Wish I had his confidence, that assurance, that I'd be safe 'cause of any parental protection. "Psh, yeah right. Couldn't get into the house." Richard sounded completely unimpressed and not threatened. Confidence'd never been my thing, not like Kylie'd always had 'til recently, not like he had right then. Was one of the ways I shared jack shit with Rotanu, considering even he's more confident than me. Yet another of his many lies.

"Perhaps you'd like to share the other day then?" Did they just switch again? There's something dangerous and knowing in that tone that hadn't been there a second ago, something closer to the amused tone I'd heard from Saite toward me and Kylie earlier, but far less friendly. "Then I will, sounds fun." His eyes — gonna just assume it's Saite but fuck knew for sure — moved to me. "Absorption devices. Gets a bit dangerous, we've already learned."

"Uh?"

Rotanu snickered, making a "hmm" sound as he did so. Again, how the fuck'd any of that work? Why was I the only one who didn't seem to know what's going on? I mean, maybe Richard didn't either, but Saite's comment'd been rather pointed and if not to me, I'd guess it's to Richard.

"Two lessons, actually, thinking about it." He stepped closer, pointing to below my chin. "What happens if someone besides you touches that?"

I glanced down, saw the old shirt I had on. "Uh? Nothing?"

"Means your absorption device." Rotanu actually being helpful for once, pigs gonna fly soon. Prob'bly's just to cooperate with Saite since he's so buddy-buddy to him and Siani.

"O-oh. Uh." I stepped back. "S'fine for me, but..." Rotanu'd healed Father's hands once when he'd come in contact with that damn pendant. I'd seen Father's hands burn with fire and ice and'd been lucky as hell Father passed out drunk and didn't remember shit when he woke up. Made sure to keep it under my shirt at all times now, and prioritized keeping people away from it. Another damn headache with magic I'd never asked for. "Fucks people up. Fine for me though."

"Very good. Guess who also learned this lesson recently?" Wait, it wasn't something Rotanu'd fucked up on with that? "Along with why we don't *remove* absorption devices."

That one Siani'd made sure I knew. Sounded fuckin' terrifying to break contact, and no matter how pissed I was, ain't even attempting that one. But that meant... "Wait, Richard...?"

Annoyance flashed across Saite's features. "I already told you, it's unreasonable to expect I'll wear *these* damn earrings the rest of my life. I have hundreds of other pairs, why would I stick with *these*?" Oh, back to Richard. Guess they did this instead of internally talking to each other? Or maybe it's a way for Rotanu and me to stay in the conversation? Fuck knew, just's confusing as hell to keep up with. Almost'd rather just miss half the conversation like happened with Kylie and Siani.

"Left earring. As far as I know, can't split load on absorption devices." Didn't ask for the explanation, but I wondered how that worked so wasn't complaining 'bout him being somewhat helpful for once in his life. Twice so close together prob'bly meant it'd be another year b'fore it happened again.

I noticed more of a trend than I'd expected, with a firm but less strict posture from Saite compared to Richard. Hypermnesia helping for once in my life. "And when we're making out, we make sure to keep wandering hands *off* the absorption device, we've learned now, haven't we?"

My cheeks darkened as I'd glanced away. Hadn't seen him with his normal array of women since a day or two after Act, actually. Since he'd been so invested in magic, thought was distracted, but uh. Saite's comment there implied there'd been less choice than I knew.

Choice... magic took that away from even *Richard* of all people. What chance did someone like me have if both Kylie and Richard had their choices taken away? It really didn't matter if it's here, at home, at school, with Emily, fuck even with Kylie now — it's all 'bout what everyone else wanted. And all I wanted was...

What'd I want?

Not to be involved in this shit show, of course, but beyond that, I ain't sure. Just one day at a time's enough, isn't it? More than anyone ever thought I'd be.

More than even I thought I'd ever be.

Chapter Forty-One

figure it out

Kylie | April 14
Rae Residence

I just wanted this year over already. I wasn't exactly sure how next year would be better at this point, but I'd reached the conclusion it couldn't be *worse*.

Every second I was on guard. Sia couldn't cover for me; it was all up to me now. She provided information — if she wanted, of course — and was the closest thing I had left to someone looking out for me. Mom was still so disappointed, conflicted, emotions she'd never had with me prior to this year. I let her down just by existing.

Jordan barely said a word to me when we were at the training house; he wouldn't even look at me. I felt it so clearly, him being uncomfortable and hesitant as he let Sai and Sia do all the talking. Sia had me help Richard and Sai in the first place, even after everything he'd said this year. It was as if him being a mage was supposed to make up for everything else, some special exclusion.

But he wasn't just a mage: he was the same as Jordan and me somehow. It'd been all but said that spell and Riyati were just for Jordan and me until Richard had Act. He wasn't like Dani or Amalia; he had Sai like I had Sia and Jordan had Rota. And she'd made me help him have an alt form like it'd be some grace to us.

All he wanted to do was show off; he didn't understand how it felt at night to keep one eye open, terrified of being captured, of being attacked. Of being too difficult to be around so no one tried anymore.

Yet again, I didn't want empathy or sensory precognition. My body had been wracked with pain earlier, the episodes becoming more prominent the more mana I obtained. Sia couldn't stop them anymore, just provide some element of buffer, she said. I didn't know if it was true but I had to believe it because what other choice did I have?

And now... well. Lianne very clearly didn't want to be working on this project or around me. I felt it in my stomach, this consuming anger, the likes of which I'd only felt from Sia the few times Sia slipped while talking to Kisate. But this time, the anger wasn't at Kisate. It was at me. I didn't know why or how or anything. She said nothing to me outside of the bare minimum.

I just wanted the year to be over.

Typing out a few more words of the final paper we had due this year, I asked, "Can you look something up?"

After she said nothing, I glanced over. She was on my bed laid down, tapping her screen with increasing intensity. Once she noticed me looking at her, she huffed before snapping, "What?"

"What genus were frogs again?"

She rolled her eyes. "Rana. Are you done now?"

What was her problem? I just wanted to get through the year. Why was that so much to ask? I wasn't that terrible of a group project partner: I did the majority of the work. In fact, I *still* was doing the majority of the work. Her irritation flooded my mind, suffocated air from my lungs. My cheeks flushed further despite my desk fan already blowing air on me. "Would be, if you actually helped." I didn't mean to say it, just kind of slipped out a bit louder than under my breath. Her irritation fed into me and made me just as upset as she was.

"I don't like liars," she said.

Fully turning to her, I stared. I saw her glare at me, a scowl on her face. Her eyes met mine as her anger flooded even further into me, maybe even mixing with my own irritation. She somehow suspected I was a mage; she was likely one herself and had alluded to what I'm pretty sure were my aura and Jordan's auras. But I wouldn't end up like Amalia. Dani knowing was already a mistake that'd effectively killed our friendship and put us both in danger — maybe all of us, even Jordan and Richard. I wouldn't — couldn't — allow this opening. Too many people wanted me dead; I didn't need to be put on the radar so that people knew to capture and send me off to who knew where. "I still don't get what you mean. What am I lying about?"

Li tossed my textbook onto the carpet, a muted thud from the book colliding into the carpet. "I'm done with this charade."

She left my room, left down the stairs.

My heart raced, my mind conflicted: should I chase after her? We were supposed to present this together. What would happen if she wasn't there? I couldn't fail this, Mom wouldn't let me.

"That was a bit melodramatic."

I was still upset with Sia for the stuff with Richard and Sai, but that was distant compared to minutes prior. Instead, I nodded in agreement, startled from watching her storm out as if she was a child throwing a tantrum. "Guess I'll just... figure it out."

Once again, it was just me and Sia in this room, something of a recurring trend since last June.

Chapter Forty-Two

gone

Ain't many blessings this year so far, but at least the weather's decent for once. Ain't stupid hot, but not freezing my ass off either. Was humid, but that's always the case in this damn town. Made times like now, where I waited outside, more tolerable. I stood over in my usual spot, out of the way of other students leaving the school grounds.

Glancing away, I saw police officers talking to a few students — looked like Steve and MaryAnne, both frequent offenders with me in detention. Why're cops here though? Seriously doubted either of them'd done anything worth calling authorities over; both usually just bitched how they got caught with cell phones out and written up.

I bit back a jump as I felt arms around my shoulders. "Surprise," Emily said, as if I ain't been waiting on her.

"H-hey." I kinda hated when she snuck up on me like that. I mean, most guys prob'bly would've liked it, just's a me thing and I knew it. Just ain't comfortable with touch in general, let alone from someone behind me that I hadn't known was there.

"What's going on?" she said as she moved her head to the

side. Emily was taller than me with the boots she had on right then, so wasn't hard for her to see over my shoulder where I'd been looking. "Oh, I bet they're here for what's-her-name that's gone missing."

Someone'd gone missing? My heart raced, flashes to when I'd seen Kylie the other day. Sia wouldn't've let things go that far, right?

Wasn't like it'd stopped them last June.

"Who's...?" My lips were dry. Didn't want to ask the question to her, didn't trust what answer Rotanu'd give in her place — or more likely, whatever bullshit excuse he'd provide. He'd been quieter than normal lately and it'd been a damn blessing, but ain't like he'd ever spoken up ahead of time for important shit to begin with.

"Oh, you should know her pretty well." Emily's tone was mischievous, like this was a game. "Been in a lot of classes with you, if I remember right."

Rotanu said nothing, no assurances, no confirmations. Never's useful when he fuckin' could've been, and I saw Kylie tied up once more in that damn castle, her skin pale.

Richard walked over, nodding to me. "Yo." I nodded back, not sure what to say. Was Saite as bad as Siani and Rotanu with hiding shit? Then again, I was assuming he'd go outta his way for Kylie, and Richard sure as fuck wouldn't, so why would Saite? "Who fucked up?" he asked as he glanced over to where Emily and me faced.

"Like I was just telling Jordan here, it's someone he should know pretty well." Her tone's even more playful, grabbing tightly on my arm as she stared at Richard.

Yet I saw someone walk past us, reddish-brown hair and teal eyes glancing momentarily at me b'fore rushing away. Kylie. Yet she didn't stop to even talk to the officers, and she definitely ain't missing. Didn't seem involved at all, walking off without looking back, without a word to me. Guess I understood, in a way: words'd been so damn hard lately, just didn't know what to say. Siani and Rotanu'd made things so goddamn complicated, magic fucked our lives more than we could've thought.

But if Emily ain't talking about her, then who? Who else

would I've "known well"? Richard and Kylie'd been the only friends I'd ever had.

Richard scoffed, brushing hair off his shoulder. "I thought I asked who it was."

Emily had the slightest whimper as she nodded. "Sorry, I just thought — ." Her eyes moved away from Richard as her voice softened. "It's that girl, Lianne Payne, been going all around the school past few days."

Guess she ain't wrong I'd been in classes with Lianne over the years, but not like we'd ever really talked. Whatever's going on ain't any of my business then though, best to let the cops handle it. Just glad for fuckin' once, it ain't Kylie involved. Ain't goddamn magic ruining our lives again.

"Jordan and I have somewhere to be," Richard said. I didn't even nod in agreement: if he's kicking Emily out, it meant I'm getting dragged back to that damn training house. "Later." He pulled his phone out as he walked off.

Emily stepped forward. "Oh, I'd love to come too," she said as she tried to keep pace with Richard. He didn't even glance up to her as he kept walking. "Or not," she mumbled, a momentary glare at me.

Rubbing the back of my neck, I glanced away. "I'll, uh, see you later." And like that, another afternoon's gone to damn magic.

Chapter Forty-Three

responsibility

It's almost a year since I "woke up" in this time. Was a special kind of ironic hell I wanted to go back to when Asuza's the biggest problem, when he's where all my attention and anxiety went. Everything'd gone perfectly, just like she wanted. Just like I should've expected. I'm the only one who wanted change, I realized now, and it ain't for the selfless reason of wanting her not to get hurt: just didn't want shit on my conscience, wanted to write over my regret where it no longer existed, even if it cost Richard ever having Act and friendship I'd gained from Sai. Even if it meant Kyle never met one of the most important people to her. Tried to dress up my guilt by wanting to *save* her, but...

Both Kyle and Sai'd accepted it long ago. Maybe b'fore we'd even come here. She'd said our mistakes defined us, and maybe my refusal to accept that'd just been a sign of how much I wished I ain't me even now.

Kinda sucked having all this time to think. Sure's fuck didn't want it. Jordan'd been around Richard, but I couldn't reach out to Sai to talk. Hadn't been able to say a word to Kyle since that night except through relays between Jordan and Kylie, which'd been shot to fuckin' hell and back with how they couldn't say two words to each other now.

I felt alone. Made me resent Jordan even more, even if I finally understood her warnings to be nicer to Jordan: in my less-positive traits, I'd always kinda been a passive-aggressive jackass, and it'd gotten the best of me. She kept her head when I didn't. I knew how each stab hurt like fuck, and it'd just edged me on more and more — finally a way to get back at myself for all the dumbshit it'd done during this time of my life. Thought as long as I planned around the one event, kept him from blowing up the day Kylie triggered NEO, could get out all the pent up anger I'd had at myself for years.

She'd fuckin' warned me it wouldn't work, and she's right.

It's a truth I didn't wanna face: I'm just as responsible as Jordan for Kylie triggering NEO. If I'd done like Kyle and Sai and hadn't gone out of my way to spite him, he'd prob'bly listened to me more. Fuck knew he ain't secure enough to be confident in his own decisions since he just recoiled to damn near everything 'cause he's in free fall, not understanding a damn thing going on.

Even if I tried to explain now, I'd burned the bridge too far.

Jordan unloaded the groceries Elaine brought back; I'd otherwise walled myself off, only keeping vague awareness. Minutes, hours, days, they all blurred together. Wiped my eyes from where I'd been crying while locked away in my subcon. Jordan didn't ask questions — the less of me, the better.

Sai's the one that'd finally made me realize I was wrong: he clearly's on the same page as Kyle, and if they're on the same side, either hell's freezing over or I'm the one who fucked up. And either the best or worst thing 'bout hypermnesia's the ability to replay every damn interaction I'd experienced since Act, where I'd simultaneously experience both the past and now — be both Jordan and Rotanu at once.

It's so damn clear.

"When d'you get out of school?" Jewel asked Jordan. I braced for the conversation. Ain't like it's worse than others that'd already happened, just the same bullshit, different day, and I ain't in the mood for it.

"End of May. Why?" Jordan didn't turn around to face her, instead pulling shit from the grocery bags onto the counter. We're on month seven of this apartment, so only 'bout two more months left b'fore the next move. Was one of the longer apartments of my childhood.

She placed something on the counter. Jordan turned his head, seeing sheets of paper — job applications. "Have this in 'fore you get out. Preferably earlier than later."

He stared at the applications, no words forming. Was overwhelmed, felt pulled in all directions. I bit back yelling 'bout why didn't he snap at Jewel, at Richard, fuck, at Emily?

Why's Kylie the first one he abandoned? Why wouldn't he cuss any of them out?

There's no point in me saying shit: he'd ignore anything I said. And even more so, I knew why he pushed her out first: he ain't willing to confront his own emotions, ain't willing to admit magic'd benefited him, ain't willing to say anything I'd said's right.

Ain't willing to admit he hurt her in the first place, continuously placing weight on her being *strong* instead of her being a damn woman who'd been tortured and expected to walk it off like nothing'd happened.

I missed Kyle so goddamn much right then. Wanted to have an actual conversation with Sai instead of relayed through Jordan if not Jordan and Richard. Less than one month left. Just needed to keep shit together 'til then.

Jordan said nothing as he turned back around and put the rest of the shit up.

"Did you hear me?" Jewel asked, her tone even bitchier than normal. "You have to help too."

Jordan's right fist balled. "I heard you. Can I finish this now?"

"Quit acting like a child. I'd already started mid-year, not dragging my feet like you're doing. I actually *wanted* to help this family. Maybe we wouldn't have to move so much if you bothered to ever pull your weight."

I barely caught Jordan's elemental control slipping, his fingers nearly gaining a spark. Should've expected that given how fast his heart raced right then, how shallow his breath became at the thought of juggling a full-time job this summer, of being forced into the same system of dead-end jobs his father and sisters'd gone into.

I remembered how I'd thought — he thought — how it ain't fair, no one understood what's going on and not like he could talk to anyone 'bout it either.

Maybe that's one of the things I hated the most 'bout myself, the inclination to think things're outta my control when it's a conscious choice. Yet for all the bullshit I'd given him this past year, I'd done the exact same thing every time I spited him, passive aggressively stabbed at him.

In a damn painful example of irony, I'd been doing the exact fuckin' thing I'd been bitching at him 'bout: avoiding responsibility and instead lashing out at others. Guess for all that'd I'd changed, some things'd stayed the same despite everything.

I remember thinking 'bout how Rotanu'd being silent meant *I'd won*. That's what he thought now, that he'd successfully punished me by ignoring me. I wish that's what'd happened. Would've saved me the struggle of wanting to do it to myself but being unable to.

Jordan went into his and Thomas's bedroom, pulling out a textbook as he flipped through it. Ain't like he's gonna actually read it, but'd learned how to skim enough to refer back during tests for hypermnesia to kick in. Should've been called out for potential cheating but teachers didn't give a damn to look into why a student who never turned in homework and historically'd barely passed suddenly started aceing tests.

He huffed, flipping one page with more force, the crinkle sound of the textbook page the only other sound in the room. "Just one more fuckin' thing," he said under his breath. "Ain't like I got ten other things going on I wanted nothing to fuckin' do with. No. Let's just add another fuckin' one in."

Maybe he should've looked into why he hated his life so much. If he hated spending time with his girlfriend, maybe it's a sign she ain't the one for him. Maybe if he felt pressured by Richard, it might've been a sign he needed to actually open his damn mouth and say something instead of passively agreeing with every damn thing.

And maybe if he resented Kylie only thinking about magic, he should've thought 'bout how she felt and realized she grasped for survival with no one around to listen.

Then again, what right did I have to lecture him? Maybe if I'd been honest — with him, with myself — , I could've had a genuine conversation with him. Just one. Maybe I'd still see Kyle on Saturday nights, maybe I could've had an actual conversation with Sai.

I'd always been told I'm a shitty liar, but apparently, I lied to myself entirely too easily.

Chapter Forty-Four

center

She took a deep breath, forcing the air down her lungs. It was a valid attempt to steady herself, but it didn't completely work. Her left hand tightened its grip over Isare. Kylie worked through strikes with the weapon, but I had to keep bringing her back to the moment — her mind was very obviously not in this training house, even if she insisted she wanted to train.

To be fair, I knew she did. It's just distractions only worked for so long, and in this case, what she wanted to think about and what she needed to process most certainly didn't align. She didn't want to think about the fact Lianne had been reported missing and she'd last been seen leaving our house that day, never reaching her parents' house. She didn't want to think that there was yet another missing teenage girl in Opal Pines.

No one else's emotions could crowd into her mind; the training house was the only place that happened now, only place with so few people around. A sensation that comforted her but was strangely silent to me since I only felt her emotions and a few faint others.

Kylie attempted to rotate Isare between her hands but

winced as she hit herself on the head — at least the blades weren't out. The potential concussion was enough for her to wince, dropping Isare to the concrete. "You made that look a lot easier," she said.

"I've practiced a fair bit more than you have. Heal up and try again. Go slower this time. You'll build speed once you understand the movement."

Sighing, she nodded as she healed her head and picked Isare back up. "Are you ever going to tell me why you can't take control anymore? That feels like something I deserve to know now. Really could use extra direction on this stuff."

"The only way you're going to really get things is by trial and error. And error's part of that process, hence why it's in the name." I intentionally didn't answer the first part, and she noticed but said nothing. We both needed each other, though in a different way than a year ago; before, I needed her alive to exist, and she needed me to stay alive. Now... I couldn't talk to anyone else, and she didn't want to talk to anyone else.

This year had given me closure in ways I hadn't known I still needed. Things would make sense in time, and she'd get there. I knew that best, after all.

"Yeah, but it'd be *really helpful* to like... show me, like you used to."

She still thought she lied better than she actually did. Unfortunately for her, she needed far more practice on that one. *"You're not steady. Center in your mana, because if you're not centered, you'll struggle to maintain focus — especially for surrounding auras and emotions."*

Kylie nodded, taking another deep breath. "Okay."

She began twirling Isare too fast for her reflexes again, so I said, *"Steady, slow down."* Her movements immediately slowed, the strength of her grip increasing as her confidence built.

The training house was silent outside of her movements and few words. There was nothing and no one else around, after all. And that meant that without me, her thoughts would've filled the gap, been entirely too loud and overbearing. She thought she wanted silence, but really, she just wanted to run from her own emotions.

One day she'd have to face them, but today wasn't that day, and I'd provide distraction until I no longer could.

Chapter Forty-Five

interest

"Yeah, and that's when Richard said..." Emily'd mentioned Richard eight times in the past fifteen minutes. I started counting after the fourth one, and it's another instance I kinda wish I didn't have fuckin' hypermnesia. Generally's the least of magic-related things I'm complaining 'bout, but I'd rather just think I'm paranoid than know it really'd been that often. I shifted my weight as she held out another shirt on a clothing rack for me to hold — this one black with some type of lace trim. How many more damn shirts did she even need? I held eight right then, and she bought ten last trip. Just this month alone, think she's bought more clothes than I got in total. Not that I bought clothes often, or like, ever, but still.

Goddamn, what'd she even do with all this shit? I started scanning my memories, and yeah, she'd never worn the same top twice. Like we'd been going out for months now, and I'd never seen the same anything but shoes and I guess socks twice. Did it go into some clothes hell vortex or something? I couldn't imagine buying this much shit. Wasn't even sure why I'm needed here to begin with. Richard never did shit like this;

barely took them to eat, and for that matter, had distanced himself from women in general. Was bored with them and magic's more interesting, he said, but I ain't sure I completely believed that's the full reason. More likely, I wondered if what Saite'd said 'bout his absorption device played in more than he'd admit. "Are you even listening to me?"

I quickly replayed the last few words in my head 'cause I absolutely ain't. "Uh, science class, right?"

She rolled her eyes, tossing another shirt at me. "Yeah, this slut came up on him like she has the right to touch him. Probably never even went out to eat with him. He even jerked her hand off of him, which was *so valid*."

Was him buying a meal the defining "know Richard" standard? Wondered if she knew 'bout magic, 'bout Richard and Saite, if she'd still think he's so awesome? Prob'bly actually. I kinda saw what he meant with the having confidence thing now, I just ain't got it though. It'd been part of what made Siani so mesmerizing, how Richard got away with shit. Well, outside of that suggestion ability, which actually looked useful as fuck. Saite actually seemed competent like Siani too.

"Yeah, for sure." Agreeing seemed the safest option regardless of it being a strange as hell metric to use. 'Specially since I'm pretty sure he jerked away 'cause of whatever happened with that incident and his absorption device, not 'cause he disliked that one chick in particular.

She nodded in approval as she came close, taking the hangers from me as she kissed my cheek. I did my best to hide how much I tensed, but every time she did that, got these goddamn weird visions — some of Kylie or of Rotanu and Siani the past year when they'd been together. Visions of girls that looked similar but different to Kylie, like that girl Asuza had on the altar, but she's actually alive in the vision.

As I'd come to brace for, it happened again: this's one of the other girls — closer to Siani in age, but hair pulled up in a long ponytail, super fancy clothes on. As she pulled away from my cheek, she had a shy blush, her bright blueish-green eyes emphasizing the redness of her cheeks.

I felt disoriented as it wasn't those eyes I saw, but Emily's brown ones. Why would I've expected different? Kylie ain't interested. I'd had my entire life thus far to more than demonstrate that. Rotanu ain't me, and Siani's hot but she'd never go for a guy like me — needed someone that'd keep up with her, which I'd more than demonstrated I ain't able to. Emily's the closest I'd had to my own decision in almost a whole fuckin' year, one thing in my life that Rotanu ain't controlled or manipulated and's separate from god fuckin' damn magic. She'd been amazing, so patient when I'm obviously such a shitty boyfriend, was objectively cute and hot. Barely even said anything now when I recoiled as she grabbed my hand and pulled me away to the checkout line. Didn't even expect me to pay now, understood that ain't something I could do.

"When're you seeing Richard next?" she asked as she laid her head on my shoulder, pulling her hand from mine as she circled the edges of hair on my neck — hadn't had time to get a haircut with all the shit going on lately.

"Ah, uh, not sure." Tomorrow, but that's when he'd drag my ass to the training house and I got to be miserable in that shitstorm. Wasn't exactly something Emily'd attend or even know 'bout.

I wished I didn't know either, but that ship'd sailed around the world fifty times over now.

"Well, we need to go out for lunch again, just the three of us."

Ain't lunch s'posed to be the two of us? Why's Richard coming? I never got it, but ain't worth the fight. "I'll, uh, I'll ask him. Maybe next week?"

She nodded, pointer finger tapping my cheek. "That's a good idea."

Chapter Forty-Six

time's up

Kylie swung down with Isare, working in her own form to increase the force while maximizing speed with each strike. Her head tilted up as her grip tensed; she picked up on Jordan and Richard's auras edging closer to the training house. She didn't want to say she was terrified at whatever Richard would say this time, at Jordan's awkward bashfulness. I chose to pretend I didn't notice.

It was one kindness I could give in all this, let her think she actually was able to block emotions from me. Today was the day, after all.

"I'm going," Jordan said, grumble heard through the door as he turned the doorknob. Richard still wouldn't touch the doorknob it sounded, much to Jordan's irritation. Emotionally loud irritation at that.

Yet Rota was the opposite, a sense of relief. I wondered if Sai knew, if Rota'd been able to tell him somehow.

The game was won, outcome decided.

The training house's door opened. Jordan saw Kylie and immediately averted his eyes. "Oh, sorry," he said. He wasn't

251

willing to redirect his inability to cope with the awkwardness to anyone but Rota, but he still hadn't had a real conversation with Kylie after the day with NEO.

Richard pushed past him. "She still doesn't own this place."

Neither did he, but Kylie didn't bother putting up a fight. This house might've been the first thing in his life Richard hadn't owned, and it showed as much as ever.

I noticed another aura nearby — bright red. Kylie stepped back, also detecting it as she shook her head. Her eyes dashed around, trying to discern its exact direction. The aura came from an incoming teleportation, so it wasn't a surprise she had trouble — mana materialized prior to a body. She'd learn right then was an excellent place for a mine to happen appearing; teleporting mid-fight without careful consideration was a rookie mistake, left the body open to ambushes. From there, the other two began materializing as well; we needed a full audience for this show, after all...

Sai must've taken control when he noticed the incoming teleports since he pushed Jordan to the side; I was fairly certain Richard didn't know how to read auras, especially not accurately enough to predict where Nimaka's teleportation finished. Even if Richard somehow had figured auras out, he wouldn't have had the experience to push Jordan out of Nimaka's lance blade which would have otherwise impaled him. Granted, that attack wouldn't have taken Jordan out, but I doubted Richard or Jordan would've known that. Jordan was just the opening, though, since her target wasn't him: he would've been collateral at most. Sai knew what he was doing, a nod to me as he effectively stared through Kylie: he pushed himself and Jordan near us, forcing all three bodies within one glyph's diameter. That meant he was aware after all. I guess that was easier for him than myself, only having one attack between his Act and now.

"You fell for it," Nimaka said. Her voice was arrogant, almost gleeful. She thought she'd finally won. A glyph went under Saite and then expanded out to Kylie and Jordan. The other two were behind us, as if to pincer anyone daring to leave the glyph — they might've been more convincing if they weren't still terrified from the last time Rota and I went round with them. The air became thick with mana as Nimaka needed more of her active supply than she'd ever want to admit; she tried to hide the pants escaping her lips, fatigue from the spell's intensity. "You won't pull those stunts ever again. I'll show them how weak you all are." Sase and Zimihe didn't feel particularly hopeful for her strategy. They were behind Kylie so I couldn't see if they pretended to be confident, but it definitely would've been a front if so — Nimaka must have near dragged them out here for this.

"This is like..." Kylie winced, dropping Isare as she bit down on her lip, hand moving over her heart.

It felt similar to the undead dismissal spell that we used almost a year prior on Asuza, on Kisate and Takite's lines for prior incarnations. That wasn't quite right though, as that spell wouldn't work on myself, Rota, or Sai: we weren't dead, after all. Nimaka wanted to play with her food, and she should've at least had the decency to do it correctly instead of missing half the facts.

My vision doubled, seeing from Kylie's eyes and my own concurrently. But my vision wasn't from my actual body in the future. It was in this time but separate from Kylie, this new line of sight steadying more as Kylie's vision disconnected.

A fake body, unable to cast magic. Nimaka hadn't realized Rota and I couldn't take control of Kylie and Jordan's bodies any longer, and Sai was by far the least threatening out of us three. We were at our weakest as we'd been, locked away. If either Rota or I could act, we could easily kill them. She didn't know that part, but then...

That had been by my design, after all. I could no longer terminate the connection tying myself, Rota, and Sai to this time period; I lost the ability to do so when I locked Rota and myself from controlling Jordan and Kylie's bodies. Only Kylie could've, and she neither knew how nor would've willingly done so. I needed an external force capable of pulling more mana than Richard would safely be able to for a while yet, even if he utilized Sai's form.

In other words: Nimaka. It was the whole reason I'd let her live through that first attack back in the fall, all for this moment.

"How...?" Richard said behind me. Rota and Sai were now beside me, generated copies of our alternative forms. She'd pulled from our memories instead of hers, which made it all the more entertaining.

Jordan said nothing but his anxiety was impressively high, enough that Kylie winced. I could no longer buffer any of her empathy, so that wasn't much of a surprise.

I glanced toward Rota, nodding. It was the first interaction we'd had in months, since I lied and locked us both from control. He nodded back: it was time to go home. I couldn't pull from Kylie's mana supply, only from the bit this body had. And even aura reading pushed the bit of mana in this body, a limitation Nimaka was smug about. It wasn't as if she did anything special — that limitation was part of the base spell, a feature to help conserve mana requirements. I picked Isare up from where Kylie had dropped it, the weight comfortable in my hand. "This one's mine. I've been waiting a long time for this."

Nimaka sneered, as if I was the one who didn't understand the current situation, as if she'd come up with this plan all by herself and I was trapped by her genius. "You can't do any of your tricks this time!"

I licked my lower lip. She thought I needed magic to take her down. Adorable.

Rota sighed as Sai gestured dismissively at me by waving his left hand in the air. Sai would've struggled without magic against her, but Rota barely used offensive magic as it was. And me...

Well. This is what I lived for now, after all.

Sase and Zimihe just watched, not acting as they observed Nimaka. A rare bright moment from them. Rota — and Sai, if Rota got overwhelmed for whatever reason — could deal with them well enough to protect the younger ones.

This was something I'd been waiting on a long time now, and I planned on relishing every second of it.

I stepped forward. "You think you've made your own choices, don't you? That you came to these conclusions all by yourself?" I released the blades on Isare's ends. "You little naive child, you just danced to the song I gave you. But your part's over. I've no more use for you."

She directed an attack spell, ice shards hurling toward me and me alone, so there was no need to dodge. I took the attack in full, shards cutting against skin, stinging blood seeping down. This body probably had a fractured rib from the energy blast at the end. I didn't budge; her eyes widened. Little did she know, I'd missed this so much. "You..."

"See, your theory is flawed. And flawed theories become flawed executions, unable to ever reach their desired conclusion." I stepped forward, pain shooting through each of the twenty or so incisions along my arms and legs, endorphins nowhere near strong enough to mute the panic signals my nervous system sent, a rush I'd not indulged while being *Sia*. "The first mistake was assuming that I was a dead incarnation. Fun fact, this wouldn't have even worked if I was dead because you can't permanently interrupt the soul's connection if there's a host present. As soon as this body expired, I'd go right back. This means you'd have to win against the host, not the replica. As you might realize, the host still has full access to mana because you did nothing to limit the supply." I took another step; she physically held her ground but the panic had set in. I could almost taste it, fear tangible in her eyes. I relished the horror from Zimihe and Sase who knew this had gone wrong but had no idea what to do, no panic response to attack any of the others. They just stood, watching my casual steps to Nimaka. "Second, you thought we were being sloppy instead of very intentionally placed little cues for you to pick up on." She shot another attack spell. My lip busted and right eye swelled. "The third is you thought pain scared me. Pain is what makes things *exciting*." I rushed forward, stabbing through her mid left breast, close to her underarm: her symbol, which I'd discerned back at our first post-Asuza meeting months ago. That was why I used such an intense symbol scan then, preparing for this moment. I needed her mana completely severed, and nothing severed quite as well as a broken symbol. "But now, you've served your purpose. Time's up."

Nimaka clawed at her throat, lungs shutting down from a

lack of mana to sustain them. I felt it through my empathy, heard Kylie gasping and wincing behind me, unable to stomach the empathic reads. I withdrew Isare from Nimaka, preventing her from using it as a crutch. She collapsed onto the concrete, blood dripping from us both and mixing into yet another blood puddle that'd dry the gray concrete red. Unlike myself, she couldn't take the pain, didn't appreciate experiencing what she'd almost forced on Kylie near a year prior.

I refused to mercy kill her, wanted every last moment of suffering her body would give. For what had already happened and what would happen. For the nightmares I'd had and Kylie would have. Even this was too polite but I only had minutes left now, couldn't toy further than I already had. Her death meant my own time was essentially up, after all. For their part, Zimihe and Sase bailed on her, teleporting off, back to wherever they hid.

Her fatal mistake wasn't to be their deaths, not today at least.

Chapter Forty-Seven
grand schemes

I couldn't even pick myself up from where I'd fallen onto my knees. I didn't know what was happening or why or how. Pain consumed everything, spots filling in my vision, ears ringing, it getting harder and harder to swallow. This intense throbbing pulsed throughout my body, everything hot yet cold and sweat drowning my lungs.

Jordan — no, not Jordan. Too calm, steady. Rota. He offered his hand out to me, helping me to my feet, his hands on my shoulders grounding me in the moment as the pain began lessening.

Sai had his arms crossed over his chest, head tilted as if bored. "Can she quit fucking around?" he grumbled.

"I heard that," Sia said. I didn't know how she stood so easily, how her empathy hadn't drowned her in emotions, in pain. So effortlessly, she walked over to us, not even a limp.

"I wasn't hiding it," Sai said. "Took you damn long enough."

Rota rolled his eyes, releasing my shoulders and turning. "*Children*, if you wouldn't mind for five fuckin' minutes?"

Sia stuck her tongue out at Sai.

How could she act so casual, so playful to him? Her emotions were fully readable to me for the first time, which meant it really had been her blocking them when she shared a body with me. She didn't hate Sai; she didn't even really dislike him, mild annoyance at best. And then... for the first time, I saw her and Rota from a third perspective. Their eyes were soft as they met. "I'll never apologize," she said, a gentle stubbornness in her voice.

He sighed, bringing his forehead against her own as he tightly hugged her. "I know."

Their lips quickly met. I couldn't look away, couldn't ignore how happy, or no — I didn't understand their emotions. This warmth. It was terrifying somehow. They parted not even a second later, Rota's right hand going to her left.

All their of their forms flickered momentarily. How? How were they even separate from us to begin with? Their souls were tied to our bodies; that was how they were even in this time, with us. Sia's eyes met mine, a warmth I'd seen only once or twice with her in subcon. She shook her head softly, braided-hair swaying, a smile on her lips. A peace I didn't understand.

Their bodies gained a translucence to them, as if they were fading. But how? Were they coming back to our bodies? "What's...?"

"It's time," she said. "This is your game to command now."

Time? For what? And my *game*?

Her words right then intermixed with something she'd said to Nimaka: a deceased reincarnated soul would return to the host body, but then... what would happen to an alive reincarnated soul?

My eyes widened as I shook my head: the soul would go back to its body, needing no host.

I rushed forward, grabbing onto her. She was cold, opposite of the warmth in her eyes, opposite of how her skin had felt in subcon. Her free hand ran through my hair. "You-you can't... I can't do this." She couldn't leave me like everyone else had. She couldn't leave me completely alone in a world where everyone wanted me dead. The other two had left now but they'd be back, and what then?

She shook her head, that soft smile still there. "You need truths now, not more lies. No more grand schemes someone else's planned for you. You decide things now, so stand tall, and never bow to anyone again." She tucked hair behind my ear before her hand became intangible, passing through my cheek. Rota and Sai were similar as their forms were barely visible even just a few feet off. Rota glanced to Jordan before nodding to me; Sai crossed his arms over his chest as he stood to Rota's side.

Water rose to my eyes. She nodded at me as her barely visible hand moved away. My lip quivered, my throat dry, stinging. The last I saw of her, her eyes were peaceful, her hand tightly gripping Rota's. Sai didn't try to intercept them like Richard did anytime I wanted to talk with Jordan. He was amused even, somehow content — as if that was normal, as if that's how they're meant to be. Soon, they had vanished, nothing remaining of where they'd stood.

"They're gone..." Jordan said. "No more bullshit with them gone, it's finally all over." He was excited. How could he be *excited* we were left to handle things ourselves? "We're finally free from all this shit." A breath of relief from him even. "Finally." He left before Richard even did. He didn't say anything to me, as if I wasn't there. Richard closed the door a minute later, dazed, following Jordan.

It was just me. I dropped to my knees, vision blurry for tears. Nimaka was only one of the women that wanted me dead. How could he think it was *over*? "Free"? For them maybe. But the other two would be like Nimaka had been, they would want revenge. And now...

I was alone for real this time, wasn't I?

Chapter Forty-Eight

the dark sky

Maya | July 18
South Georgia Tram Line

More people stepped off the tram. I wasn't getting off yet though, not yet. I needed to go as far away as I could: I couldn't ever be found. There were still two more stops after this one, another town or city or county over. I didn't know the stop's name; I just saw it was the third to last stop. I didn't even know where I was besides in the Georgia state lines. There had been a direct line from DC into Atlanta, and easily eight hours had passed since that I swapped from that connection to this one, which went from Atlanta to... somewhere.

What was I even doing?

I was a teenager, not even legal yet, not for many more months. I stole my adoption certificate, which had my birth name instead of the legal name I'd had after my adoption. I'd stolen four thousand from Father's savings, and I didn't want to imagine what would happen if he caught me now. My stomach and collarbone throbbed even considering it, reminders of not even a week past; my lower right forearm stung from a cut that had at the time taken my mind off my stomach and collarbone bruising but now ironically reminded me instead.

The doors closed; the bus resumed moving. My mind begged for rest, but I couldn't. I needed to stay alert, had no one looking after me. I wasn't naïve: I was a young woman at night on a dimly lit bus in a state I'd never visited. Even awake, I was in a dangerous position, let alone unconscious.

I saw more trees — how many had I passed since I left home? All were different kinds I'd never seen before. The trees were lush, growing more and more green the further away from the last stop we went. The bus's windshield fogged, driver grumbling as he flipped a few switches to defog the windshield.

The only sound in the bus was the hum of the engine. Driver didn't have the radio on loud enough for me to hear it in the back of the bus. I saw the full moon, lighting up the dark sky. It seemed brighter now that I was away from the crowded building lights in DC.

I didn't even have a phone, left it at home so I couldn't be traced. I *couldn't* be found. I had to make this work or die trying because death would be more pleasant than whatever waited for me if I ever went back now.

The doors opened to the bus again, lights turning on overhead — it had already been another hour? Time blurred this many hours on a bus. I read the overhead: Opal Pines.

I didn't know why, but this was where I needed to get off, not the final stop as I'd intended. I stood, legs cramping from sitting so long, humidity hitting me as I approached the bus door. I stepped off the bus ramp and into the bus stop covering. No one else had gotten off, and the bus doors creaked shut behind me, shutting off any second decisions I suddenly felt. This was it then. I tightened my eyes, taking in a deep breath. This was my new home.

Opening my eyes back, I glanced up to the arched wooden sign above the stop covering:

"Welcome to Opal Pines."

thanks for reading!

Thank you for reading until the end! If you enjoyed this story, please consider leaving a review on Goodreads, TheStoryGraph, BookBub, PageBound, or on your favorite book retailer — as you've likely heard many times, reviews are exceptionally important for indie authors, and each one both means a ton and is super helpful in helping others decide if this book is right for them!

Check riyati.ink/rivals for a handy list of review sites & retailers!

acknowledgements

Much like I said in *Riyati Rebirth*'s acknowledgments, there's so many people I need to thank for the opportunities I had while writing *Riyati Rivals*. Of course, I have to thank my husband and closest friends, both who have given me the time, space, and grace to even be able to write this book, and the cats (who did not give me time, space, or grace, but all slept on me at one point or another during the drafting, editing, and publication process of this book). I must also thank Alli Rense and Ellie Sigsbee, both of who graciously beta read for me; their suggestions helped refine *Riyati Rivals* into the book you're reading today. As well, I'd like to thank Kate for proofreading *Riyati Rivals*, helping to assure 100% fewer typos because I always miss them somehow. Finally, I'd like to thank Cait (Kanao7) for the *Riyati Rivals* character art that's on Riyati's Library Archive, and amagren for the glyph illustrations used in the cover art.

I'd additionally like to thank the numerous discord servers I'm in; without the experience of authors far smarter than myself, I'd still be lost in the forest of details I still am learning about every day. And of course, if you've read *Riyati Rebirth*, I must acknowledge you as well — thank you so much for taking the time to read this series I've wanted to share for so long, and for continuing to do so with *Riyati Rivals*!

Sincerely,
Kai Zeal

about the author

Kai Zeal (she/her) is a queer, disabled writer, academic, gamer, cat mom, and, most recently, content creator. She got her start writing fanfiction as a child, creating an awareness of tropes, characterization, and the importance of retellings. From there, she refined her analytical skills both in academia and through fandom with critical analysis of media to gain a better understanding of how the parts of a work come together to form its whole.

She has degrees in psychology, writing, higher education administration, and is pursuing a PhD with a research focus on critical disability studies through a queer, feminist lens. In her free time, she's a lifelong gamer, particularly of JRPGs, many of which have shaped her storytelling strategies and love of media.

Want to know more? Check out her personal website & sign up for her monthly newsletter at https://kai-zeal.com/. For *Riyati* specific information, check out https://riyati.ink/

interested in more riyati?

If you'd like to further explore Opal Pines and the *Riyati* universe, sign up for my newsletter to receive *Riyati Origins*! You'll also receive behind-the-scenes updates, previews, and deals for *Riyati*. If you're more of a Discord fan, join Riyati's Official Discord server — on top of a great community and instant Riyati updates, subscribers get access to Riyati's Archive Library, a *Riyati* hub for bonus short-stories, alternative PoV chapters, and character art!

Newsletter: https://riyati.ink/newsletter

Official Riyati Discord: https://riyati.ink/discord

Long before Kylie Rae ran into the forest that fateful day, there lived another woman — Kisate Riyati, crowned princess to the Royal Kingdom of Riyati. This is her story, of how kingdoms fall and dreams are dashed.

Just before Kisate's twenty-second birthday, she received word that the man she'd secretly loved for many years was now arranged to be her eventual husband, Takite Tanoti. Yet this news sets in motion a series of events that would not just be life changing, but ultimately instigates the destruction of the kingdom she was to rule. What was meant as a kindness to Asuza Nuueti, her primary servant and a man that long since had unrequited feelings toward her, will both save her and damn her.

Explore the beginnings of the Riyati universe, back when the Ancient Kingdom of Riyati still thrived — and see Kisate, Takite, and Asuza as they once were, long before the events of *Riyati Rebirth*.

Get *Riyati Origins* for free today @ <u>https://riyati.ink/ newsletter</u>!

Riyati Ripple Preview

chapter one: fresh start

Maya | August 13
Matthews High

I just needed the damn piece of paper. That's all that mattered. I could do this, *would* do this. Yet despite telling myself that more than once in the past few weeks, I still wondered if this had been nothing but a massive mistake. I pulled my jacket tighter around myself. Outside was like a humid swamp hell, but they must've had the AC running full blast inside. It worked for the best since I preferred long sleeves, but outside of work, I hadn't been in an AC'ed environment in weeks now — nearing a month. It brought me back to the question I'd asked myself so many times now: how *was* I going to do this?

Just as predictably, there was only one answer as well: it didn't matter; I had no other option.

More people filed in, all laughing and talking to each other. Likely, I was the only one here that didn't know anyone, but that made sense. They'd probably been together for the past three years, maybe more. Even at my old high school, so much larger than this one, I still was aware of the people in my grade level. Really, I wasn't sure why there were so many high schools in this town to begin with. Three felt like overkill if this one's size was anything to go by.

More students — my classmates, I assumed — shuffled in, wearing short sleeves and shorts, not at all phased by the difference between outside and inside temperatures.

"Why's it so hot out there?" I heard one girl say. Others voiced agreement. I pulled my eyes away, reminding myself that I wasn't here to make friends. Friends only caused problems, so it was better I didn't have them in the first place. Hell knew I'd learned that lesson my fair share already.

Someone finally sat to my right, interrupting the mindless sketch of the classroom I'd been working on. Turning my head, I saw her take in a deep breath. Why'd she sit beside *me*? There were still *plenty* of other open seats literally anywhere else in the classroom. I was in the second row, off to the side, near the window. Most of the students wanted to be near the door so they could rush in and out later, which was why I'd picked the exact opposite.

From the corner of my eye, I saw her pull out a planner, running her eyes over a piece of paper I couldn't read because it was too far away. She wore a t-shirt and jean shorts and had some type of markings around her wrists. Not a tattoo, closer to a scar. Old though, nothing new.

Guess if she's leaving me alone, at least the seat was taken so no one more talkative could occupy it.

I turned my attention back to the sketch. The perspective on it was off; it bothered me, but I didn't want to put the effort into actually fixing it. I hadn't tried to draw anything complex, just what I saw in front of me — the desks, the board, the entrance to the room. Something in my line-art was off though. It was too flat with no depth. Maybe I could hide it with shading. This was yet another thing to pass time until the school day was over and I went back to work.

"Are you new here?" my now-talkative neighbor asked. I nodded, hoping that'd satisfy her curiosity. "I thought so. It's kind of obvious we both are, isn't it?" Her voice softened at the end, so I pretended to not have heard the question. It sounded like she was a talker after all, which was not what I wanted to deal with. Instead, I kept sketching, my eyes on the paper instead of anywhere that might invite further discussion. "My name's Kylie. Nice to meet you."

I glanced at her from the corner of my eyes; if I directed my whole attention at her, she might take that as an invitation for more conversation. "Maya. Same, I guess."

Her head tilted, catching a glimpse of the sketch I'd been working on. "Oh wow, that's amazing. You drew that?" Apparently she wasn't an artist either. Other artists knew better than to snoop on people's sketches. I again nodded. Homeroom hadn't even started yet, and I wanted it over like I wanted this whole year over already. Her voice was contemplative as she glanced around at others in the classroom. "I kind of envy them right now, to be honest. They're with people they know, have known for years, probably."

"Mm." People just got in the way. But I wasn't wasting time arguing with her on this; it wasn't worth either of our times.

An adult walked in, a woman with blonde hair tied in a bun. She went to the teacher's desk in the corner by the entrance door. The student conversations hushed, their attention half focusing on her. This had to be her classroom then. I glanced at the clock above the board: eight thirty-five in the morning. She was late. Hopefully this was just a first day problem and not something that'd be a recurring trend. I wanted her to talk more so that everyone else talked to me less. She calmly walked to the front of the room, saying something to the two students closest to the middle of the room in the front row. A brown-haired girl with gray eyes and thin-rimmed glasses — likely another student since she looked similar in age to the rest of us in here — walked in right as the teacher closed the door, sliding into the seat behind me. I saw my talkative neighbor's posture suddenly stiffen as she turned around to look at her. To her credit, they looked like twins — maybe they were sisters? She turned back around to face the front of the classroom a moment later, her eyes staring at her planner with a perplexed expression. Weird, but whatever. Maybe she'd be distracted with that person instead of talking to me now.

The teacher introduced herself: Mrs. Carslie, who was one of two history teachers in the school. Of note to me, she was the one that taught AP World History, which was my first class after homeroom. I could just keep this seat and didn't need to worry about moving to another. There weren't any morning announcements today, she said, but they would start tomorrow. She said to use the time to check our schedules among ourselves and get to know those around us, so I was stuck with more socializing, the last thing I wanted to deal with.

"Hey," the girl behind me said. "I'm Ashley, new here."

Great, *another* talkative one. Maybe I'd get lucky and they'd entertain each other so I'd be left out of this small talk social dance thing. Kylie turned around and nodded to Ashley. "Wow, I didn't know so many people would transfer senior year. I'm new too. My name's Kylie."

Three people were *not* that many. It really was a small town here, wasn't it?

"What's your story?" Ashley asked, and I unfortunately could tell it was directed at me.

"Maya. Just here because I have to be." I didn't turn around; maybe she'd get the hint. Besides, things would be better once I was out of high school hell. College had to be different. People would leave me alone there.

Ashley snorted. "Aren't we all?"

I thought as social and peppy as both of them were at this hour of the morning, she'd be thrilled to be in high school.

"Anything has to be better than last year," Kylie said, but I wasn't sure she meant for us to hear it since the comment had almost but not quite been under her breath. Her left hand moved to a pendant — no, a ring on a necklace, weird fashion choice — that had been tucked under her t-shirt. Her eyes shifted over to me. "Oh, you're left-handed — me too. I'm excited to have a seat neighbor that doesn't bump into me every two minutes."

"Really?" Ashley said, her foot kicking the back of my chair as she leaned closer. Could they both go somewhere else? "I'm left-handed as well — what a coincidence." Good, they had something to bond over now, and we could all move on with our mornings.

Kylie dropped the ring back under her t-shirt as she turned around to see Ashley better. "Wait, seriously? That's funny."

The bell finally rang, and almost everyone in the class stood up, including Ashley. Unfortunately, that meant only one of my problems left the classroom. Kylie didn't move. I saw her schedule sitting on the corner of her desk and glanced over as subtly as I could.

Great. I shared like half my day with her somehow. So it seemed she was academically intelligent but couldn't take a hint, particularly about how much I wanted to be left alone. She pulled the schedule from the edge of her desk as she wrote something down in her planner before reaching down to her backpack and grabbing a notebook that she flipped open to a blank page. She glanced around, eyes stopping on me. "You're still stuck in here too, huh?"

That was one way to put it. "Yeah."

Her head turned back to the seat where Ashley had been, not yet filled with the students coming into the room now that Ashley had left. "That's so..." she mumbled. I almost asked her what she meant, just because she obviously hadn't intended for me to hear it so maybe she'd understand how it felt to be stuck in conversations she didn't want. With my luck, she'd take that as an invitation to talk *more* though, so I decided against it. Everyone was so damn *talkative* down here. I missed being somewhere where we all ignored each other. She shook her head, as if trying to remove thoughts by doing so. "No. It's a fresh start for the final year."

Every act of defiance steers you into the person you were always meant to become.

After Nimaka's death and the older selves returning to their own time, Kylie ran from all she'd known and grown up with at North Opal Pines, but she soon learns she can't run far or fast enough.

She thought she could leave it all behind: go back to being a normal high school student, make new friends, keep her grades up and her mother happy. But Nimaka's death has only rallied the two others, and now they've stalked Kylie to her new school. Even worse, they have a mysterious new leader who no longer seeks to just kill Kylie but all those she knows and loves.... and the body count is rising.

Kylie can't get by on "just surviving" anymore: to protect herself — let alone those around her — she must become as strong and cunning as Siani was, or everyone she's ever known and loved will die with her.

Check out *Riyati Ripple* @ https://riyati.ink/ripple!